SAVAGE SINNER

Sinfully Savage: Book Four

KRISTEN LUCIANI

Savage Sinner © 2021 by Kristen Luciani

This book is a work of fiction. Names, characters, places and incidents are the product of the author's imagination or are used fictitiously. Any resemblance to actual events, locales or persons, living or dead is purely coincidental.

Except for the original material written by the author, all songs, song titles, and lyrics mentioned in this novel are the property of the respective songwriters and copyright holders.

All rights reserved. The unauthorized reproduction or distribution of this copyrighted work is illegal. This book or any portion thereof may not be reproduced, scanned, distributed, or used in any manner whatsoever, via the Internet, electronic, or print, without the express written permission of the author, except for the use of brief quotations in a book review.

For more information, or information regarding subsidiary rights, please contact Kristen Luciani at kluciani@gmail.com.

Cover Design: Book Cover Kingdom

Editing: Allusion Graphics

Photo Credit: Rafa Catala

❦ Created with Vellum

PROLOGUE

Anya

I tug hard on the brass handle, pulling open the heavy steel door that leads into the underbelly of Tatiana, Vigo Kosolov's premier nightclub and restaurant here in Brighton Beach, Brooklyn.

It's late afternoon, so the parking lot is empty save for two cars.

Vigo's Mercedes-Maybach S 560 and my Uncle Boris's Honda Accord.

I swallow hard, the ache in the back of my throat a very clear warning that this whole setup is bad with a capital B. Vigo doesn't just take quaint pre-dinner meetings with his rivals and their nieces.

Makes me wonder who else might be inside and didn't park in plain sight.

A shiver runs through me, and I adjust my glasses. I prefer to wear contacts, but the glasses give me a geeky appearance that is easily forgettable. Helps me stay invisible for the times when I need to do my job.

And by job, I mean, kill people for money.

I work for my uncle as an assassin for the Volkov Bratva. He took me and my brother, Maks, under his wing ten years ago when we escaped the Ukraine.

More specifically, when we escaped our parents' murderers in the Ukraine.

But devastation continued to follow us.

Six months ago, my brother Maks fell prey to the bratva life and was shot to death in a parking lot for being in the wrong place at the wrong time.

I've been picking up the pieces of my shattered existence ever since, but my heart?

No amount of the strongest Gorilla Glue can patch it back together.

My best friend is gone.

Forever.

And my time since then has been spent extinguishing the lives of scumbags like the guy who pulled the trigger.

I guess maybe in some sick and twisted way, it's been therapeutic.

But the only real way I can move on is if I find the person responsible and slit his throat from ear to ear. I keep thinking my Uncle Boris will uncover a name and an address and give me the order.

I've been holding on to that hope for a long time.

Maybe one day it'll become a reality.

My sneakers squeak against the polished floor as I venture slowly into the labyrinth underneath the restaurant. My hand is closed tight around my gun as I walk. Vigo runs an underground casino here, as well as his own sex trafficking ring. Girls are brought in under the guise that they're interviewing for waitressing positions, and he puts them to work so that his patrons can put in their bids.

It's disgusting, and I've toyed with the idea of killing him several times since the big boss, Ivan Volkov, brought him up the ranks, trampling my uncle in the process.

Vigo's fucked with my uncle plenty and deserves to have his lips pulled through his asshole.

But I stand down because Uncle Boris has been in enough trouble lately, most recently because of an altercation he had in Manhattan with the Villani crime family.

Vigo is one of the bratva's top earners and is considered untouchable.

At least, that's what he tells everyone.

I'd like to prove that claim fucking false.

I knock at a large red door at the end of the hallway, cringing at the loud crash that follows.

What in the *fuck*?

The door swings open, and I'm yanked inside of the room.

"You thought you could pull this little partnership off on your own, Boris? Huh? After you fucked up so badly last time?" Vigo bellows as one of his guys shoves me into a chair, holding me down as Vigo hurls another glass against a wall.

"You're fucking old, sloppy, and a goddamn pussy to boot!" He thunders as shards fly all over the floor.

"Leave him the fuck alone!" I screech, struggling against the grip of the men holding me down. I have no idea what partnership he's talking about, but I'm willing to bet he's pissed off and wants a piece of it because he's such a greedy fuck.

Vigo looks up, a murderous glimmer in his eyes as he walks toward me. "Anya, I'm so glad you could join us. I wanted you to hear why your brother walked into a trap that got him killed, and why your life is a fucking dead-end!" He smacks his hand hard against my uncle's head. "It's because of him. Your dear uncle who couldn't stop the shit storm from raining down on you both! You think he can protect you? You think he gives a flying fuck about you?" Vigo screams into my face. "Well, he doesn't. He only gives a shit about himself and about how much money he can fuck people out of. What kind of a future do you think you're gonna have with this guy dragging around behind you like a ball and chain?"

"He does plenty for this organization!" I shriek, thrusting my shoulder backward into the chest of one of the guys. "And you're a fucking scumbag pig! He didn't have anything to do with the hit on Maks!"

Vigo chuckles, but it's a low, ominous sound. He drags the back of his hand down the side of my face, and just as my leg is about to jut out and kick him in the balls, two of his guys shove me back down into the chair. He leans over me, his stank cigarette breath making my stomach roll. "You'd better remember who the boss is, sweetheart. Because I will tear the skin from your body before I drive an ice pick through your heart if you ever mouth off to me like that again."

"Goddamn you!" Uncle Boris yells, kicking over a table and pulling Vigo away from me. "Don't you fucking touch her!" He goes to grab the knife he's always packing around his right calf, but Vigo's guys are faster and they have their guns pointed at him before he can grip the blade.

Vigo closes his hand around my uncle's throat, pushing him backward against a wall. "The only reason why you're still alive is because Ivan hasn't given me the go-ahead to kill you," he seethes. "Family loyalty or some shit like that. But it'll only get you so far. I'm taking the reins, Boris, and nobody can stop me. You had so many chances to prove your strength, and nobody gives a fuck. Nobody is threatened. The Villani family kicked you out of Manhattan, do you remember? You went there with a kill order, to take out the people who murdered your nephew, and you couldn't even finish the job! Those greasy bastards cut you down in front of your guys and sent you back to Brooklyn with your dick in your hand. They may as well have sliced off your balls! You're pathetic! You couldn't even avenge his death!"

Vigo turns to me. "And you. You're his muscle. A fucking bitch! He needs you because he can't deliver! He uses you, Anya!"

"You drove him into the ground!" I screech. "You came in here and took everything that belonged to him!"

"If he was a real contender, he'd have stomped me into the fucking dirt when I showed up on the scene. But he didn't. He couldn't. And he never will because I am going to be king!" Vigo glowers at my uncle. "If my nephew had been slaughtered like that, I'd have made damn sure anyone who got in my way of revenge was next." He glares at me. "Now you know the truth!"

This time, I make it on top of him and spit in his eye before his guys pull me off.

He rakes his beady eyes over me and licks his chapped lips. "Play your cards right and you'll be my queen."

I throw up in my mouth before lunging for him a final time.

But Vigo just laughs as his guys drag me back by my long blonde hair. "Be very careful, Anya, or I'll sell *your* tight pussy to the highest bidder."

****

I pace around the kitchen while Uncle Boris stitches up one of the gashes he couldn't manage to escape at Tatiana. So many thoughts are racing through my mind right now. Vigo spat out a lot of information that I have yet to process.

And he was right. I will destroy anyone who had a hand in my brother's death.

Maybe my mind is rebelling because deep down, I'm afraid that it's all true. Why else would Uncle Boris keep it from me?

We're all we have left now that Maks is gone.

I scrub a hand down my face, taking a few deep breaths to calm the blood simmering in my veins.

I watch my uncle working the needle. My eyes narrow at his shaking hand. Nerve damage from a stab wound years back. "Here, let me help," I snap, reaching out for it.

He grunts and gives me a slight shove backward. "No!" he thunders. "I can do it myself!"

I should have known better. There's not much he despises more than being perceived as weak, and Vigo has made that his new reality.

"I hate that bastard," he mutters, taking a break to swig from the bottle of Stolichnaya vodka.

I tug at my ponytail, anger bubbling in my chest as Vigo's words pummel me like an all-consuming wave and I can't hold back the questions for a second longer. "Why didn't you tell me about the Villanis and their involvement in Maks's death? You knew how devastated I was, how badly I needed answers. How could you keep that from me? You lied to my face every single time I asked if you knew anything! He was my best friend!" The scream gets caught in my throat, tangled with a gaggle of tears.

He rubs a hand over his shiny bald head, letting out a deep sigh. "Things got out of control that night. The Villanis needed to pay for their part in your brother's murder. I went there for revenge, to make them suffer the way we had, but we were outnumbered. I didn't finish the job and they threatened me with a war if I didn't leave. I had no choice unless I wanted Volkov to put a bullet in my brain for opening the bratva up to a bloody battle with the Italians."

"You should have set fire to their territory before you left!" I screech, slamming my hand onto a table. "How could you just walk away, knowing what you did about them? And that you haven't gone back to finish the job?"

"Because I knew it was only a matter of time before we'd get our chance to make them feel our pain," he hisses through gritted teeth. With a harsh glare, he pins me to my spot. "We have to be smart and do things the right way to get the revenge we both want. And what did I tell you about questioning me, Anya?" He shoves back the chair and gets up from the table, his blue eyes darkening. He stomps toward me with his wound half-stitched and murder in his gaze. "I gave up a lot for you and Maks," he growls. "For ten fucking years, I watched over you and trained you to become the person you need to be in order to survive this life! And I never got anything in return! Don't you ever challenge me!"

I stare at him, the words playing on my lips...the same words that run through my head most times we talk business since we really don't talk about much else. "What about what I've done for you? I never wanted this life! You turned me into this person! I have so much blood on my hands, I can never wash them clean!"

I was happy in the Ukraine with my parents and my brother and my school friends and my warm and safe home.

But someone else decided that my life was no longer mine.

"You did it to survive, because it was the only way to survive. Maks was weak. Do you want to end up like him, too?"

"How can you say that?" I yell. "He was your family! He did everything you asked!"

"Not everything," Uncle Boris grumbles. "He didn't listen to me that night, and for a lot of nights before it. You work for me, and part of your job is to take orders," he snarls, so close to me I can smell the stale alcohol on his breath. "He didn't do his fucking job."

The words hit me in the chest like a sledgehammer, knocking the wind clear out of my lungs.

He is a fucking insufferable asshole sometimes.

Okay, most times.

But the reality is that now I have nobody except my unhinged and vodka-soaked uncle, so I cling to this dysfunctional relationship, looking for any crumbs he's willing to drop for me. And he knows it, too.

I sink into a chair, covering my face with my hands. "How am I supposed to trust you when you keep so much from me? How can I not question you?" I ask. "I'm always running in blindly to save you without any knowledge of why you were attacked in the first place!"

"I give you the information you need when you need it in order to survive, Anya," he says, averting his gaze. "When you know too much, you take rash actions that can be dangerous. And deadly."

I tap my fingernails on the tabletop, avoiding his hard stare because I don't want to see the infuriated expression on his face when I ask my next question. But I can't sit on it any longer. If I don't have trust...well, shit. Then we really don't have anything at all. *I* don't have anything at all. And that's something I just can't accept. I don't want to know that I'm really all alone in this toxic world. "Did you tell me the truth, Uncle? About Maks? And the Villanis? Or was Vigo right?"

I look up, hesitant to see his face because I'm afraid to see something I'm just not prepared to accept.

"Of course I told you the truth," he says in his gruff voice. "And I didn't tell you about the Villanis because I was embarrassed. Like Vigo said, they chased us out of there, and because I was worried about my own ass, I left without avenging Maks's murder. I didn't finish the job I went there to do." His forehead creases. "And that bastard Vigo just loves to tell the story. It's bad enough he's taken over my role as *brigadier* in the bratva."

"But you said you had a plan," I say slowly. "Maybe we can fix this and change the way Volkov sees you."

"I waited for months to come up with it." His eyes glaze over, his expression pinched. "And now that I have one, the Villanis will be assaulted and decimated by the pain we've suffered, trust me."

"Are you going to tell me about this grand plan?" I ask.

He shakes his head. "Not yet. I need to work out a few last details. And Vigo..." His lips curl upward into a menacing smirk.

"What about him?" I ask.

"Before we move forward with the arrangement, you're going to clear a path for us using your very special talents."

I rub my hands together, a smile spreading across my face. "Does that mean what I hope it means, Uncle?"

He gives a quick nod. "You will handle Vigo for us."

"But what will Ivan Volkov say? He's never going to be okay with anyone taking out his number one."

"Fuck him," Uncle Boris grunts, bristling as he continues to stitch the wound. "If Volkov wants his cut of what I'm gonna offer, he'll have no choice but to deal with it. It's time for *me* to take over as Ivan's fucking golden boy. And you're gonna help me do it."

ANYA

TWO WEEKS LATER

"Enough of the Little Miss Innocent bullshit, sweetheart. This dick ain't gonna suck itself."

I force a smile, even though I'm practically choking on bile at the thought.

Still, my disguise is perfect.

He has no clue who I really am.

Vigo Kosolov reaches out and grabs one of my boobs, which is dangerously close to the neckline of my low-cut dress. I level him with a stare as he fondles it with the grasp of a man who never bothered to learn how to properly pleasure a woman.

Well, fuck him.

Looks like I'm about to do the entire female population a favor.

But there's no way on this fucking planet that I'm serving *him*.

Vigo is absolutely one of the most vile men I've ever encountered. He sticks his dick into anything with legs, and preferably only those below the age of twenty. He takes advantage of young girls, addicts them to drugs, and then pimps them out for cash... cash he can pump into his underground casino. The illicit business he's built in Brooklyn has made him wads of money.

It's why the big boss, Ivan Volkov, keeps him in power.

And I'm so excited to finally knock him off this throne.

I grit my teeth, the tense conversation I had with my uncle a couple of weeks ago looping through my mind. We'd just gotten home from that standoff with Vigo, and all of the memories of that horrific night had bubbled to the surface again, threatening to spew out at any given second.

The night my brother died.

The night he was *murdered*.

I tuck a strand of dark brown hair behind my ear, gripping his legs and pushing them open in a way that has him frothing at the mouth. He has no idea who I am under the wig, the makeup, and the clothes.

He will soon enough.

Before the light goes out in his eyes, I want him to know who's responsible.

I inch closer to his stubby cock, which is barely hard since he's high as a kite on drugs...drugs that don't belong to him.

Drugs he stole.

Drugs he's been stealing for a while.

The bastard is selling them, too, and skimming the profits. And Volkov has no idea he's being robbed blind.

But the big reason why I'm here tonight isn't to make him pay for screwing over his boss and the bratva.

It's to make sure my uncle has a clear path to execute his master plan, the details of which are still under lock and key. I have to trust that he will tell me everything I need to know when the time comes. Blind faith sucks, but it's all I have right now.

The first part of the plan...*my* part...is to make sure Vigo gets what's coming to him, that the slimy, thieving bastard is exterminated.

Permanently.

And I'm perfectly positioned to slaughter.

I run my fingernails down the front of his beefy chest, trying not to gag as he thrusts his hips toward me. A quick glance confirms that my lips will not come anywhere near that shriveled up, old ass dick.

My knife, on the other hand, will definitely make an impact.

Talk about him getting the biggest possible bang for his buck.

Ha! Pun *so* intended.

I posed as a hooker to get in here since I can't take a chance that someone will recognize my face. This hits way too close to home, and if I'm spotted, it will bring hellfire to my doorstep.

I've already lost too much.

I won't risk my uncle's life.

And I also can't take a chance of being outed.

"Suck it, bitch. I don't got all night to play cat and mouse with you."

"Oh yeah?" I say in a sultry voice, sliding closer. "What else do you have to do tonight? I thought for sure you'd only be doing *me*."

I knew just where to go and how to dress to make sure he picked me out of the crowd of girls just waiting for a chance to get fingered by the legendary Russian gangster.

They don't realize I'm about to do them a huge favor.

"You're a hot piece of ass, but I got business to take care of," he grunts, grabbing me by the back of my head and forcing my face between his thighs.

I yelp at the sudden force, and a flutter of panic explodes in my belly when I realize my wig has slipped from its pinned position and is now hanging off the side of my head.

Dammit.

I wasn't planning to do this just yet, but...oh well.

Plans change.

More specifically, plans go up in fucking smoke with the snap of a finger, just like everything else that's good and perfect.

And just like that, realization seeps into his pock-marked face.

"Anya," he growls, clutching the armrests and pushing his body to an upright position. "What the fuck do you think you're doing here? Did your fucking pathetic uncle send you here?" He reaches out and grabs me by the throat. "Or are you just hard up for cash, because nobody wants to work with either of you?" He pulls me closer, hissing right into my face. "You know your uncle is a fucking has-been. It's just a matter of time before someone drives an ice pick into his heart and tosses his ancient body into the New York Harbor. If you need money, I can take care of you. I got a lot of clients who'd pay plenty for a taste of that pussy if you wanna work for me. It's the only way for you to get anywhere in this life," he grunts, grabbing my boob and squeezing it hard.

Okay, really? Is he trying to milk a goddamn cow right now?

I force a seductive smile, ignoring the fact that he's got his grubby hands on me. He'll never get a chance to put them *in* me, that's for damn sure.

"Tell me about how you can take care of me," I murmur, fluttering my eyelashes at him. "How much can I make?"

He chuckles. "Depends. How tight is that pussy?"

I avert my eyes, trying like hell to appear demure when really I want to hurl all over him.

He lets the wig fall to the floor and grips the back of my head, pulling me toward him. "You a virgin?" he hisses.

"Y-yes!" I yelp as he fists my real hair harder.

Another sinister laugh escapes from his lips. "Well, then, I'm gonna have to give it a test run to make sure you know what you're doing. I can't charge top dollar for a bitch who doesn't know how to fuck."

The knife strapped to my upper thigh is pressed tight against my skin, my fingers itching to grab it and plunge it into his chest.

But first...

"I can do whatever you want."

"Oh yeah," he mutters. "You fucking will. Now start by taking my cock in your mouth, or I'll kill you and your uncle!" When he swings the palm of his hand against the side of my face, I lose my balance, cursing myself for not seeing that coming. The side of my face is on fire from where one of his ridiculously gaudy rings catches on my cheekbone.

Oh, he did *not* just do that!

I grit my teeth and he smiles, his yellowed, gapped teeth flashing in the dim light of the room we're in.

"How does it work?" I gasp in a desperate voice, ignoring that he just bitch-slapped me. "You're right! We're broke! Vigo, please, I really need the money, so what would I have to do?"

Vigo's smile widens. "I like a girl who's hopeless. Makes me wanna do things to her, things no decent woman would ever allow, but because she needs me to save her, she'll let me. Just thinking about it makes my dick drip." He snickers. "Maybe I'll invite your pathetic uncle to come and watch me fuck his niece. Just knowing you came to me because he couldn't get you what you need…I fucking love it."

Uncle Boris is a lot of things, but he saved my brother and me from our own personal hell. Yeah, my life here in Brooklyn is far from glamorous, but it's better than being dead.

Most days, anyway.

There are always exceptions.

Like the day I have to swallow a cock like Vigo's.

"He is over, Anya. The Italians fucked him over and humiliated him. Volkov almost had him killed after starting shit with the Villanis over your brother. And I know he's suffering because he doesn't have a pot to piss in now. He's hurting and he's taking you down in flames with him." Vigo settles back against the chair. "But I can fix all that. For *you*."

I swallow hard. Yes, my uncle made a dumbass move by going after the Villani family and then walking away. Yes, we've been struggling to make ends meet for far too long. And yes, I'm here tonight to help him get back in good with Volkov so he can start getting the big jobs again.

Volkov has two loves — power and money.

And I'm the only one who can help fix my uncle's shitty situation and get Volkov more of what he wants.

It's all part of this secret fucking 'plan'.

I allow the corners of my lips to curl upward as I grip Vigo's cock, running my hands up and down the shaft. My stomach roils, but I do it because I owe my uncle.

God, I owe him so much...

He's the only family I have left.

I need to do this.

Vigo will pay for everything he's taken from us.

It's my personal mission to make sure everybody suffers that fate they deserve, and my list of targets is *long*.

But first thing's first.

This piece of shit has to go.

"There's something I'd like to do...for *you*," I say. "To thank you for helping me...help my uncle." And with my free hand, I grab the blade from the Velcro holding it to my upper thigh and drive it into his chest. The shocked expression on his face assaults my heart for a split second, the unwelcome sensation all too familiar to me every time I do a hit.

The excruciating memories always bubble up to the surface right about now, when I'm watching the life drain from the eyes of my kill. It's then when I wonder if my parents' killers saw the same horrified looks the second they took those machetes to their throats.

Did they feel anything? Or was it all just business to them?

Because even though Vigo is the dredge-of-the-earth kind of bastard who had to be punished, I still feel a twinge of remorse staring down at him.

My parents were good people. They were sweet, loving, and kind; the best parents I could ever ask for.

Did their killers feel that same twinge? Did they have any remorse for stealing them away from me and my brother?

Or was it just business?

Because, to me, it's never just business.

It's always personal.

Chapter One
DANTE

"Something is up with Conor. I just don't know what the hell it is," my friend Patrick Mulligan mutters as we walk down Brighton 6th Street in Brighton Beach toward our destination.

I rub the back of my neck, thinking of the flight I have back to Las Vegas tomorrow morning and how I'd really like to get at least an hour of sleep before I have to drag myself out of the hotel to head for the airport.

But, duty calls.

I came out to New York City for a few days at my brother Matteo's request to do a little investigation. And to be honest, I needed the break. I've been out in Vegas for months now as my niece and sister-in-law's personal bodyguard. Matteo has been focused on all of the threats to our family that have surfaced over the past couple of years, and since I'm paid very well to eliminate them, he asked me to provide my own brand of security for his family.

And I've been a good soldier because family comes before everything. There's nothing I wouldn't do to protect them.

But I'm getting damn tired of my life out there in the sweltering desert heat.

There's no action, no suspense, and definitely no sniper rifles in my midst.

Christ, I haven't even spotted anyone cheating in our casino.

At least then I'd have the chance to smash in some skulls.

But my life has become as stagnant as the thick and heavy air out there.

I miss the thrill of the hunt and with each passing, boring-as-fuck day, I'm losing my edge.

So I was happy to hop a flight out here to stalk my family's latest threat.

Conor Mulligan.

But he's not just any enemy.

He's the worst type — a fucking lunatic with a serious grudge and a taste for bloodlust.

He also happens to be my sister-in-law Heaven's estranged and seriously disturbed brother.

After being forced to marry my oldest brother, Matteo, Heaven's relationship with her family pretty much went to shit. Her father is a controlling, sexist asshole, and her brother Conor snagged her spot as underboss of the Mulligan family only because he's got a dick.

I look up at the nondescript sign next to the door to the restaurant and nightclub. If you look fast, you'd completely miss it.

Tatiana.

This is it.

I did my own investigating when Patrick gave me the name of the place Conor was planning to visit tonight and found out there's an underground casino in the hidden lower level of the place run by the Russian bratva *brigadier*, Vigo Kosolov. He oversees an elite group of soldiers and runs his businesses on behalf of Ivan Volkov. Volkov is the *pakhan*...the boss of this bratva. But casinos aren't Vigo's real game. His big businesses are drugs and prostitution, and he uses the girls to mule his product. He sends them to nightclubs all over the tri-state area to distribute them.

Working with the Mulligan family wouldn't do anything for Vigo.

They have nothing to offer him. They don't deal in pussy, and they've gotten burned by one of the biggest cartels in the area.

They're the ones who really need the strong backing.

But why keep the meeting with Vigo a secret from everyone, Conor? What the hell are you really up to?

Vigo is a dangerous motherfucker, too. He'll set fire to your life if you cross him.

Your life and the lives of everyone you love.

And Conor doesn't have a great track record of playing nice in the sandbox, which means anyone associated with him has their necks on the chopping block.

One wrong move and the machetes will fly.

And because I like my head attached to my body, I agreed to check things out before going to Conor and putting him through a brick wall.

"Tell me again what you heard, Patty," I mutter as we walk inside of the restaurant. Red floods my vision. The walls, floors, and much of the décor have red tones and gold accents. The lights are dim enough that you can't exactly make out faces, which is very good for us since we both play roles that require us to fly under the radar.

I am paid very well to take care of "problems."

And part of that job description is to be invisible.

Unfortunately for us, Patrick is a little more well-known in the city, especially since he looks like the rest of the Mulligan brothers. But he refused to let me go in alone. If Conor is pulling something with the Russians, he wants to see it for himself.

Patrick's jaw tightens as he takes in the scene. The bar is packed and loud, the restaurant overflowing with patrons.

But we're not here for food or drink.

What we're interested in is what happens beneath all of this drunken chaos.

I lead the way to the bar where we find a spot on one end. The bartender is a tall blonde with clear blue eyes and deep red lips. She saunters toward us, and I order two double shots of Stolichnaya vodka on the rocks.

Patrick grins at her and I roll my eyes once she walks away. "Dude, we're not picking up tonight."

"Sorry," he says with a sheepish smile. "Couldn't help myself."

"Well, try," I grumble, rubbing the back of my neck. "Now let's go through it all one more time."

"Like I told you, he didn't tell me anything direct. Shit, he barely talks to me at all anymore because he knows I report everything back to Heaven, and that pisses him off to no end."

"So who knows?"

"Quinn," he says, nodding at the bartender when she places our shot glasses on the bar.

"He overheard Conor on the phone in his office, talking about a new business opportunity in this area. He'd just gotten there for a meeting, so he hung around outside the office to catch any bits of information since Conor never mentioned Brooklyn, or the Russians, to any of them. He heard the names Tatiana and Vigo and today's date. Then when the call ended, he waited a few minutes and went inside. He asked some vague questions, just to see if Conor would give anything. He didn't, so Quinn got suspicious and came to me."

"He was smart to do that. The last thing he should have done was to tip Conor off." I rub the back of my neck. "Vigo Kosolov is the right hand to Ivan Volkov. I'd bet my left nut that's the Vigo he was talking to. Conor is too much of an egotistical prick to talk to anyone low level." But that connection has warning bells going off in my mind. I'd heard that the Russian bratva is trying to edge into Manhattan, and Matteo doesn't want them closing in on our territory, especially since there's some bad blood between us. My brother Roman and I had an altercation with some soldiers from the Volkov Bratva months ago, and while we haven't gotten caught in each others' crosshairs since then, this hits a little too close to home.

It could just be Conor building himself up, looking for quick cash opportunities with new partners whom he hasn't yet fucked over.

Or it could be something else.

Either way, I don't want any of his dealings to touch my family.

I'll fucking kill him if his poison seeps into anything of ours.

That's why I'm here, to make sure that doesn't happen.

And by that, I mean presenting Vigo with a very clear picture of what will happen to him if he tries to invade the empire we've built. A little charge zips through me when I think of pulling the trigger of my Glock 19...

It's been too fucking long.

"Yeah, but then why not tell us? Why hide it?" Patrick asks.

"Well, that's what we're gonna find out, yeah?" I toss back my shot and slam the glass on the table. The bartender catches my eye and walks back over, with a seductive swing of her hips. She leans over onto the bar, her tits practically spilling out of her tiny top. "What else can I get you gentlemen tonight?"

I run a hand through my longish hair and lean toward her. "We're looking for a seat at the chef's table," I murmur. "Can you get us in?"

Her eyes sweep over us both, and a slow smile lifts her lips. "Let me see if there's space." She backs away and picks up a phone hidden behind the alcohol bottles, speaking into it as her eyes travel back toward us.

"I didn't think we were gonna eat, Dante," Patrick mutters. "I figured we were gonna do a little recon."

"Relax," I mumble. "And finish your shot."

The bartender comes back. "They're holding a spot for you downstairs." She nods toward the far right corner of the place. "There is a staircase beyond a black and gold door down that hallway. It will lead you to the private dining area."

I flash a grin and drop a hundred-dollar bill onto the bar. "Thanks."

"If you want to come back for a nightcap..." She grins at me. "I get off at two."

Ah, fuck it. Who needs sleep?

I wink at her and give a small nod.

Patrick grumbles the entire way to the back of the restaurant. "I thought you said no hooking up tonight. And what the hell are we doing at the chef's table? I didn't come here to eat! I came here for fucking answers!"

I grab his arm and pull him toward me once we're out of sight. "There *is* no goddamn chef's table," I hiss at him. "It's an underground casino, for fuck's sake. You have to ask for the chef's table to get entrance." I shake my head. "Jesus, Patty."

He lets out a snort. "Look, I don't do all of the business-y shit for my family. I'm a fixer, not a fucking secretary."

"Well, if you wanna save your ass and your family's livelihood from one of Conor's fuck-ups, you'd better start paying attention. Take some notes, bro." I pull open the black and gold door and step onto the landing, the din of voices drifting up from the lower level.

I usually work alone, so having Patrick dragging behind me is like having a ball and chain clanging against the floor announcing my arrival.

It's hard to be invisible when you have a six-foot-six, blue-eyed blond guy who looks like a young Brad Pitt bringing up the rear.

I square my shoulders and walk down the stairs. Wall sconces line the hallway, giving off a golden glow to the surrounding deep burgundy décor. The floors are black marble, our shoes clicking along the shiny polished surface as we approach the main room.

"I was able to get my hands on a floor plan of the place," I hiss over my shoulder at Patrick. "Vigo should be here tonight. He only shows up one night a week, usually Wednesdays. But my sources tell me he switched things up tonight."

"So that means he might have switched things up to meet with Conor," Patrick mutters as we enter the large space. There are dice tables lining the perimeter of the room, blackjack tables in the center. Ornate bars are set up at each corner, and scantily-clad cocktail waitresses are carrying trays of drinks to the crowds of men in their midst.

"Exactly." My eyes sweep the entire room, from the crystal chandeliers hanging from the ceiling, to every possible exit I can make out. I'm not planning on having to make a fast getaway, but in my line of work, you have to be prepared for anything.

"Hey, did Conor say anything about a—?"

I don't even get a chance to finish my question before the barrel of a gun presses into my back, accompanied by a voice that slithers over my skin like a snake. "Don't fucking move. Don't fucking speak. Just fucking *walk*."

A quick glance to my right confirms that Patrick is also being discreetly shoved toward a darkened doorway just outside of the main gaming room. I don't know who these guys are or what they want with us, but I don't argue.

I never argue.

I only ever annihilate.

Once we're out of the view of gamblers, the short, stout guy who stuck his gun into my spine shoves me against a wall, and the other guy throws Patrick right next to me. "So, Mulligan," one of them says in a thick Russian accent. "Vigo will be very happy to see you here. He expects full repayment on the debt your brother Conor owes."

"I don't know anything about a fucking debt," Patrick grunts, struggling against the guy who has his gun pointed right at his throat. "We came here to play."

"Nobody just comes here to *play*," the guy in front of me hisses. "You're here with an agenda, just like everyone else. You know what's on our agenda? Taking your money and then leaving you for dead." He narrows his watery blue eyes, his fat face twisted into a grimace. "Nobody fucks with Vigo, do you understand?"

I can't even start to process all of this shit, but one thing is clear. Conor Mulligan is on Vigo's hit list. He's not looking to partner with them. I should have known he'd have never been able to pull off a business arrangement with the Russians. He's probably up to his eyeballs in debt because he's a gambling addict.

And now that there's a debt to pay, someone is gonna have to fork over the cash. These people won't rest until they get their money, that's for shit sure.

Conor is a selfish, self-centered prick!

I should find him and put a bullet in his head myself.

Christ, I'd do it very happily, too.

Looks like Vigo and I need to have a little conversation, the kind where he assures me Conor's dealings won't blow back on my family and that I don't put a bullet between his eyes.

And there's no way I'm gonna get dragged into his lair like fucking cattle going to slaughter. I'm walking in there on my own two feet.

I don't waste a single second. I drive my elbow into the throat of the guy in front of me and my knee into his groin, sending him crashing to the floor. Then, I swivel around, and with a palm heel strike to the nose of Patrick's assailant, send him flying backward against a wall.

I pull out my gun and fire off two shots to the head of each one of them.

Thank fuck for silencers.

Patrick smirks at me. "You can never just go out, can you?"

I avoid his question and ask one of my own. "Why is it that whenever your family is involved, I end up with blood on my hands?" I grunt. "Come on. Let's find Vigo and figure out what the hell is going on."

"Are you nuts?" he asks. "If *these* guys recognized me, there will be more on the lookout. Are we just supposed to kill everyone who gets in our way?"

I level him with a stare. "That *is* my MO. You got an issue with that?"

He shakes his head. "Jesus Christ..."

"What's the matter? You too pretty to get dirty?" I lift an eyebrow. Patrick isn't known for being the most prepared gangster on the planet. Maybe that's why he decided to go the *GQ* path. He can fire a gun, but isn't great with hitting his targets. I mean, for fuck's sake, he and Heaven once got jumped right next to his car in a park one morning after a run. Broad fucking daylight and he completely missed the ambush.

And this is exactly why I prefer to work alone.

But he's here so he's in this, too.

Besides, it's his fucknut brother who put us on Vigo's radar in the first place.

Patrick clenches his jaw. "Fine. Let's go."

I creep down the darkened hallway, hoping like hell we'll find who we're looking for before I have to set fire to the place with my gun.

"What in the fuck has Conor gotten us into this time? And why the hell are we going to find Vigo, by the way? If Conor really did screw him over, he's not gonna be very welcoming," Patrick mutters as he follows close behind me. "Besides, Conor isn't supposed to find out that I know anything about him being involved with Vigo. He'll fucking roast me if Vigo tells him we showed up here."

"Relax," I grunt. "I've got a plan." Which, if translated, actually means I have no plan at all.

I didn't come here tonight expecting to find out that Conor stiffed Vigo. I just figured Conor was running some scam with him, a scam I'd have to expose for all of our safety.

But if Vigo has it out for Conor, then he definitely has it out for the rest of the Mulligans, and that includes Heaven and my family, by association.

It's only a matter of time before he launches an attack against us all, and while I want to see Conor go down in flames, it's my job to worry about everyone else.

Although, I'm hoping we can avoid the hellfire. If this is just about money, let the Mulligans pay him back.

If it's just about money, that is.

My reconnaissance activities usually involve some sort of torture techniques. Cutting throats, tongues, cocks, fingers — I do whatever I need to get whatever I need.

And I'll make sure Conor never knows we were here. That'll keep Patrick from getting his ass chewed out...or worse.

We creep farther down the hall and a door suddenly swings open to reveal a young, topless girl, shaking uncontrollably. A thin stream of blood trickles out of the corner of her mouth, her blue eyes wide with fear.

Some guy inside of the room growls at her in Russian, but she makes no move other than to shake her head. She is yanked backward into the room, a thick hand slapped over her mouth before she can let out a scream.

"Fuck," I mutter. What in the fuck else do they have going on in this place? That girl has to be fifteen, for Christ's sake! "I'm going in."

"Dante, don't forget why we're here. This isn't about starting a war with the Volkov Bratva!" Patrick hisses, pulling me backward.

I shake off his hand, glaring at him over my shoulder. "I didn't start this fucking war, Patty, but now that I'm here, I'm gonna make sure these assholes don't take one single prisoner on my watch."

Patrick rolls his eyes, throwing his hands into the air. "Fine! Go!"

I kick in the door to find the beefy Russian straddling the girl. She struggles against his massive body, his hand still cemented to her mouth.

"Hey, asshole," I bark, coming up behind him, my gun pointed at the back of his head. "Get off the girl now or I blow a hole through your fucking skull."

The man turns slowly with a sick grin on his face. "Pull the trigger, bitch." His words are heavily accented and he doesn't make a move to get off of her.

"Dante," Patrick mumbles. " I hear footsteps. Plug his ass and let's move!"

I keep the gun pointed at the fat Russian. "Get the fuck away from her and I'll let you live."

"Fuck you, pussy. You won't shoot me. If you wanted me dead, I'd already be—"

Pop!

"Yep, you're right," I say as he tumbles off of her, landing on the floor like a bag of cement. "Dead."

I hold out a hand to the girl, pulling her up. I slip off my jacket and toss it at her. "Do you speak English?" I say.

She nods, her skin ghostly white. "Yes," she whispers.

"Get out of here now. There's a staircase at the end of the hall. Take it upstairs to the restaurant and disappear. Don't look back." I grip her shoulders. "Forget you were ever here and that you saw any of this."

She nods again, her teeth chattering as she puts on the jacket and runs out the door. I don't have time to make sure she gets to the stairs. I guess I'll find out when we get there ourselves.

After we handle Vigo.

"Okay, Good Samaritan, now what? Who do we take care of first?" Patrick grimaces as several pairs of footsteps thump along the floor. Shit. None of this has gone the way I planned. We've wandered into some kind of elaborate labyrinth that is separated from the casino, and right now, our escape route is blocked. I shove Patrick aside and crouch low, pointing my gun in the direction of the approaching sounds. As soon as they appear, I fire off some shots. Bodies land in a heap in the middle of the floor and I jump over them, running down the hall with Patrick huffing behind me. "You need to get in some more cardio, man, and I don't mean the kind that involves hooking up with random women," I grumble as I stop next to another closed door, grasping the knob and pushing open the door. I hope this is it. Vigo has plenty of security hawking the casino floor, and if any of those guys wander back here, we'll be outnumbered.

I twist the doorknob, shocked to find out it opens without me being forced to kick it in, but thankful because I'm really trying to limit the noise. I walk inside the darkened room blinking fast as I process the bloody scene splashed in front of my eyes. Vigo Kosolov is on the floor, face up, with a knife sticking out of his throat. "Looks like someone beat me to the punch," I mutter as Patrick inches into the room behind me.

"Beat *you*?" he says, quirking an eyebrow. "You mean us, right?"

I scrub a hand down the front of my face. "Don't flatter yourself, Patty."

"So now what?" he asks, narrowing his eyes at Vigo's blade-torn neck.

"We get the fuck out of here."

"Great, how the fuck is Conor not gonna be fingered for this, especially if he's already on Vigo's shit list?" Patty groans.

I hear a soft whimper from a corner and I step farther into the room, peering into the shadows. "Who the fuck is there?" I growl, pointing my gun into the empty space where the sound pricked my ears.

"P-Please," a heavy female Russian accent responds in a quivering voice. "Don't hurt me. I am innocent! I need help!"

I toss a glance at Patrick over my shoulder. "Cover me," I mouth to him before creeping closer to the voice.

"Come out," I say gruffly. "Or I start shooting."

A rustling sound follows as the shadow morphs into a body...a fucking incredible one, not that I'm paying close attention to that fact. We're on borrowed time, and who knows for how long it's gonna last?

A girl who looks to be in her early twenties inches toward me, teetering on heels she probably has no business even wearing. My throat tightens. Is she one of Vigo's girls? An innocent victim whose life he stole away?

He's lucky he's dead already.

"Please help me get out of here," she cries. "He almost...he started to..." She breaks down again, choking on a sob as she recounts her story. "He told me I'd have a good job and make lots of money, but then...then..." She starts to sink back onto the floor again, but the clock is ticking and our window is closing fast.

I hold out a hand to her, and she steps over his body, her shoulders quaking as the tears stream down her face once again. Her eyeliner is smudged under her brown eyes and her dark hair is matted to her face.

But she's alive.

Still, even though she looks like a hot mess right now, I don't lower the gun. The reality is she probably just narrowly escaped being sold into some sex trafficking ring, but I don't like to take unnecessary chances.

"Put up your hands," I say as she moves closer to me.

She recoils. "I just told you that I'm—"

"Yeah, innocent. I heard you the first time. Put up your hands. I don't have all night, sweetheart."

The girl slowly puts up her hands, her confused gaze traveling from me to Patrick and then back again.

So I quickly frisk her, ignoring the way her curves feel under the pads of my fingertips because above all else. I'm a goddamn hitman. Eliminating risk is a big part of my job, and until I can prove otherwise, that's exactly what she is.

Hot as fuck, but still a risk.

Once my hands have completed their task and no weapons are found, I grasp her hand and pull her close. "I don't know who you are, but if you wanna live, you'll keep quiet and run fast. Got it?"

"You can help me get out of here?" Tears pool in her eyes, but there is a flicker of hope in the depths. "You can save me?"

I nod, pulling her close, her fresh floral scent wafting under my nostrils. I drink it in, unable to help myself, and for a split second it clouds my mind.

I grit my teeth. Assassins don't get sidetracked by perfume, dammit!

I nod toward Patrick. "Go. I've got your back. We have to get the hell outta here before someone wanders back here to find Vigo."

"Wait, I need my bag!" She grabs a small, beaded handbag and I grab her wrist, dragging her out of the office. I don't bother to check it. Any good assassin would have a weapon on her person. You never know when your purse might get lost or stolen or confiscated by an enemy.

We tear down the hallway, searching for the entrance to the casino floor since that's where the staircase is located. I pull the girl behind me, checking constantly to make sure there is nobody skulking around behind us, ready to take us out.

Patrick rounds a corner and a shot explodes into the air. I back the girl against the wall, covering her with my body as Patrick fires off a couple of retaliatory shots. A loud thud confirms that he hit something, which is good. Of course, it would be better if there was only one person shooting at us.

I clench the gun in my hand, sliding against the wall to shield the girl when another shot sails past me and lodges itself into the wall. I twist around and fire two shots into the head of the guy who crept up behind us. I throw open the door to the staircase and shove the girl in front of me. She clambers up the steps, practically tripping over her feet to escape the dungeon where she'd been trapped only minutes earlier.

"Patty!" I hiss. "Now!"

He darts across the hallway and disappears into the stairwell with me right behind him.

Jesus Christ, what in the hell did we walk into and manage to escape?

Vigo Kosolov is dead.

The powerful Russian mafia *brigadier* is lying on the floor with a knife sticking out of his throat.

I should feel good about the fact that the piece of shit is in hell where he belongs.

But there are too many nagging questions eating away at my brain right now to feel like we dodged a bullet.

And the biggest one is poured into a tight red dress a few steps ahead of me.

Chapter Two
ANYA

I scramble up the stairs headed toward the restaurant, not bothering to look back at the two guys who pulled me out of that room.

I don't need them.

I'm perfectly capable of executing my own escape plan.

I didn't intend to cower in a corner of that room like some panicked little bitch who'd just witnessed a murder, but in the end, it worked out in my favor.

An easy out if someone happened to come into the room to check on things. They'd have never expected me to jump out and snap their neck, which I most certainly would have done.

It was a smart move to leave my knife planted in Vigo's throat... once I wiped off the fingerprints. It gives the perception that I am helpless, sans weapon.

I'm *not*.

Besides, you just never know when you're going to be frisked by a gorgeous yet mysterious stranger with a gun.

I know from past experience that Tatiana has a hidden exit that doesn't require you to go through the restaurant. It's usually locked, but tonight I happen to have stolen the key from Vigo's jacket after butchering him. I tucked it into my bra for safekeeping.

When I get to the top of the stairs, I swivel around, popping my eyes open wide like a deer in headlights, really playing up the role of damsel in distress. The guys totally eat it up and they flank me on both sides as we enter the back of the restaurant. The music from the lounge pulsates, vibrations rippling through me as I stand in the center of them, quivering with 'fear'.

The guy who frisked me murmurs something against my hair, and his warm breath against my cheek makes the hairs on the back of my neck prickle.

He knows about the other exit, too.

"I-I have a key," I whisper, my words still heavily accented. "It fell out of his pocket and I grabbed it. Maybe we should try it?" I've been here in Brooklyn for ten years and worked tirelessly to drop my accent. It just helps me blend better and people don't readily assume I fled the Ukraine because some psychopaths were on the hunt to destroy my family. But it comes in handy during times like these when I'm playing a part.

And doing a damn good job, if I say so myself.

The guy looks at me, his thick eyebrows knitting together. We hurry toward the exit door and I pull the key out of my bra, making sure my hand quivers just enough to be believable. It takes me a few seconds to stick it in the lock, but that's all part of the ruse. Finally, it slides in and I twist the handle.

I rub my hands down the sides of my arms once we're outside.

I need to ditch these guys fast and strip out of this costume.

I've already been spotted in the casino with Vigo tonight, so shedding this getup is the only way I can fly under the radar and avoid potential retaliation by any of his allies who might be watching.

But I can't very well do it here on the street.

My eyes scout the desolate alleyway right next to the restaurant. If they would just piss off, I could go behind one of the dumpsters and do my quick change.

But the shorter, darker guy grabs my arm and pulls me toward the street. "Let's go have a drink," he mutters. "I'm sure you can use one."

"No, no," I say, holding up my hands in protest. "Please, I just want to go home. Thank you for saving me, but—"

He stops, his deep blue eyes narrowing. "It wasn't a question."

"But I'm not thirsty," I say weakly.

"I'm not used to women turning me down." A small smile quirks at his lips, but there's something behind it. Suspicion, maybe. This isn't a social call. For fuck's sake, he and his friend came barreling into Vigo's office toting Glocks. He's not just trying to be nice and helpful, and that knowledge has my skin crawling. "You're taking a sledgehammer to my self-esteem right now."

I highly doubt *that*.

His fingers dig into my arms, gripping me tighter. "Don't walk away. I'm the kind of guy who will be able to find you no matter where you run off to."

Shit.

Looks like I need a Plan B.

Between them, they're a combined total of about four-hundred pounds of cut muscle *and* they have guns.

I have some pretty lethal moves, but they'd draw too much attention to me out here in the open.

So I expel a sigh and nod.

I guess it's story time.

They keep me positioned in the middle as we walk down the street toward the strip of bars in the next block. It's unusually quiet tonight, and I was hoping to get in, carry out the hit, get out, and be in bed before eleven. Who the hell knew my plans would get thwarted by these two?

I bet any other girl on the planet would be thanking her lucky stars for a chance to be sandwiched between them, but as far as I'm concerned, they're just super-hot obstacles I need to kick out of my path.

The taller one pulls open the door to the first place we come to called Velvet Lounge and I let out a shallow breath. Good fucking pick, guys. It's dark and private, which is a very good thing for me, especially in terms of a quick exit.

My throat tightens as I step inside the door.

They're not letting me go.

If I were them, I'd keep me close, too.

They obviously had business to take up with Vigo, so naturally, they'll want to know who butchered him. And I can't very well tell them the truth, that tonight was a setup to lure Vigo to Tatiana so a killer queen could go in and slay the bastard.

I have to focus on getting the hell out of here and disappearing into the night, leaving their questions hanging in the air.

This girl, this wig, this dress...none of it can exist outside of Velvet Lounge.

And if I want to stay alive, I need to bury it all immediately, if not sooner.

Lucky for me, I have the perfect out. I just need to get to the ladies' room.

I clutch my bag, holding it tight against me as my heels click against the floor of the lounge. Part of me wonders why they haven't tried to snatch it from me, not that they'd find anything interesting.

But they seem awfully trusting of someone who was just found crouched in the same room as a murder victim…a dangerous scumbag murder victim who'd committed too many crimes against humanity to even count.

I guess I'm a better actress than I thought.

They don't seem the least bit threatened.

The shorter, dark-haired guy points me in the direction of the bar, giving me a little shove to move forward, and I grit my teeth.

Okay, really? Does he need to lead me around like I'm his fucking pet? I shake off his hand once we're standing in a somewhat private corner of the bar, unable to bite my tongue for a second longer.

"Listen," I say. "You don't need to pull me around like I'm on a leash. I did not fight you. I came here with you as you requested, even though I begged you to let me go home."

A look of surprise flits across his face and a smile lifts his lips. "Sorry. Maybe I just wanted to keep you close."

"Keep me close?" I roll my eyes. "Please. After the way you frisked me at Tatiana, I think I you owe me a freaking marriage proposal."

"Let's start with your name, and then we can see how the night unfolds," he murmurs, his lips lifting into a seductive smirk.

"Shocking." I lift an eyebrow. "There are so many other questions I thought you'd have asked first."

"Don't worry. We'll get there," he says, waving over the bartender.

"One drink," I say through gritted teeth.

"Maybe."

"Definitely," I seethe, almost letting my Americanized accent lace my words. He doesn't catch it, though, since he's too busy trying to liquor me up. Jesus. He doesn't yet realize I can drink him and his friend under the table. I'm Russian, for Christ's sake. I have vodka running through my veins instead of blood!

Although, the tall guy has the look of the Irish. I bet he can do some damage to a bottle of Jameson.

Jameson. That's the name I'm giving him since I sure as hell know he'd never tell me his real one.

The bartender places three doubles of a clear liquid in front of us, but I make no move to grab my glass. Instead, I fold my arms over my chest.

"Is that the game we're playing?" Blue Eyes says with a chuckle. I study him hard. Let's call him Gio. He looks like he could be a Gio. I get that whole slippery, slimy, yet sexy and seductive vibe from him.

Gio hands Jameson one of the glasses, and both of them tip them back, gulping down the liquid and then slamming the glasses back on the bar.

After the shit I've seen and done tonight, I can really use a shot.

Or twenty.

But I don't want to give this guy the satisfaction of knowing any of that.

I do, however, want to find out exactly who Gio is and why he was looking for Vigo. As far as anyone knew, he wasn't supposed to be at Tatiana tonight, so I'd like to know why they were skulking around.

That means I've got to pack up my inner snarky bitch and bring out my weepy damsel alter ego again.

God, I fucking hate her.

But good that I can play her so damn well.

I force tears to my eyes and take a quivering breath before taking the glass Gio holds out to me. I release my arms, gazing up at him through my glued-on lashes. Can I just say the glue must be of the Gorilla variety because I can't figure out how the hell they're still adhered to my eyelids right now after all of the bullshit crying I've done.

Pretty impressive if I say so myself.

"If you only knew what I've been through tonight, you'd understand why I am being a little difficult."

"Tell us," Jameson says. "How the hell did you end up there?"

I raise the glass to my lips and take a tiny sip of the vodka. Mm. So smooth. So crisp. I want to toss it back in the worst way but I restrain myself.

I'm restraining myself a lot right now.

Self-control is something I struggled with for a long time after we escaped our hellish existence in the Ukraine, when I was angry all of the time and wanted to unleash it on anyone who got a little too close for comfort.

I've since learned how to channel that hostility in more productive, cash-generating ways, thanks to Uncle Boris.

"I was interviewing for a job," I say in a shaky voice. "A cocktail waitress job in the casino. A friend of mine works there and she set me up with Vigo. But when I got there, he had something different planned for me. He brought in another man who pointed a gun at the back of my head and ordered me to take off my clothes." I cough up a sob to make shit really sound legit as I spin my bullshit tale. "He told me he would shoot me if I didn't. So I...I..." My shoulders quake and I weep into my hands, biting back a smile when I see the look of rage flit across both of their faces. I mean, yes, Vigo was a total pig and he deserved to die. But these guys are more than a little pissed off to hear how he came damn close to violating me. "I took off my dress and Vigo did...things. He touched me, made me touch him, and then he pulled off his pants and forced my head between his legs." Bile genuinely rises in the back of my throat when I recall how very close my lips were to his diseased cock.

Gio slams his large fist on the bar, his full lips twisting into a grimace. "That fucking bastard," he mutters. "What else?"

I balk. "That's not enough?"

He shakes his head. "I'm just trying to figure out if he hurt you. In other ways," he says vaguely, motioning for me to continue my story.

"If you're trying to find out if he raped me, the answer is no," I say. "I guess you could say I was one of the lucky ones who escaped that fate."

"Lucky how?" Jameson asks.

I furrow my brow. "Someone killed him before he could do anything else. You saw his body when you pulled me out of there. The man with the gun left the room, and not a minute afterward, someone came in with a knife and plunged it into his throat while I watched from that corner."

"But the killer left you alone," Gio says.

"Yes. Like I said, I was lucky. I could be dead right now. And before you ask, he was completely covered so I have no idea what he looked like." I quirk an eyebrow at the guys. "Okay, so I gave you a lot of information right there. Now tell me why you were looking for Vigo. Do you work with him? For him?"

"Fuck, no!" Jameson grumbles. "We'd never get involved with that piece of shit!"

"Okay," I reply, taking another sip of the vodka. "So why were you there? With guns?"

"Let's just say Vigo did some business with a friend of ours," Gio says in a low, gravelly voice. Cone to think of it, I should have named him Mr. Dark, Dangerous, and Delicious. It totally fits him. "And he didn't pay a debt. So we were there to collect."

I nod. "Explains the guns. Sorry you didn't get your money."

Gio shrugs. "We didn't exactly walk outta there empty-handed."

"Yeah, but you're walking out of *here* empty-handed. I can assure you of that," I snap, allowing the scathing words to slip out before I have the chance to bite them back.

"Another blow to my self-esteem," he says with a playful grin. A shiver runs through me as he shifts away from the bar, his muscular bicep brushing against my side.

Jameson grabs his phone from his pocket and peers at the flashing screen. He holds it up and looks at his friend. "I'm gonna take this outside." He disappears through the front door, leaving me with he who shall remain nameless.

Gio has a hint of an Italian accent, so I know he's not American. And my God, I've never seen eyes like his. They pop against his deep olive skin, so mesmerizing, I find it hard to drag my own gaze away from his. They root me to the spot, so piercing, so penetrating, sizzling every inch of skin as they travel the length of my body.

In another life, one where I have a normal existence and backstory, I would melt under his fiery sapphire stare.

But in my current state, I can't give in to the temptation, no matter how strong it is.

My job is too important, and it doesn't make accommodations for low-level thugs who carry out petty revenge plots.

I don't know why they were really looking for Vigo.

And since Vigo is dead, I guess it really doesn't matter.

I accomplished my objective, and that's the most important takeaway.

He leans toward me, close enough that his spicy cologne wafts in the air between us, intoxicating me to the point where if he asked me my name, I'd have to force myself to recall my alias.

"So, I saved your life tonight," he murmurs.

"It would appear so," I rasp as he trails a finger down the side of my arm.

"It's interesting that the killer didn't slit your throat, too," he whispers against my ear, sending tiny chills shuttling down my spine.

"I begged him not to," I say. "And I guess he wanted to get out of there fast."

"Still." His fingers scorch a path down the back of my dress, stopping right at the small of my back. "Even a complete amateur wouldn't have left the murder weapon behind, especially with an eyewitness."

I recoil, my eyes popping open wide. "What the hell are you implying?" I gasp.

Gio shrugs, looping his fingers into the shoulder straps of my dress. My nipples peak under the fabric from the chills induced by his persistent and deliciously invasive touch. "It just seems odd that he didn't kill you, too." He stares at me, those blue eyes darkening with suspicion. "But who knows? The guy could have been a complete fucking moron who'd never done a job like that before. There are plenty of sloppy hit men. They don't last too long in the field, you know what I mean?"

"Yeah, I've seen a lot of—" And then I snap my mouth closed, realizing I just took his fucking bait. Sonofabitch! Two sips of vodka plus a goddamn lusty haze and I'm rendered a complete airhead?

"I bet you have," he growls, pressing himself up against me. I swallow a yelp as he backs me against the bar, something thick and hard pressed against me. Is that...?

Oh, yes, it fucking *is*.

I bite down hard on my lower lip, locking my legs together. Holy Christ, what is happening to me right now? Inexplicable desire for this stranger floods my body, heat swirling in my belly and exploding out to every extremity under his hungry stare.

"What are you doing?" I gasp, making sure that my words are thickly laced with my accent. I may be overcompensating a bit, but I have to keep up this ruse if I have any shot of getting out of here.

His hands attach themselves to my hips and I flash my eyes in defiance. "You already know what's underneath this dress," I hiss, unable to control my temper this time. "Remember?"

"Maybe I wanted to do a second check, just to make sure," he grunts in reply, his fingertips digging into my flesh.

"Do you second guess yourself often?" I ask, his lips hovering over mine.

"Never."

Oh, *no*...

I take in a sharp breath, drinking in his masculine scent and letting it infuse me, one cell at a time. Goosebumps shoot up my arms and down my legs, and my hands suddenly find their way around his waist, then around his back...

Shit, this has to stop!

But I am rendered utterly powerless under his hungry gaze because my body's appetite is equally voracious.

"Tell me who you really are." His voice rumbles through me like a wave gathering force as it barrels toward the shore.

"I never told you who I *wasn't*."

Oohh, that was a dangerous move right there. Why can't I stop myself from speaking?!

This salacious cat and mouse thing we've got going on has every nerve on high alert. I'm not above using my body to get what I want from the slimy bastards I deal with on behalf of the Volkov organization.

But this is me using my body to get what I want...period.

I haven't ever felt a connection like this, the kind of touch that ignites my insides. It's electric, explosive, and all-consuming.

It has the power to sizzle my brain waves and turn me into some kind of lusty vegetable.

Argh! No!

Not tonight.

Not ever!

I swallow hard, running my fingers over the gun tucked into the back of his pants. I quickly debate my next move, and judging by the way he's looking at me, he's questioning the same things I am.

But there's a reason why I didn't take the knife with me.

If I want to make a clean escape, I won't be able to stash a weapon.

Besides, he clearly doesn't trust me right now, so he's fully expecting me to try and pull his gun on him.

My mouth stretches into a tight line as my fingertips slide away from the gun and from his taut torso. Just an aside, in another life, I'd spend hours tracing the outline of his muscles with my tongue... "I don't know what you think you're doing, but I'd like you to take your hands off of me right now," I say in a menacing whisper.

"That's what you say, but is it what you really mean?" He presses himself tighter against me, forcing himself between my legs and I have no choice but to grab onto him, otherwise I'll lose my balance completely. He grins. "Yeah, that's what I thought."

"You know, I just told you about a traumatic situation," I say, trying like hell to make my lip quiver. "And here you are trying to take advantage of me. In public, no less! You knew how scared I was. What kind of an insensitive asshole would play on that fear?" I shove a finger into his chest. "I don't know who you are, but you're not collecting a prize tonight because you did a good deed by saving me. Just so we're clear!" I grab my shot and gulp it down. "And now, as you can see, I've finished my drink, so I'll just be going now." I shove my hands against his chest and... nothing. He doesn't even blink.

And his chest is like a massively thick wall of cement. It's going to take a hell of a lot more of a quick shove to get him to move.

I know why I agreed to come in here.

What I question is the reason why I'm still standing here when I should be on my way home right now!

I'd always prided myself on getting a job done without being sidetracked by distractions, no matter how deliciously decadent they may be. And tonight, I am just failing on all fronts.

Epically.

"I don't think so," he says.

"Fuck you," I seethe. "What, are you part of Vigo's sex and drug trafficking ring? You brought me here to get me drunk and finish the job he couldn't?" I don't really believe that, but as I speak the words the thought percolates...I mean, anything is possible in the mafia underworld.

Too bad this jackass doesn't see what's about to happen next.

"Quid pro quo, sweetheart. You want answers? You'd better start giving them."

"I already told you what happened to me! That's all I know!"

"I don't believe you."

"Okay, then, Columbo, why don't you tell me what you think?"

"I think you want something, something you didn't anticipate," he breathes as he leans back into me. "And that's why you're still here. You say one thing, but then you do another. Why is that?" He backs me into a literal corner, the wood bar pressing against my spine.

I square my shoulders. "You don't know anything about me. Don't pretend to guess what's going on in my head."

"I know you haven't made a move to leave. And you had a chance to grab my gun but you didn't."

"So what, that makes me a glutton for punishment, doesn't it?" I flutter my eyelashes at him. "In which case, how could I be anything but innocent?"

"No innocent would be able to handle the punishment I'd deliver," he snarls, lowering his forehead against mine.

The cloud of desire swirling around me is so thick, I may just choke on it.

"Is that a threat or a promise?" I murmur as the door opens as Jameson struts back into the lounge.

His expression is pinched and he looks seriously pissed off.

May be just the break I need to cut ties with The Italian Stallion.

And that time could not come soon enough.

Uncle Boris wouldn't be happy about this little detour I've taken.

The job was to kill Vigo, not trade sexual innuendoes with a man who may possibly want to kill *me* if he finds out my true identity.

I shove my shoulder against Gio and he finally backs away, a wicked glimmer in those deep blue pools. "No need to be rude."

I lift an eyebrow. "I'm going to use the restroom."

"Sounds good. I'll join," he says.

I balk at his words. "You're a really sick bastard, aren't you?"

"Relax, I'm not coming in. I'll just stand guard outside." Gio leans toward me. "You never know who might show up, and I wouldn't want that to play on your..." He trails a finger down the side of my arm. "*Fear.*"

Jameson looks between us a couple of times before rolling his eyes. "I don't wanna know, do I?" he asks, hailing the bartender over.

"No," Gio says, never moving his gaze off of me. "We'll be back."

I grit my teeth, holding onto my bag as I stomp through the place in the direction of the restroom. I push through crowds of people dancing and pawing at each other without so much as a look back at the sexy anchor I'm dragging, even though I'm fighting the temptation to pull him close and pin him against a wall so I can show him how much he can do to help alleviate my 'fear'.

I think that's what has me the most pissed off right now...the fact that I let way too much slip in the small amount of time I was under his devious spell.

Okay, and maybe also because this mysterious, yet potentially deadly, stranger totally has my thong in a twist and has me caught in a loop of X-rated fantasies.

For all I know, he's planning to slit my throat once we get to the darkened space at the back of the lounge. He hasn't let me go for a reason, and I'll bet it's not because he—

A determined force jerks my left arm, pulling me around a corner. I gasp, stumbling into a column before my back is slammed against a wall. But before I can utter a single sound, his lips crash against mine, his needy tongue plundering my mouth, tangling and tussling with my own in what can only be described as a frantic feeding frenzy.

Not that I can imagine ever being sated by this delicious assault on my mouth.

Goddammit!

I was so close to escaping…

But the taste of the forbidden is just too sinfully sweet to resist.

He presses his chest against me, his hands sliding up the sides of my torso — so powerful, so demanding, and so unbelievably in control, which is more than I can say for myself right now.

Then again, my objective is complete for tonight, so why not engage in a little release?

His knee forces my legs open, his lips scorching a path down the column of my neck toward the neckline of my dress. I lean my head back against the wall, my eyes floating shut as his devious hands knead my breasts, lapping at my exposed flesh without a single care about anyone interrupting our erotic little tryst.

Oh God, he is *so* good at this.

So much better than that fat fuck Vigo was.

I run my hands up and down his spine before gripping his waist. His mouth has moved up to my ear, tugging at my lobe and teasing the area behind it. I let a tiny mewl slip out as I cup his dick, stroking it through the fabric of his pants. So it *is* true what they say about Italian guys.

They really are massively hung.

Heat pools between my legs when I feel his fingers slide up the sides of my dress. He presses against my clit through the lacy fabric and I squeal as he slides it to the side, plunging his digits into my pussy. He drags them out slowly, agonizingly, and methodically, rubbing against my clit before shoving them deep once again. I clench around his fingers as he taunts me with the push and pull. I lift one leg and snake it around his waist, drawing him closer so I can slip my own hand into his pants. I fumble with the button, finally able to grasp his throbbing dick. I rub my finger over the tip, sliding the slick precum up and down his shaft as I stroke him.

He crushes his lips to mine once again, groaning against my mouth as I tighten my grip around him, running my hand up and down with increasing speed as my body quivers and trembles against him. The orgasm rips through me, paralyzing every movement to the point where I can't even move because the rush is so intense.

And that's just what his *hands* can do.

Holy hell, this is bad with a capital B.

When my eyes finally flutter open, I see the smug, satisfied look on his face. I let my leg fall back to the floor and pull down my dress, my short, sharp gasps making my chest quake. "So that was your plan all along? Pull me into a dark area and finger fuck me?"

He shrugs, a wicked twinkle in his eye. "It's not like you stopped me."

"Maybe I was due for a little release," I grumble as he puts himself back together. I chew my bottom lip. And it was great, but I'm a little defeated, to be honest. He was able to make me come undone faster than I'd ever thought possible, and I just get a little pre-cum in exchange?

I wanted to see him unravel the way I just did.

The way I want to again.

The way I never will, though, because I've been here for far too long.

I put my hand against his chest and push him away from me. "Thanks for that," I say, with a flip of my fake hair. "Now, if you'll excuse me, I'd really like to use the ladies' room, the whole reason why I came back here in the first place." I smirk at him. "See, I wasn't actually trying to get off."

"Shocker," he murmurs, reaching around and grasping my ass. "I guess I had you pegged for a different girl."

What in the hell is that supposed to mean?

He stands back and nods toward the door next to us. "I'll be waiting."

I allow my lips to curl upward in a seductive grin. *Yes, sweetie, but you have no idea how long of a wait you're in for.* Then, I pull open the door and walk inside.

When the door closes, I quickly lock it. Thank God it's a one-person restroom with a window, a fact Romeo may have wanted to check before he let me come in here. I guess he thinks if I come out with some kind of weapon he might have overlooked, he'll be prepared because he's in the offensive position standing out there like some kind of sexy AF bodyguard.

But I don't plan on ever seeing him again.

I quickly pull off my wig and all of the hair pins that were keeping it in place, allowing my light blonde hair to tumble over my shoulders. Then I pluck out my colored contact lenses and strip off my dress and heels, shoving everything into the trash. I squint at my reflection in the mirror.

I open my bag and pull out my phone, eyeglasses, a rubber band, a pair of tiny Nike pro Spandex shorts, and a pair of mesh sneakers that I can literally roll up and stuff into my smallest bag. In less than a minute, I look like I'm just out for a brisk jog on this balmy summer evening in Brighton Beach.

Then I unlock the window and lift it slowly, giving myself just enough space to slip out of the room and into the darkness. Luckily, the side of the bar the bathrooms is on is a relatively quiet cross street, so nobody is there to witness me shimmy out of the place in basically glorified underwear. I look left and right, tighten my ponytail, and adjust my shorts before trotting down the street, away from Velvet Lounge away from Vigo and Tatiana, and away from the most erotic experience I never should have had in the first place.

It's about damn time I closed the book on tonight.

My phone vibrates and I hold it to my ear. "Hi."

"Anya," Uncle Boris hisses into my ear. "Is it done?"

"Of course," I say in a perky voice as I keep up my brisk pace.

"Good," he replies. "It's time to discuss the next part of your job. I'll meet you at home."

"Perfect, I'm on my way."

I peek over my shoulder but I'm still by myself. And even if I wasn't, I look nothing like the little tart who just got finger-fucked by a slick Italian guy who may or may not have been waiting to ice me back at the lounge.

"And be prepared. This one's gonna take a little time," he says gruffly. "You'll need to pack a bag because you're headed to Las Vegas in the morning."

Chapter Three
DANTE

How fucking long is this gonna take?

I peer at my watch.

Five minutes have passed.

Feels like hours.

And I can't hear a goddamn thing from where I'm standing outside the door.

I rake a hand through my hand and lean back against the wall. I tailed her to make sure she didn't pull a fast one and escape out the back door, yet something inside of me snapped as I followed her.

Watching her stalk through the crowd in that tight red dress, her perfect ass swinging with every angry step she took, dark hair my fingers itch to fist cascading down her bare back...I couldn't help myself.

And *she* couldn't pull off her little shrinking violet act, hard as she tried. That woman killed Vigo — I'd stake my life on it. The reason why is still eluding me, and it makes me wonder who else might be on her hit list.

Because if I know one thing, she's Russian mafia.

I saw the star when she pulled the key out of her bra at Tatiana, and again just now when I was feasting on her tits.

That kind of ink can't be mistaken for anything other than a rite of passage.

She's killed for that five-pointed star, more than once.

And her sob story about that 'interview' gone wrong was complete crap.

The only thing Vigo interviews women for are his very special positions, and I guarantee none of them involve walking around his casino slinging drinks.

Knowing all of that didn't stop me from kissing her, though, or from launching that erotic invasion against her. I can still feel her slim leg snaked around my hip, clenching me tight as I drive my fingers into her soft, wet pussy.

My cock jerks at the thought and I swallow a groan.

This was not the goddamn plan!

All I needed to do was find out what the hell Conor was up to, eliminate the threat to our families, and hop a flight back to Vegas.

Now I've got a gorgeous bratva assassin to contend with, and she has information I need.

Information I was supposed to get from Vigo before his throat was impaled with a steel blade.

The big question is, can I get what I need from her without getting stabbed myself?

Or worse...

My phone vibrates against my pants and I pull it out, stabbing the Accept button.

"Yeah?" I grunt.

"Did you take care of things?" It's Matteo. I squeeze my eyes shut and press a clenched fist against my forehead.

"No. Someone else did," I say in a low voice.

"Fuck," he mutters. "Conor?"

"I don't know." I stare at the closed door, willing it to open as Matteo unloads on me. "We got there too late."

"Do you know anything, Dante?" he yells. "I sent you in there to collect information!"

"Yeah, well, I got some information, but it wasn't enough, okay? I didn't get to the target in time." I let out a frustrated sigh. "Listen, we can talk tomorrow when I get to the hotel. I'm still working an angle here."

"Don't fucking tell me that angle is lying spread-eagle and naked on your bed!"

I roll my eyes. If only. But I don't tell him about the girl. Not yet. I still don't have a clear-enough read on her or why she killed Vigo, and even though I want to bend her over a couch and fuck her until she can't remember her alias, I plan to get the information I need before this night is over. "No, I'm still out with Patty. But I may have a lead." That's all I offer right now. I know my brother, and if I gave him anything more, he'd keep me on the phone hounding me for details I just don't have to offer.

"You'd better grab hold of that goddamn lead before you get on the plane. We need to know what we're up against. That's why I sent you in, Dante. I didn't send Roman, I didn't send Sergio. I sent you because you're the best at what you do. Please don't fuck with my perception of you."

"Look, this is a sensitive job, Matty. That's why you wanted me to handle things. I could set fire to the whole fucking place, but that wouldn't get us any closer to the truth. We found out Conor owed a debt. That's it. I don't have the details, though. Vigo's vocal cords were, ah, a little bit compromised, you know what I'm saying?"

Matteo lets out a snort. "Great, so what the hell do we do now? If someone did that hit, they might have been trying to set it up so Conor takes the fall. Then we're all up shit creek."

"Look, Patty is gonna be watching closely and he'll let us know if anything points in our direction."

"I don't like this, Dante. What in the fuck would Conor be doing with the Russians? Because I seriously doubt it was just a gambling debt that degenerate owed them."

I scrub a hand down the front of my face. "I don't know. But let's face it. He's too much of an idiot to carry out that kind of a hit on his own."

"What are you thinking?"

I sigh, leaning my head back against the wall. "Just so we're clear, I'm not usually the guy who comes up with the theories about 'who' or 'why'. I just carry out the 'what' and 'where' parts of the plan, you know?"

"I know, thinking isn't your forte." Matteo's dry laugh makes me cringe.

"Fuck off," I grumble. "I just don't have enough information, and since you need me back in Vegas, I don't have time to pull it all together.

"So you don't think you should high-tail it to Hell's Kitchen, find Conor, and put him through a little rat torture to get him talking?"

"As satisfying as it would be to make the cocksucker suffer like that, I think we pull back on the reins a little bit." I shake my head. "And by the way, you don't sound like a boss right now. You sound like a guy who wants to make his wife's enemy suffer."

"He is a common enemy, as much to us as he is to her," Matteo grunts. "And he should fucking suffer. Him, his father, and his other schmuck brothers."

"Easy, bro. "You know Niall and Quinn can't do anything in their positions. They aren't gonna stage a coup or anything. They're being led around by their dicks because they have no other choice."

"Patty did," he says darkly.

"Patty is a different guy. Plus, we both know he's not gonna do anything to get his pretty face smashed in. So, right now, we watch and wait. I guarantee it won't be long before Conor pulls something and I'll be all over him like fucking flies on roadkill."

"You'd better be right," Matteo says. "If anything happens to Heaven and Aisling—"

"Nothing will." My jaw tightens. "That's why you have me." And as I say the words, I know it's only going to be that much harder to tell him I'm moving on after we handle this business with Conor. I need my life back — outside of Sin City.

And not just because I'm perpetually on the run from my own demons.

Killing is what I'm good at, the only thing I'm really good at, for that matter.

I don't allow myself to ever get comfortable in one place.

Not anymore...

Matteo is silent for a second. I know he wants to tear Conor apart with his bare hands. I don't blame him. But if we want to see the bigger picture, we need to keep him alive.

For now, at least.

His time will come.

Fuckers like Conor always go down in flames because they can't see past their own noses.

And if we're talking about noses, Conor is the type to do more snorting than looking, anyway.

"Okay," he finally says. "We'll do it your way."

"Good. Now take the rest of the night off, have few drinks, and fuck your wife. I'll see you guys tomorrow."

"Fuck my wife. That's a good one. Sure, I'll see if I can slip something in while the baby sleeps for like an hour. Christ, we need this au pair so badly."

"Oh pair of what?" I furrow my brow.

"Not 'oh pair', dipshit. An au pair, you know, like a nanny." He groans. "Maybe then I can have sex again."

"So you're not getting any." I smirk. "Makes sense why you're wound tighter than usual."

"Screw you, Dante."

"Yeah, see, I'm not the one having an issue with that."

"I'm flipping you off right now," Matteo says with a loud yawn.

"Okay, so you go to bed and not fuck your wife. I'll wrap things up here." Speaking of wrapping things up, where in the fuck is my killer kiss?

"See you tomorrow. Safe flight. I had one of my guys drop off your car in short-term parking at the airport."

"Good," I reply. Matteo doesn't know it yet, but I've got a side job to handle once I get back to Vegas, the first one I've taken in months. And an Uber won't give me the fast getaway that I'll need.

Soon enough, I'll get instructions for the hit and I'll finally be able to scratch the damn itch that's been plaguing me for months.

I click to end the call, letting my hand drop to my side. I look over my shoulder. Nobody is coming. I could just peek my head inside the bathroom—

I shake the door handle.

Locked.

Dammit!

I stuff my phone into my pocket and rap on the door with my fist. I don't really want to attract any attention to myself, but an uneasy feeling eats at my gut as I stand there with my ear pressed to the door.

I don't hear a thing.

Of course, the blaring music could be the reason for that.

I jiggle the handle again. It's not strong. Flimsy, at best.

I take another look over my shoulder and kick open the door, figuring I'll deal with the hellfire that erupts *after* I get some answers.

The one-person bathroom is tiny, barely enough room for a toilet and a sink.

My gaze drops on the red fabric hanging out of the trash can positioned next to the single window to the outside.

She didn't even bother to close it.

"Motherfucker!" I yell, kicking the trash can so hard, it falls over. The lid tumbles off and my mystery woman empties out of it.

Dark brown wig, tight red dress, small handbag.

She completely stripped herself bare to the point where she may as well be a ghost.

I grab the bag, pulling it open for no good reason considering the fact that anything of value would be on her person.

And that would be an interesting sight to see.

What kind of clothes could she possibly have fit into this tiny purse?

Of course there isn't a single clue in the bag. I throw it against the wall and let out a loud roar.

She played me like a violin.

And there was no way she was gonna stick around and get caught for whatever indiscretion she committed earlier tonight… like murder.

I don't think we've seen the last of her.

But since my 'angle' managed to escape my clutches, I'm not as clueless about her involvement as I am about Conor's.

I open the window and climb out of the small opening, feeling a little like a contortionist maneuvering my way out of it. I straighten up, quickly jogging around the front side of the building and then back down the side street to see if I can find… Christ, I don't even know who I'm looking for right now!

Not that there's anyone in sight.

For all I know, she could have called someone to come pick her up.

Someone she's working with.

Someone I might want to get acquainted with.

I fist my hair and stalk toward the back door of Velvet Lounge instead of shoving myself through that window again. I push open the door so hard that the girls standing right inside jump back with looks of horror on their faces.

"Watch where you're going, asshole!" one of them yells as I push past. I stop for a second and silence her with a menacing glare.

Lucky for her, she gets the message I just impaled her with.

I shove past people grinding against each other on the dance floor, my cock now limp as a fucking overcooked spaghetti noodle.

Patrick looks up from his phone with a single eyebrow lifted when he sees me.

"I thought you were with her in the back."

"I was."

"Well, where is she?"

"Gone," I say through clenched teeth, picking up my shot of vodka and sucking it down before slamming the glass down again.

"Gone where?"

I narrow my eyes. "She didn't tell me before escaping out of the fucking window!"

"So why are we still here? If she escaped, shouldn't we try to find her? We'll definitely find her in that red dress!"

"No dress," I grunt.

"What are you talking about?"

"She stripped out of it. Left it in the trash along with a wig."

"Shiiiit," Patrick mutters. "But if she left her clothes, we'd have an easy time picking out a naked chick running through Brooklyn, yeah?"

I rub the back of my neck. "God only knows what she's wearing. And as far as I could tell, she disappeared into thin air." My shoulders slump. "But one thing I know for sure. She's Russian mafia, I saw the star."

He furrows his brow. "I didn't see anything. Where was it?"

"In my mouth, along with the tit it was inked onto."

Patrick gives my shoulder a punch. "Damn, I knew you were stealth in your job, bro. When was her tit in your mouth? And how did I miss it?"

I nod toward the bathroom.

"You fuck her, too?"

"No time," I mutter. "But the bigger issue is that she wasn't working on her own tonight."

"You mean for her interview?"

Jesus Christ. Why is he so goddamn slow on the uptake?

"Patty," I say. "There was no interview. It was bullshit!"

"What are you saying?"

"I think she killed Vigo. And she might not have been acting alone."

"Are you saying what I think you're saying?"

"If you are going to say that she might have ties to Conor, then yes, that's what I'm saying."

"That's not good. Conor, in bed with the Russians?"

"Patty, if you ask me another fucking question, I might put you through a goddamn wall. I'm just saying." I swallow hard. It's insane for me to feel this way, but my gut clenches when I think about that cocksucker Conor's hands on...whoever the hell she is.

Let's call her Red Dress.

Red Death.

Whatever.

I don't even know her name, but somehow I'm all tangled up in her lethal web.

Conor.

I wanna fucking vomit just thinking about it.

For all I know, she wants me dead.

But, as much as I hate myself for it, I want *her*.

"Okay, so lemme phrase this as a statement so that you don't bite my head off about answering another question," Patrick says with a smirk. "You're going back to Vegas tomorrow and I'm staying here in the city. I'm gonna keep an ear to the ground and see if Conor does or says anything suspicious, now that I know what I'm looking for. And I'm gonna keep you posted. Hopefully, I'll have something by the time I see you for Aisling's christening next weekend."

I rub my temples. "Just keep the rest of your family out of this. You're on your own here. If you need backup, you call Roman. Whatever happens, do not tip off Conor. Christ only knows what he'd do to you if he found out. I mean, he tried to kill Heaven while he was high, for fuck's sake."

Patrick's gaze darkens. "I can handle him. I *will* handle him."

"Be careful. The last thing you want is for whoever he's working with to handle *you*. Because if that happens, you can be sure as shit they'll be coming for us next." Blood rushes between my temples, rage bubbling under my skin at the thought of Conor's betrayal.

If I can't kill him, then goddammit, I need to fucking kill somebody.

Immediately, if not sooner.

The burner phone in my pocket buzzes against my leg almost on cue. I pull it out with a roll of my eyes.

I can't handle more of Matteo right now.

My gaze drops to the screen and the corners of my lips lift.

Just what I've been waiting for.

Fire and Ice. Las Vegas Blvd. Five million.

Well, feather my ass and jiggle my balls.

I'm about to scratch the hell outta that itch.

Chapter Four
ANYA

"Anya, once you get through the metal gate, run. Run like you've never run before. Run until you can't take another breath, and then, keep going. Don't look back, don't scream, and whatever happens, don't stop. Just get to the boat. It's the only way you'll survive."

I swallow a gulp of oxygen, the frigid air lancing my lungs like the sharpest icicles as my older brother Maks and I trudge through what look like mountains of snow in our path. His words to me before we started on this horrific journey are seared into my mind.

My legs sink deep into the freezing snow, the drifts so high, they reach the top of my knee-high boots. I shudder, pulling my fur-lined parka tight around me.

A lump the size of a grapefruit lodges itself in my throat.

I want to scream.

I want to cry.

The property surrounding our house is gated off by wrought-iron fences and you need the security key to open the locks. There is no escape from the front. Besides the fact that there would be too much snow lining the *driveway, whoever just massacred the guests in our family home would most likely have someone waiting for us by the road.*

There's only one other way out for us.

The lake isn't frozen over yet, so it's our only chance to survive this ambush.

Tears spring to my eyes, freezing as they slip down my cheeks.

I can't feel my fingers or my toes, and we've barely gotten away from the house. I feel the blood in my veins slow as my body temperature drops more and more with every passing second. I take in air, choking as my lungs work overtime to fuel my body with oxygen as I run. With a thumping heart, I focus on the boat swaying around on the lake.

Just a few more steps...

Almost there...

I can almost feel the wooden planks of the dock rattling beneath my feet.

"Maks," *I rasp, keeping my eyes forward. I squint into the darkness, the moon being our only source of light.* "We're close. So close! Please God... please God, let us make it before—"

My throat tightens, panic bubbling in my chest as I reach the gate and stab in the security code. Then I do the things my brother warned me not to do.

I look.

And then I scream.

———

"Mama, you look so beautiful," I say, fingering her long blonde curls. "Your hair glows like a halo."

"That's because she's an angel," Papa says, surprising us by appearing in the doorway to the kitchen. He grabs Mama by the waist and spins her around as she gasps. A breathless giggle escapes her deep red lips as Papa twirls her around the table. Her light blue dress fans out around her, her cheeks bright pink from the impromptu dance.

Mama gives Papa a playful slap. "If you want this feast to be ready on time, you'd better find yourself another dance partner."

Papa's blue eyes twinkle and he holds out a hand to me as Mama fusses over the meal she's preparing.

"It's been hours," I say to her in a teasing voice. "Isn't it done yet?"

Mama gives me a sharp look, her lips parting to speak the word burned into my memory.

"No!"

A flash of red floods my vision as the tears freeze and crackle on my skin.

It was only supposed to be a friendly business dinner.

"No!"

One swing of the machete took Mama's life.

The second one killed Papa.

"No!"

I never saw it coming.

"I'll always make sure you're safe, Anya..."

"Don't ever look back, Anya..."

"They will kill you, too, Anya..."

My head swarms with terrifying thoughts and images I will never be able to erase from my memory.

Mama and Papa trusted them, invited them into our home.

And they took everything from us that night.

"What's happening down there?" I whisper to my older brother Maks in the darkness of his bedroom. Dishes smash against walls, gunshots explode into the air, piercing screams shattering me to my core. "We need to get Mama and Papa!"

"It's too late," he says in a tight voice. "For them."

He knew this would happen.

He was ready for them.

I pull my arm out of his tight grip. "No, it's not! We have to help them!"

He grabs me by the shirt, his eyes blazing with rage. "Mama and Papa are gone. And if you don't want to end up like them, you need to do as I say!"

———

My feet pound against the snow as I drag myself closer and closer to the boat, my fingertips frozen to the point that I'm not sure I can even press the numbers into the security keypad. My breath freezes as it hits the air, my teeth chattering like I've been plunged naked into a pool of ice cubes.

I reach out to hit the buttons, the boat bobbing on the water, and I'm suddenly thrust into the backseat of a blacked-out Ford Expedition.

Maks's truck.

Pulsating electronica fills my ears through my earbuds, my eyes drooping closed as I sprawl out on the leather. "Did you really need me to come with you? You could have just brought the ice cream home, you know," I grumble, scrubbing a hand down the front of my face. I'm exhausted from doing a job the night before in a town upstate, and all I really want to do right now is burrow under my covers and sleep.

"Relax," Maks says. "This won't take long. Don't be such a bitch."

I feel the car turn right and the cool, salty air billowing through my hair tells me we're at the pier.

"Fine," I huff. My stomach growls and I rub a hand over it. It's officially rebelling against me. I guess some ice cream would be good after all. "You need me to come with?" I ask with a loud yawn once the truck comes to a stop. "I'm fresh off a killing spree, so I'm still a little jacked up."

He snickers. "Thanks, but I've got it. I don't need my baby sister backing me up."

I sigh, a smirk tugging at my lips. "Suit yourself. Don't say I never offered." I'd do anything for my brother and he knows it. He and my uncle are all I have left.

He opens the door and hops out of the truck, leaving me with my thoughts.

Most of the time, I can deal with our shitty circumstances. I mean, we're still alive, so that's a big bonus. A few years ago, I didn't think we'd survive for this long. But thankfully, our Uncle Boris had taken us in after we fled from our home. He brought us here to the States and gave Maks a job working on his crew.

I was too young and inexperienced, though, so he trained me. Turned me into his own personal weapon. Years later, I'm more lethal than my brother.

Uncle Boris never misses an opportunity to warn us that word travels fast, and the same people who killed Mama and Papa are still hunting for us. So most of the time, I keep my head down, flying under the radar and doing my work for that asshole bratva boss Volkov, hoping that one day, I can finally look up and see the light at the end of this dismal and dark tunnel.

Maks has promised me that we'll be able to write our own ticket wherever we want to go after a few more 'jobs'.

I've heard that before.

Papa used to make that same promise to Mama.

Unfortunately for both of them, he never got a chance to make good on it.

Crack! Pop! Bang!

I sit straight up with a gasp, the exploding sounds blasting through the music.

Holy shit! Did he seriously just shoot someone?

Did he kill someone?

A scream bubbles up from my lungs, but I bite down hard on my lower lip to prevent it from piercing the still air.

Oh my God, Maks!

Two more shots are fired and I strain my ears to hear voices.

They're yelling something in a different language...

And it isn't Russian.

My throat tightens, blood rushing between my ears.

Maks...

Police sirens sound in the distance and a car door slams, tires squealing on the pavement outside. The engine fades and my world is plunged back into an eerie stillness, save for the approaching cops.

I try to swallow, but the gaggle of tears in the back of my throat chokes me to the point that I can barely squeeze out a breath.

Maks never calls out to me.

He never opens the back door.

Minutes later...or maybe it's hours...I reach up, my clammy, shaking hand gripping the door handle and pushing it open. I am greeted by a black sky and a desolate parking lot in the middle of an overgrown tree field near the water. I shakily get to my feet, gingerly stepping onto the pavement as if my legs might give out at any second.

My mouth falls open, but I can't say the words that hover on the tip of my tongue.

My pulse throbs against my neck, heart galloping like a thoroughbred as I creep around to the back of the truck.

I fall to my knees, crashing hard against the concrete, bits of gravel digging into my hands as I collapse onto my brother's bullet-torn and lifeless chest.

"Don't look, Anya."

"Don't scream, Anya."

But I can't help myself.

I do both...

Again.

"Maks!" I gasp, sitting straight up in my airplane seat, my heart throbbing so hard, I press a hand to it to make sure it stays in my chest.

Yeah, I'm still alive.

I made it out that night.

I survived and my brother...didn't.

After all we'd been through together...losing Mama and Papa, being forced from the only home we ever knew, on the run and living in hell with our uncle in a shithole apartment in Brooklyn...he was gone.

Forever.

Those splintered memories come back to haunt me pretty frequently, even though it's been almost a year since he was murdered.

The book I'd been reading right before I fell asleep...when my mind was filled with steamy rock stars, hot surfers, and swoon-worthy FBI agents...falls to the floor. I let my eyes flutter closed for a second, trying to calm my breathing before I bend over to pick it up. Beads of perspiration pebble on the back of my neck as I force the images out of my mind.

Hence, the reason for the book.

It's one of the reasons why I became such an avid reader over the past few years. It's my only real escape...when I'm awake.

But once my eyes droop closed, the demons take over and my sexy romance fantasies morph into gruesome horror story plots with me as the main character.

"Oh dear, I think you dropped this." A kind old lady next to me nudges my arm with the fallen book.

"Thank you so much," I say, forcing a smile as I clutch the book tight in my hand.

"It certainly looks like an ...interesting read," she says with a little chuckle. "I love romance novels, too. I read at least three a week! Although, not this week. Oh, no. This week, I'm going to be parked in front of my favorite slot machines at the Excelsior!" She clasps her hands together. "It's just going to be such a fabulous trip! My girlfriends and I are all meeting at the luggage carousel since we're flying in from different places. And we're so excited..."

The woman continues to talk and I just smile and nod, my mind tripping back to the handsome stranger who managed to get caught in my crosshairs last night.

I'd much rather think about him than about my sordid past, not that there's any shot I'll ever see him again.

When I ran away from Velvet Lounge last night, it was partly because I was afraid he could see right through me. He called me out on so much and came damn close to connecting the dots that were never meant to be linked.

I stayed with him at the bar last night and let him in further than I have any guy in what feels like forever.

And I knew if I stayed for a single second more, he'd have peeled away enough of my layers to find what lay tangled and twisted inside of me. And I'm not just talking about my clothes either.

I couldn't allow that to happen, especially after our hot little tryst outside of the restroom.

He had...has...the power to undo me.

And I can't afford to unravel like a cheap fucking rug.

Not now, not ever!

I've played that role and it almost got me killed.

I suddenly feel like one of the toxic heroines in the romance novels I devour, the ones who can't let a guy get close because they don't trust anyone, the ones who are so emotionally damaged that they want to rely entirely on themselves and not get into any romantic entanglements with hot as fuck strangers.

That's where the similarity ends for me.

The difference for those other girls is that they eventually bend...then bend over...and let the guy in — literally and figuratively.

And that's just not me.

My past is too littered with death and devastation for anyone to possibly break through. Right now, I feel like an empty shell, void of everything except hatred. And that shit is debilitating.

The only way I think I can actually move on is to make sure that the people who hurt my family feel the same pain.

Because I feel it all the time.

A sharp pain assaults my chest.

I can't even look at mint chocolate chip ice cream anymore without dissolving into tears because it's the guilty pleasure Maks and I had always shared. It was our tradition to go out for it once a week and to talk and laugh and act like somewhat normal people for a little while.

On those occasions, we'd remember our parents and our lives back home.

Even though things came to a tragic end, there was still so much good and I always vowed I'd remember it all. Maks knew how much I needed to talk about them, that if we didn't, I was petrified I would forget.

He knew me better than anyone and he always promised to find us a way out.

And then he died.

My best friend in the whole world left me, and I never even got to say goodbye.

Through all of my splintered thoughts, the woman keeps chatting. I don't want to seem rude, although I hope she doesn't ask me a question because I haven't heard a single word she's said in the past couple of minutes. I keep smiling and nodding, realizing that she only wants someone to talk to, and I silently thank God when the stewardess's voice comes over the speaker.

"Ladies and gentlemen, we're going to begin our descent into McCarran International Airport in our destination city of Las Vegas. The local time is two o'clock in the afternoon and the temperature is one-hundred-and-two degrees. Please fasten your seatbelts and put away all electronic devices. We will be on the ground shortly."

My fingertips turn white as I clutch the arms of my seat.

"Oh, are you afraid of landings?" the woman asks, noting my death-grip on the armrests. She reaches out an pats my hand. "No worries, dear. It's all computer-based, anyway. These planes don't even need humans to fly them! The computers are even smarter than the pilots, if you ask me," she says in a conspiratorial voice. "We'll be on the ground, safe and sound, soon enough!"

I sit back against my seat and let out a deep breath. It is actually nice to listen to someone drone on about innocuous things like a weekend out with the girls, winning slot jackpots, and which hotel has the best buffet for the money. The conversation pales in comparison to the fantasies I've had looping through my mind about mystery man Gio from last night, but then again, maybe it's time to shove those into the dark recesses of my mind where I lock up all of the other shit I can't control.

I need to clear my mind of everything other than the job I was sent here to do.

Forget the fact that I have no clue how to *do* said job, but I'll just worry about that when the time comes. The most important thing is making sure I get the damn job in the first place.

The plane finally hits the runway, bouncing a few times before gaining traction on the pavement, and I let out a huge sigh of relief, gathering my stuff together so I can make a run for it as soon as the doors open.

The woman next to me, who introduced herself as Dottie, busies herself with putting her own bags together while she prattles on about the jerkoff husband of one of her friends who wouldn't let her join in the weekend fun. I swear, she hasn't taken a single breath since she started this one-sided conversation. She also hasn't asked me a single thing about myself, which is fine by me. The last thing I need is for some lonely old woman to interrogate me about my own life choices.

I get enough of that at home from Olga, the seamstress I've been working with over the past few years. She taught me to sew when I first came to Brooklyn at thirteen and it helped calm the demons battling inside of my head and heart. It became therapeutic for me to work beside her, and I learned to use the needles in all sorts of creative ways. I even took up crocheting to get comfortable using the larger, longer variety.

Olga is now my only friend aside from Uncle Boris.

It's a self-imposed occupational hazard.

I try to keep my circle small. Makes it easier to slip in and out of my everyday life to handle a hit when there aren't many people interested in my whereabouts.

I never get caught in a lie because Olga is the only person who ever asks about things I can't actually divulge. My stories are simple and straightforward, and I never mix up details because there is only one narrative.

But it's damn lonely.

I'm suddenly a little jealous of Dottie and all of the girlfriends she'll be spending the week with here in Vegas.

I guess it's just not a life I was ever meant to have.

Building big circles of friends means willingly putting trust in people, and I just don't have that luxury.

When the door opens and people begin filing out of the plane, I expel a grateful sigh. I need to get my head screwed on straight, and getting out of this airport is step one. I sling my bag over my shoulder and turn to Dottie and give her a cheerful wave.

"So great talking to you," I gush. "Have a great time with your—"

Then she grabs my arm and links it with hers, tugging at me as I try to walk up the aisle. "It was so rude of me to not even ask your name, dear!"

My lips stretch into a tight line. "It's Anya," I say.

"Anya! What a beautiful name! Just like you," she says, patting my arm. "Now, Anya, I would be so appreciative if you could help me carry my things to the baggage claim area. I'm afraid if I have to lug them myself, my friends will leave me here!" She chuckles. "I move so slowly these days, you know, because I had a hip replacement not too long ago..."

Fuuuuck.

How can I leave her now?

I grit my teeth and hoist her bags over my free shoulder as she yammers on about her bionic hip.

Eh. This won't set me back too much and hey, I need all the good karma I can get, especially with this new job hanging in the balance.

Speaking of which...I really need to binge watch some *YouTube* videos before I head over to the interview.

I've given good performances before, but this one will have to be the best one of my career if I can pull it off.

Dottie clings to me like Saran Wrap as I guide her through the throngs of people in the terminal. We sidestep men, women, wheelchairs, wayward kids, and rows of slot machines. That's when I almost lose Dottie...and my mind.

I can tune out her nasally voice, but I refuse to chase her around the slots like a kid let loose in a goddamn candy store.

So I firmly place a hand over hers, keeping it stuck to my arm as we wind our way around the airport toward the luggage carousels.

I search the origin points for JFK International Airport. "There it is!" I exclaim. Carousel 3. And as luck would have it, the bags are already circling. Dottie really *is* a pretty slow walker.

Now is my chance to make a break for it.

"Dottie!" Another woman calls out from a neighboring carousel. I turn around to see another Estelle Getty lookalike waving her hands over head.

"Bette!" Dottie says in an excited voice. "Anya, look, it's my dear friend, Bette!"

I smile and walk Dottie over to her friend. "It was such a pleasure to meet you. Best of luck for a fun weekend!" I say with a bright smile, backing away.

Thankfully, Dottie and Bette are already talking and laughing like I've disappeared into thin air, which is exactly what I'm about to do.

I swivel around and dash out of the first door I can find, a blast of dry heat pummeling me like a huge hair dryer that opened fire on humanity.

Holy shit.

My skin almost instantly pebbles with perspiration, making my clothes stick to me like I've just been dunked in a vat of water. I fan myself as I drag my carry-on behind me in search of a taxi stand.

I didn't have a chance to schedule an Uber because I had Dottie to contend with, and if I need to wait out here for a second longer than necessary, I'm afraid I might just evaporate. I pick up the pace, ready to cross over to the other side of the street outside of the Arrivals gate when a cherry red Ferrari Testarosa squeals to a stop in front of me as I start to cross the street and I yelp, jumping backward.

"What the fuck, you lunatic?" I yell, flipping off the driver whom I can't really see through the shaded windshield. "You almost hit me!"

The door opens and my spine stiffens as one long leg climbs out of the driver's seat, followed by another.

My breath hitches when I see one of the most gorgeous men in my entire life smirk at me. Oh, sweet Jesus.

It's Gio.

How the *fuck*?

And why? Here, now?!

"You saw the 'no crossing' light flash, didn't you? I had the right of way," he says in his low, gravelly voice. Good God, I remember that voice...it caressed my ears the way his mouth and hands caressed so many other parts of my body.

"Oh, so if I was lying on the ground in a bloody puddle, would that have been your defense?" I snap, so flummoxed that the memory of him has such a strong hold on me.

And maybe a little bit angry because he doesn't seem to recognize me at all, which tells me he's a total scumbag who didn't see anything besides a hot piece of ass.

Of course, I *am* yelling at him sans accent, and I look completely different than I did last night.

Here I was, thinking he might have actually seen right through me if I gave him the chance.

What a fucking joke!

I slam my hand on the hood of the car, letting some of my pent-up aggression seep out and he snickers. How can he not recognize me? Are slutty clothes and makeup all he took away from last night?

I mean, not that I actually want him to recognize me.

It would just be nice to know that I left an impact on him.

The way he did on me.

"Rage," he says with a wink. "I can sense you've got a lot of it."

"You might feel the same way if you'd almost been bulldozed by an arrogant asshole who doesn't even have the decency to ask if I'm okay!" I tug at my ponytail. God, something about this guy gets me so fired up...must be because he's the devil with that mouth and body.

"Sorry, that was wrong of me." He flashes his movie star smile and I swear my heart jumps in my chest. "Are you okay?"

"Yes!" I scream, stalking across the street because if I stand there for a second longer, I will launch myself at him like a wolverine, and that just would not be the persona I'm trying to adopt right now.

Besides, if given the opportunity, I might get arrested for assault, and Uncle Boris would not be happy about that. I'm also thinking that a rap sheet might prevent me from getting the job I've been sent here to do.

I take a few deep breaths, letting my eyes flutter closed as I get in line to wait for a cab.

"Can I give you a lift somewhere? It's the least I can do since I almost killed you."

My eyes fly open and I gasp at the delicious interruption. "What?"

"I asked if you needed a ride," he says again, a twinkle in his bright blue eyes.

"Are you serious?" I ask. "You're a stranger!"

Not that that stopped me from letting you finger me at the club last night, but now, I guess I have limits.

"I am a stranger," he says, acknowledging my words with a nod. "But I'm not the kind who's gonna drive you to the middle of the desert and chop you up into a million pieces, if that's what you're worried about."

I look at him like he's grown multiple heads over the past few seconds, one more gorgeous than the last. "No. I don't want a ride. I'll be just fine, Your conscience is clear. Be gone!" I wave him away and turn my back toward him.

But I can still feel his gaze on me.

As if my body can stand to be flooded with any more heat right now.

"Anya!" I jump, startled to hear my name being called.

"Shit," I mutter. It's Dottie and her crew. I flash a panicked look at Gio and he folds his arms over his chest with a knowing smirk as they walk across the street.

"Friends of yours?" he asks.

"Not exactly," I say under my breath, craning my neck to see if there is any salvation in the form of a cab for me on the horizon.

"Anya! I'm so glad we found you! We can share a cab together! Let's get one of those fancy SUVs!" Dottie exclaims, clapping her hands together as her friends squeal with excitement.

I feel bad. They obviously don't get out much, but I don't really have time to be a tour guide right now.

I sneak a glance back at Gio and bite down hard on my lower lip.

He doesn't know who I am and let's face it, if he tried anything, I could end him in a hot second, even without a gun.

It's what I do.

But before I can respond to Dottie, Gio appears next to me and snakes an arm around my waist. "Babe, I'm sorry I was late. Come on, your chariot awaits." He grins at the older women. "Sorry, ladies. My car's a two-seater, or I'd take you all with us."

Lust beats out my better judgment and I let him lead me away from the cab stand and out of the sweltering heat.

His familiar scent wafts under my nostrils, and for a split second, it weakens my knees.

Until I remember why I'm here and what I have to do.

"Wait," I say as we walk away. "If you only have a two-seater, how are you going to pick up whoever you're here to pick up?"

"I'm not picking anyone up. I flew in and my car was waiting in short-term parking. I made a wrong turn and ended up in front of you." He winks at me. "Lucky for me. And you since I was able to rescue you." Gio puts my bags into the tiny trunk and pulls open my door, slipping a bill into the hands of the cop who is currently writing him a ticket for double-parking outside of Arrivals. The ticket disappears as I slide into the cool luxe leather bucket seat, and the cop tips his hat at Gio before walking back to his car.

"That still remains to be seen," I mutter under my breath.

Gio jumps into the car next to me and presses his foot on the gas. The car lurches forward as he shifts, swerving around cars.

"I guess I should have been more worried that I'd end up a mangled wreck in a tragic car accident than being chopped up into a million pieces," I say.

"So tell me why you were so desperate to keep away from *The Golden Girls* back there," he says, zooming onto I-215 toward Las Vegas.

I twist my ponytail around my finger, trying not to stare at his profile and the chiseled jaw I long to graze with my fingertips. "I wasn't desperate. I just have someplace to be."

"Like the rest of us," he quips, signaling and swerving into the left lane.

"She was kind of a talker, too," I say, stretching my legs out as far as they'll go in front of me.

"And what's the problem with that? You don't talk back?"

"Well, I wasn't really given the chance." I smirk, shielding my eyes with my hand as the sunshine beats down on me through the window. Even though it's tinted, it isn't enough to prevent the light assault on my eyes. "She was hard to stop once she got going. I got a little tired of listening. Whatever. Call me a bitch for it. Still…" I sigh. "She was so happy to spend some time with her friends. Except for the one whose asshole husband wouldn't let her come out here."

"I bet she's the hot one," he muses, a sexy smirk lifting his lips. "Husband is jealous, doesn't want her picking anyone up at one of the early-bird specials or slot tournaments."

I giggle. "Yeah, maybe. It's just cool that she has a group of friends to hang with. Sounds like they'd been friends for a really long time."

"So you're a busy lady, you don't like to talk, and you have no friends." He lifts an eyebrow as he turns to check me out again.

"And you were suspicious of *me*?"

I roll my eyes. "I have friends, thank you very much. Just not, you know, super close ones I grew up with. I keep a very small circle." Like so tight, nobody other than Olga and Uncle Boris can push through. Let's face it. Nobody else could handle me, and I'm not so sure I'd want them to anyway. "How about you? How tight is your circle?"

He flashes me a sidelong glance. "Damn tight. I don't really have friends either. I have business associates. And brothers."

I nod. "That must be nice," I say. "How many?"

"Three. It gets loud when we're together."

"Well, you're Italian, so..." I snicker, kind of startled that I made a joke. I'm not really the jokey type.

"Aha, so you picked up on my accent."

"The accent, the clothes, the car, the..." I twist around, pretending to get a closer look. "Wait, are you wearing the Italian horn around your neck? Or a cross?"

"Oh, shit. You've really got me pegged, don't you?" He chuckles and the sound reverberates through my insides, just like it did last night. I take a deep breath, inhaling his spicy scent. I bite back the moan that threatens to slip from my lips.

I don't have him pegged, actually, but my God, I wish I did...

And then anger clutches me, forcing the thought out of my lust-filled mind, and I want to punch him in the arm and ask him why the fuck he can't see who I really am?

This little back and forth banter...how can he not remember?

Argh!

I feel less than invisible right now, and while it is exactly what I'm going for, work-wise, it makes me feel small and insignificant to Gio. I ran away from Velvet Lounge last night...ran from him...and he doesn't seem affected at all, even after what we did.

That makes me feel nothing short of pathetic.

Like I wasted the hours tossing and turning and replaying our salacious encounter.

"I guess everyone needs a good party now and again."

"What?" I ask, his voice yanking me out of my frenzied thoughts.

He turns to give me a quick look. "I was just saying that everyone needs a little bit of Vegas every once in a while, even *The Golden Girls*. Must make them feel younger, zippier, peppier." He flashes a sidelong glance at me. "You don't like to talk, but you're not so great with the listening thing, either. Just saying."

"Sorry, I'm just a little preoccupied." I tap my fingers on the screen of my phone, anxious to find out more details about this job. Uncle Boris told me to call him once I was settled at the hotel and he'd give me the details.

"Hey, I didn't ask you where you're going," Gio says as he pulls off of the interstate heading toward the Vegas Strip.

"You didn't."

"I also didn't ask your name."

"Right again," I say. "You look a lot smoother than you actually are, just in case you were wondering."

"I don't get out much."

"I find that highly unlikely," I say with an eye roll. "But fine, I'll play. My name is Anya and I'm headed to the Bellagio."

"The Bellagio?" he snips. "Why the hell would you go to that shithole?"

"Because that's where my reservation is," I say. "Why do you think it's a shithole? It's gorgeous!"

"It's so fucking twenty years ago!"

I snicker. "You sound like a hotel snob."

"I just know what I like," he says, slowing to a stop at a light. He winks at me, a wicked twinkle in the depths of his bright blue eyes. "Now, Anya, what are your plans while you're here in town?" He pulls the Ferrari into the long driveway leading up to the Bellagio and slows next to the curb, the red and gold overhang packed with people and cars and rolling luggage carts.

"Well, the plan is to nail an upcoming job interview." I stare at him, hard, my eyes searching for any sign of recognition in his expression.

Nada.

What the hell?

My ass, he doesn't get out much.

Guys who don't get out much would definitely remember something about the face and body of a girl they hooked up with the night before!

"Then what?"

My breath hitches as his blue eyes darken and he leans toward me the slightest bit. "Then I guess I'd start work."

"You gonna be shacking up here for long?" he asks, nodding at the hotel.

"I guess I'll find out in a few hours," I murmur, my eyes dropping to where his fingers sit on the floor shift. Such long, thick fingers. I remember them so very well...

"I guess I will, too," he says with a smile that makes my heart hammer against my chest. What does that even mean? And why do I even care? I have one objective while I'm out here... and it doesn't include this guy.

Or any guy, for that matter!

I have to keep my head focused.

Uncle Boris needs me. I have to do this for him...and for Maks.

I need to remember who I am and what is expected of me.

I don't have the luxury of getting tangled up in some hot guy's web.

I'm the black widow, for fuck's sake!

Then Gio backs against his door, shoves it open and hops out, stopping to grab my bags from the trunk. Then he jogs around to my side and pulls open the passenger door. When he holds out his hand to help me out of the car, despite myself, I take it. The immediate electrical current that shoots up my arm almost makes me gasp as I step onto the cobblestones.

Holy crap, he *had* to have felt that!

I place my hands on his arms, stepping toward him, completely consumed by his fiery irises. I can feel his biceps tense under my fingertips and his hands move to my hips, seemingly oblivious to the hustle and bustle around us.

We're standing in our own little blissful bubble, caught in each other's gazes, his still searching...still questioning.

But I don't have to question.

I already know.

"Excuse me, you're going to have to move that car," an intruding valet voice shatters the carnal haze that has since settled in, but I'm not ready to let it dissipate quite yet.

"Yeah, in a min—" Gio starts to say, but I swallow his next words when I grab his head by the back of his neck and crush my lips against his.

A rush of heat blasts through my insides, just as it did last night, when he moves his hands to the sides of my face and plunges his devious tongue into my greedy mouth. He drinks me in like we're in the middle of the desert and I'm a tall glass of ice cold water.

Funny.

We *are* in the middle of the desert.

And we both clearly have an insatiable thirst...for one another.

I run my hands down his back, the tight, muscled one that once again ripples beneath my palms as his explore the sides of my torso until the annoying-as-fuck valet pipes in with his own commentary.

"Good thing we're at a hotel so you can get a room," he snaps. "Now, move it!"

Gio breaks away from me, his eyes heavy with pent-up desire, and I am so tempted to forget about my interview so I can take him inside and ride him like the fucking stallion he is.

"Hey, you never told me your name," I say breathlessly, sweeping a few stray hairs out of my eyes.

His lips curl upward. "It's Dante," he murmurs.

I grin back. "Like the inferno."

"You'd better fucking believe it," he growls with a wink, backing away as the valet impatiently taps his wingtips on the cobblestone driveway, waiting for us to say goodbye.

Goodbye...

Dante.

He opens his door and flashes one last wicked grin at me before climbing inside. "Your own hellfire blazes pretty damn hot, too, *Anya*."

A shiver...ironically...rushes through me at his words and I stand here with my bags at my feet, staring at the Ferrari as it peels out of the driveway and disappears onto the Strip.

Holy crap, I'm in Hades.

And that's a gross understatement.

Chapter Five
DANTE

I pull my Ferrari into the self-parking lot of a restaurant down the block from the nightclub, Fire and Ice. It's off the beaten path, so there isn't a whole lot of foot traffic around the place. It's also overgrown with weeds, and there's a chain link fence around the dilapidated building.

All good for me.

I get out of the car, the hot air damn near smothering me as I walk in the direction of the club. I've been down here before, so I know exactly how to navigate the area as a ghost.

It's pretty deserted on this side of the Strip. None of the big money is down here. It's all at the other end.

Also good for me.

Nobody gives a shit about the places around here. They only exist for derelicts and criminals.

Hell, the cops barely come down here.

I skirt around some unwieldy bushes and take a quick look around before hopping the fence. I don't love doing hits during the day, but this is the only way to stop the scumbag from snatching any more innocent young girls.

He's expecting to auction them off tonight, and the only way to prevent the sales from taking place is to pop a cap in his brain.

Five-million dollars.

That's what I was paid to terminate him.

Hell, I'd do it for nothing to rid the world of this piece of shit.

The money was already wired to my account by the requestor who goes by an alias.

We all do.

The requestor knows I'm not on the job right now, so he upped my price to sweeten the deal for me.

But I only had to see the name of the target and I was all in.

Miguel Rivas is an infamous sex trafficker who operates between Los Angeles and Las Vegas. He imports kidnapped women on vacation in Mexico and harbors them in LA until the auctions are scheduled here in Vegas. He's got a lot of guys on his payroll, but they'd scatter like cockroaches if the big fish suddenly gets his head cut off.

And that's exactly what I plan to do to him.

I pull open the back door slowly so it doesn't make a sound. I step inside, taking in the darkness and the damp, dank air. This club is a front, and the auctions are all held in the lower level, leaving the main floor pretty much empty, save for a few tables and chairs.

I wrinkle my nose. Smells like fucking sewage.

From what I know, Miguel is only in town for a few days to handle the sales. He'll be on his way back to LA as soon as the cash from the sales hits his offshore accounts.

Or, so he thinks.

I pull out my gun from the waistband of my pants and hold it in my outstretched hand.

Tingles shoot out to the tips of my fingers, and I swear I get a cock jolt from the thought of pulling the trigger.

It really has been way too long...

I creep down a narrow hallway toward a sliver of light.

I can hear a thick Spanish accent coming from one of the rooms. I strain my ears to identify the number of voices, but there's only one distinct one I detect. He must be on the phone.

Making his deals.

Ruining lives.

Fucknut.

But, I'm here.

Now, you die.

I slide along the wall, moving stealthily toward my target when a shadow flickers in front of my eyes.

If I'd have blinked, I'd have missed it.

So I stop and wait until it moves again.

This time I don't lose a second before I fire off a few shots and hear a body drop to the floor like a bag of cement.

The silencer on my gun keeps Miguel blissfully ignorant for the time being, but I can't waste any more time. Who knows how many more minions he's got roaming the place?

That was rhetorical.

I don't really plan to hang around and do a body count.

The sound of Miguel's sinister laughter makes my skin crawl, and for the briefest second, my mind trips back to that night…

The one that confirmed my career choice.

The one that convinced me to dispose of bottom-dwelling pieces of trash like Miguel.

The one that never ceases to bring out the darkness I keep buried down deep.

My jaw twitches, and I wait for silence before I kick out my leg to bust open the door.

When it comes, I crash through the rotting wood frame

I wait until realization seeps into his fat face. He's clearly living large in his new digs out in California.

"You know who I am?" I hiss at him as I step inside the door. The place reeks of cheap cologne, cigarettes, and weed.

"No." His eyes widen when he sees my gun. "There is no money here."

"I don't want money," I say. "I've already been paid."

"What do you want?" he demands. "And how did you get—?"

I nod my head toward the door. "You need to invest in better security. I took out one of your guys in the dark, for fuck's sake. I may as well have been blindfolded and I still got him."

He narrows his eyes. "You won't get away with this. My men—"

"I will fuck your men up," I growl, stalking toward him. Right now, I am completely violating the job requirements. You never speak to the target. You just blow their skulls open.

Period.

But rage floods my insides, and I remember the screaming and the cries for help.

And I just can't help myself.

I shove him backward so that he falls into his chair, and get close enough to his face that I can smell his stank breath. My gut twists but it only eggs me on. "You're a disgusting bastard who deserves to be skinned alive for all of the travesties you've committed against innocent young women." My lips curl into a sneer. "But I don't have time for that. I only have time to shoot you in the fucking head. My loss is your gain, fuckhead." I point my gun at his forehead and his eyes widen in fear. "It'll be fast."

"P-please don't kill me," he whimpers like a little bitch. "I'll give you anything you want…everything! Name your price!"

"You can't possibly pay enough money for the wrongs that have been done by you and every other cocksucker out there who steals lives," I hiss, my breath hitching. Every time I stare one of these bastards in the face, I see *him*.

The man who destroyed so many lives and turned me into the killer I am today.

It was so long ago, but the chilling memory is so clear in my mind.

I had one job to do, to watch over my cousin, Emilia, and keep her safe.

But I lost my focus and she ended up dead at the hand of a guy just like Miguel.

I couldn't stop him and failed my family and myself.

My pulse throbs against my throat as I clutch my gun.

So, as my own form of self-soothing, I take as much pleasure as I can in eradicating the planet of the others who are just as despicable, just as deadly, and just as evil.

"Burn in hell, cocksucker," I mutter.

"Not so fast, *ese*," another slimy voice from behind me says. "Drop the gun and back away from him." I hear his gun cock and Miguel yells to him.

"Don't shoot, you idiot! If you miss, I'm fucking dead!"

My lips curl upward as I slowly turn to look at the person stupid enough to interrupt my hit. "So, you work for Miguel," I say to the peon with the gun. "You know what he does and you're okay with that?"

The guy shrugs. "Pay's good."

"Yeah, I bet. You got a daughter or a sister?"

"I have both," he says.

"You love 'em?"

"Yeah," he says.

"That's real nice," I say. "You wanna know something that really irks the shit outta me, *ese*?" I ask.

He shrugs again.

"People who get in my fucking way!"

I fire off two shots at ese and then point the gun back at Miguel as he crumbles to the floor. A dry chuckle escapes my lips. "See? I told you. Your security sucks." I bring the gun back toward Miguel, and with a jerk of my wrist, I pop a cap in his balls. He screams, clutching himself and tumbling off of the chair.

I snicker and then stomp on his bloody groin for good measure.

"I told you I didn't have time to skin you, but I made time to shoot off your diseased cock." I look down at my watch. "Shit, Miguel. I've gotta go. I wanted you to feel just a little bit of the hell all of the women you've snatched have experienced. And even though it will never come close, I want you to remember this pain for the rest of your life." I point the gun at his temple and squeeze the trigger.

"All two seconds of it," I grunt, kicking him in the head and shooting him three more times in the head and chest for good measure.

I stare at him, feeling the familiar flood of emotion ravage me. My heart thumps hard against my chest, beads of perspiration popping up along the back of my neck.

"Rest in hell, bitches," I mutter as I step over the jackass sprawled across the doorframe as I walk out of the building.

I take a few deep breaths as I step outside, feeling a sudden surge of purpose. My fingers still tingle from firing my gun. The adrenaline high has my heart racing and my temples throbbing.

I'm back to my murderous self, even if it's just for a fleeting moment.

I really do need to shoot shit more often.

Best damn therapy ever.

Chapter Six
ANYA

I slide the key card into the door and the lock clicks, opening to a modest type of room. I frown as I walk around the smallish space. It's not bad, I just expected more glitz and glam considering what the rest of the place looks like.

Dante's words come back to me.

It isn't quite a shithole, but it's definitely not the lap of luxury.

I guess the Bellagio reserves its best for the whales.

And I'm not about to be caught in their net.

I have enough of my own mazes to navigate.

I drop my bag and collapse onto the bed, kicking off my sneakers. I close my eyes for what feels like half a second before my ringtone blares in my ear. I let the phone drop next to my head and it feels like clashing cymbals are being smashed between my ears.

I flip onto my stomach, stifling a yawn as I click to accept the call. Uncle Boris's face flashes on the screen. He's always got a pinched look, and the creases in his forehead are deeper than usual.

"Anya, any trouble at the hotel?"

He's not one for small talk. He's the guy who gets right to the point.

My mind trips back to my one-way conversation with Dottie.

Yeah, sometimes a little small talk would be nice. Make me feel like I'm more than just an employee.

"No," I say. "All is good. So tell me about this job, Uncle. You didn't give me much to go on last night when we spoke."

"Your interview is in an hour," he says in his thick accent. "At the Excelsior Hotel and Casino."

I snicker. "What's the job? Blackjack dealer?"

"Au pair," he says, his brows knitted together.

I sit straight up on the mattress. "Au *what*?"

"Au pair. You're interviewing to be the caretaker of a child."

"What?" I shriek. "A caretaker? For a real live *child*? Whose kid is it? And *why*?" This is truly horrifying news. Besides the fact that I have zero experience with kids, I avoid them like the plague. You know how some girls just flock to them because they're so cute and cuddly and whatever else gets their ovaries pumping?

I'm not that girl!

I'm the one who runs because they're noisy and sticky and whiny.

How in the hell could he possibly think I could even *get* this job?

I have zero maternal instincts!

"I realize it's a little different than the types of jobs that you're used to, but you're the only one who can do it. And the Villani family is the client — the ones who were involved with Maks's murder. This is the big one, Anya. This is the job that will put me on top again. Without Vigo blocking my path, I will finally be in control again. I will finally be respected. And we will finally get the revenge we seek!"

My skin prickles at his words. I vowed to eliminate anyone who had a hand in that fateful night.

I clench my fists tight. Yeah, I'm ready to do whatever he asks.

Except, there's the whole kid thing to figure out...

"How old is the kid?" I say, sudden panic gripping me. I press a hand to my forehead, my stomach clenching.

I'm a fucking assassin, not Mary Poppins!

What the hell is he thinking?

"Five months old," he says, peering at a paper. "It's a girl."

"Five months?" I cry out, falling back onto the mattress. "That's not a kid, it's a baby! Do you realize I have never even changed a diaper? How am I going to even get this job, Uncle?"

"Anya," he says abruptly. "You are the only one who can do this."

"Except I really can't! Whoever is interviewing me will see it in a hot fucking second!"

"Then you'll have to be extra convincing," he says. "I'm sure you can find out everything you need to know on *YouTube*."

"Great," I huff. "That's just perfect." I shake my head at the screen.

He levels me with a sharp glare. "You *will* do this, Anya. It's because of the Villani family that Ivan Volkov was damn close to driving a dagger into my skull. This job will set us up for life. They took from me, now it's my turn to take from them for our gain."

"Can you please give me a little bit more than that, Uncle?" I ask, expelling a sigh of exasperation. "I mean, you never even told me about this Villani family before that day at Tatiana! I need more details about this amazing scheme of yours."

"I told you. You'll get the information when I say you need it! Not when you say you do!"

"This is insane!" I exclaim. "I could have at least prepared if you'd have told me about this last night."

"There are reasons for everything, Anya," he says coldly. "And you will do what I ask because if you don't, you will become a target for Volkov as well." His eyes take on a threatening glare. "And don't think that I will put my neck on the line for you if you challenge me. This is my opportunity to get what I'm due. What I've been waiting years for!" His lips twist into a grimace. "And you're going to help me get it because you owe me that. Do you understand?"

I grit my teeth and nod.

He stares at me for a second before speaking. "You killing Vigo cleared a path for us, Anya. You proved that you can deliver, and my contact is impressed. He is going to get us access to the Villanis' territories in Manhattan in exchange for information, information you will be able to gather once you get this job."

"Are you going to tell me who your contact is?"

"It's nobody you would have heard of," he snaps. "But just so you feel that I'm letting you in on some of the details, I'll tell you that he reached out to Vigo first about this plan to overtake the Villani territories. He wanted to partner with the bratva to expand his drug pipeline into other tri-state areas. Of course,

Vigo jumped at it because he's already got a big business in those areas, and bringing in more product would line his pockets as well as Volkov's."

"What did the contact want in exchange? What kind of information?"

"He's got some beef with the Villani family. Said they have information he can use to get access to their territories in Manhattan for more pipelines, but he can't get to it himself. So that's where you come in. He needs someone to gain their trust and get close enough to get this information for him. You proved yourself to him last night with the hit on Vigo. He was pleased."

"What kind of information am I going to be looking for?" I ask, furrowing my brow. "Like a contract or something?"

"Enough with the questions!" Uncle Boris thunders. "Get the fucking job first!"

"So I'm going to spy on this family and gain their trust under false pretenses for a guy I don't know at all."

A faint smile lifts Boris's lips. "Yes. Exactly. I need them to trust you, to give you access to private areas he can't access."

"So you think I'll find incriminating evidence in the nursery?" I snap sarcastically.

"As an au pair, you will be living with them, and as the caretaker of their baby, you will be left alone to investigate certain areas. You will learn their habits, listen to their conversations. There are several brothers who are in business together, and I am sure you will meet them all. Keep an ear to the ground."

"And what exactly am I listening for?" I ask, still flabbergasted that my life is morphing into *The Nanny Diaries*. I still don't understand how this is going to help with Volkov. What does he want with them, anyway?"

"For the last fucking time, I will let you know everything you need once you get the job!"

"One last thing, just in case it comes up," I say, pressing my luck. Uncle Boris's face is beet-red right now, but I need to ask. "How did I even get into the running for this job? You know, since I never actually submitted a resume."

"It's amazing what you can do when you have eyes and ears on everything," he says curtly. "I took care of everything through my contact. He had inside knowledge of their au pair needs and was able to slot you in as a candidate. I emailed you what you need to prep. You're a student who wants to enroll at UNLV next year. You took time off between high school and college to make some extra money to pay for school."

"And I study...?"

"International business." He lifts an eyebrow. "Because you're bilingual."

"Fabulous." I roll my eyes. "Is there anything else I need to know?"

"Just read the email. It's all in there. You're safer not knowing too much."

"Yes, I can definitely see how my complete and utter ignorance will work much more in my favor," I say with a roll of my eyes.

"Call me when you have the job," my uncle says in a tight voice.

"Yeah, *if* I get the job," I mutter, clicking to end the call. I toss the phone onto the mattress, cover my eyes, and let out a loud groan.

Okay, so I have an hour to figure out how to take care of a baby and manage to not get reported to Child Protective Services as an imposter nanny.

Or au pair.

Or what the fuck ever!

I clutch the comforter in my fists.

And I will figure it out…because whoever these people are, they're about to experience some damn severe retribution.

Chapter Seven
DANTE

"So then, I tiptoed into the room, went up behind the chair he was sitting in, and slit his throat from ear to ear!" I say in an exaggerated sing-song voice. "And a-boom! He was dead!"

Aisling's bright blue eyes light up as she giggles, her arms and legs flailing as if I've just told her the most amazing story she's ever heard. I keep my best assassin tales stored up just for her. Her plump little body shakes with laughter when I give her belly a little motorboat action.

Yes, I'm a great fucking uncle.

We're outside on the pool deck at my family's hotel, the Excelsior, and even though I'm all set up in the shade, the heat is so excruciating, I need to jump into the water every five minutes to make sure neither one of us dies of heat stroke.

I scoop Aisling into my arms and walk over to the ledge of the pool, making sure her sunhat is securely fastened under her chin and that she's slathered with sunblock.

Heaven and Matteo will skewer me if the kid shows up with a hint of pink on her skin.

I position her in my lap, very aware of several pairs of female eyes on me bouncing Aisling on my knee as she splashes and babbles. In my periphery, I can see them smiling and whispering, but I have zero interest in engaging with any of them. My mind is on one girl only...the one I just left, the one currently slumming it at the Bellagio for the foreseeable future.

Anya.

What a sexy fucking name.

That kiss has had my dick in a twist for the past couple of hours since my visit with the now-late Miguel Rivas, and I've been trying to come up with scenarios where I can experience it again without looking like a total stalker.

The other thing nagging at me is the connection I felt. It's something I can't explain...just a feeling, really...like I've met her before.

She makes me think of Red Death...Dress...from last night, and I can't for the life of me figure out why.

Maybe I'm just so wrapped up in the wanton memories from that erotic little encounter at the back of the lounge that I'm projecting them onto this other girl.

The one who is here in Vegas, not the nameless Russian mafia princess who left without so much as a 'thank you' for getting her off.

And oh yeah, she was my only lead on the Vigo situation.

I splash some water on my face and run my hand through my hair as Aisling kicks and coos.

But even though there was nothing about them that matched up physically, the feeling of familiarity sticks.

Just like the taste of those lips.

I've kissed plenty of women in my life, more than I could ever count. But something about those two was just so damn similar... in an uncanny way, not to my mind but to my body. When Anya kissed me, my body melded against her like it had been there before, like it knew exactly what to expect even though my mind had no fucking idea what I was doing or why.

I chalked it up to Red Dress being a loose end, one I have no confidence that I'll ever tie up. I mean, I don't even know who she is. Without that disguise, she could be anyone.

Invisible, just like I usually aim to be.

That makes me more than a little nervous because she can reappear as quickly as she left.

And I still don't have any trust in the bullshit she fed me last night.

We have unfinished business, in more ways than one.

Then again, so do me and Anya.

And she knows it as well as I do. Everything in her expression confirmed it...not to mention the way her body was plastered against me for those few stolen seconds.

Jesus Christ...

Without my real work occupying me, all I have is time to think. And thinking is dangerous.

I'd much rather act.

I had one job to do while I was in New York, and all I have are loose ends and a severe case of blue balls.

"You know what, Aisling? Women are the fucking devil. I hate to be the one to break that news to you since you're gonna be one of them, but they are. They have this witchy way of distracting men from things that are really important, and then they escape out a fucking window," I mutter, leaning back on one hand.

I really need to let that go. Part of me believes I let her get away without talking because I'm actually losing my edge, and that pisses me off to no end.

I haven't completely lost it. I mean, I think Miguel Rivas would agree with that.

But it's slowly morphing from a sharp, serrated blade to more of a blunt-edged butter knife.

That's bad news, not only for me but my family.

But it wasn't the missed opportunity for sex that grates on me.

It's that I let myself lose focus and without the information I need, I can't do what Matteo expects – to protect the family.

I can't protect anyone from an invisible threat.

I'm much more effective with tangible ones.

Aisling claps her hands and keeps splashing.

I sigh. "Good talk, kid. Just file it away for later."

"What, exactly, are you telling my daughter to 'file away for later'?" My brother Matteo drops next to me in the pool and picks up Aisling, holding her up and blowing raspberries onto her belly. I stifle a smirk. The girls around us have to be creaming in their bikini bottoms right now watching us with the baby.

That, or they think we're gay.

"You're in a bathing suit," I say to Matteo. "What gives?"

He shrugs. "I figured I needed a little break."

"When does the boss ever take a break?" I say with a mock look of shock on my face.

"This place is Sergio's baby," he says. "Not mine," he says, nuzzling Aisling's cheek.

It's true. Sergio, one of my other brothers, runs the Excelsior. But Matteo is still the boss, and he never lets any of us forget it.

He also never comes out to the pool. It's his wife Heaven's grand plan to stay out here in Vegas. Matteo hates the heat — dry or otherwise.

"You know, I am so fucking tired of hearing how people say dry heat isn't as hot," he grumbles, almost on cue. He says some variation of this every time he comes outside, and only seconds later, he finds some excuse to dart back in the air conditioning.

But today, he's in board shorts.

That tells me he's sticking around, something that makes my gut knot a bit. I see a cocktail waitress walk toward us and I flash her a big smile.

She grins back and leans down next to me so that I can get a clear view of her tits popping out of her bikini top. "What can I get you, Mr. Villani?"

"I'd love a Tito's and soda. Actually, make it three."

"Three?" Matteo asks, his eyebrow lifted.

"Yeah," I say with a snicker. "One for you and two for me. If you're out here, I figure I'm gonna need to be double-fisting."

"And a water, too, please," Matteo says with a smile. "Thanks." He rolls his eyes at me. "Why do you insist on coming out here? It is so fucking brutally hot, you can't breathe!"

"I think you can breathe just fine," I say. "You just don't like to sweat because you think it makes your hair frizz." I waggle a finger in front of Aisling's face and she grabs it, stuffing it into her mouth, getting it nice and wet with baby drool. I tickle her under her chin with my free hand and flash a bright smile at her. "Tell Daddy that Uncle D is right, because he's so vain about his hair."

"My hair doesn't frizz," he grumbles. "I just hate being outside in the fucking desert. It's hot and I'm sweating, even sitting here in the damn pool."

"Just let the tension go," I say, dragging my fingers through the water past Aisling.

"She shouldn't be out here. Look, she's already getting red."

"She's fine. You can't keep her in a plastic bubble. She needs to get exposed to the elements and be like a normal kid, especially since nothing else about her life will be even remotely close to normal."

Aisling smashes her fist into the water, splashing Matteo, and sure enough, the first place his hand goes to is his hair.

So fucking vain.

"Okay, so what gives?" I ask. "You're not out here to tan. What, you don't trust me with the kid?"

"I trust you more than anyone," he says. "Or at least, I did until you came back here and told me you couldn't close the deal in Brooklyn."

"I *said* someone beat me to it." I smirk. "That deal is most definitely closed."

"But you didn't tie up loose ends. Or stuff shit down the throats of loose cannons," he grumbles.

"No," I say. "You're right. Conor is still at large with his wide fucking pie hole open."

"We need to find out what the hell he's up to, Dante," Matteo says, dropping his voice.

"Look, I know you think shit will blow our way, but will it really? I mean, with Vigo dead, maybe the debt will be cleared. Besides everyone knows Heaven has been on the outside for a long time. Why come for her?"

"You of all people should know how these people operate. They go after everything and everyone." He shakes his head. "I've got a hell of a lot to protect, and I don't want any of Conor's scams to rain hellfire down on us, especially if Volkov thinks Conor may have been the one to kill Vigo."

Hellfire.

There's that word again.

Makes me think of Anya.

She was hellfire.

I could see it.

I could feel it.

And fuck, I could taste it.

But I also need to forget about it. There's a bigger fish named Conor I'd love to gut before frying him. That's the only way I get my life back.

Matteo would second that death sentence, that's for sure.

He's hated Conor ever since the guy tried to kill Heaven right before their wedding, and if it wasn't for the fact that he's her blood, I know for a fact that Matteo would have had him sunk to the bottom of the Hudson without a second thought.

But much as Heaven despises him, she'd never want her family to suffer that loss.

To me, it'd be a gain, but hey.

Not my family. Not my call.

"That's why you have me. You know I'll do anything to protect this girl. And then once we've taken care of the 'problem', I go back to what I do best," I say, lifting her into the air and dipping her toes into the water only to bring her back out again. She loves playing this game.

Matteo's expression darkens slightly, but before he has a chance to respond, a smooth female voice croons into my ear as a tanned, lithe body sinks to the step beside me.

"Your baby is so cute."

Evidently, the water-toe game makes a lot of fans.

"Thanks, but she's not mine," I say, nodding at Matteo. "She's my brother's."

Her eyes brighten up at that. "Oh, so...you guys aren't together, then," she murmurs, sliding closer.

"Most definitely not."

Matteo snorts. "What, like I'm not a good catch?"

I shrug. "I need someone who's less vain about their hair than I am."

The girl giggles and twists so I have a full view of her tits.

Jesus, Aisling is like a homing device or something.

The cocktail waitress struts over, shaking her ass in a more exaggerated way than she was when she left with my order. And I can't be sure, but I think she just mouthed "Die, bitch," to the girl sitting next to me. I bite back a smile as she 'politely' shoves the girl away with a quick little shoulder move.

Damn, she's territorial.

I'm thinking she may pee on me next, you know, to really get her point across.

"Here you go, Mr. Villani," the waitress croons in a seductive voice, handing me the tall glasses. I pass one over to Matteo and pull out a fifty-dollar chip from the pocket of my board shorts and drop it on her tray.

She shoots one final glare at the intruder before swiveling around and stalking away from us.

I pick up one of the glasses and hold it out to the girl, but before she has a chance to take it, it's swiped right out of my hand.

"That looks good," my sister-in-law Heaven says, taking a long sip and letting out a moan.

"You know, your husband has one of his own," I say. "Why'd you go for mine?"

She gives a pointed look to the girl. "Because I was trying to save you, pumpkin," she says in a very fucking fake-sounding voice.

"Do I look like I need saving?" I hiss at her. The girl's lips twist and she jumps up, taller than Heaven by about six inches.

"There's no need to be so rude," she snips, creeping toward Heaven, her arms folded against her chest. "But then again, if I was wearing that kind of getup out here, I'd be pretty crabby, too," she says, pointing at Heaven's sundress.

Okay, it's not really so much a sundress as maybe a muumuu.

Heaven is extremely sensitive about her post-baby body. I don't dare tell her that getting up in the middle of the night with Aisling doesn't have to mean that *both* of them get a yummy snack.

For nine months, she had chocolate soft-serve ice cream with butterscotch sauce three times a day. It became a new food group for her, and I guess she hasn't lost the taste for it.

And this girl literally just took her life in her own hands when she made that crack at Heaven's wardrobe choice.

I'm kinda interested to see how far it goes before I need to step in.

Heaven gasps, recoiling with that drink still clutched in her hand. "Excuse me from trying to protect my brother-in-law from some almost-naked slut who can't even keep her tits in her bathing suit top! I mean, there are *children* out here!" she yells, waving her hand around her. "And you are clearly a gold-digging whore!"

The girl swings out her hand, I guess in an attempt to slap Heaven.

That's just stupid right there because what she doesn't anticipate is Heaven grabbing her wrist and bending it back so hard, it's on the brink of snapping.

That's exactly what she does, too.

See? So not fucking normal.

My poor niece.

"Whoa," I say, jumping up from the ledge of the pool. The girl is screaming bloody murder, and a few security guys are hurrying over.

I peel Heaven's hand off of the girl's wrist and she glares at me.

"I was in the middle of something, thank you very much!"

The girl clutches her wrist. "You're a crazy fucking bitch!" she shrieks. But she hightails it away from us as quickly as she can.

I'm clearly not worth the potential for bodily harm.

Eh.

I've already got a girl.

She's easy to please, too, and happy to be flailing around in the pool. She's got no idea her mother just committed assault.

"Heaven, babe, you can't just go around attacking people like that," Matteo says.

"The fuck I can't!" she bellows. "That skank called me fat! What was I supposed to do?"

"Is everything alright here, Mr. and Mrs. Villani?" One of the security guards asks as he approaches. "Looks like there was a bit of a commotion."

I bite back a smirk. He knows all too well what the commotion was all about. Hell, I think everyone on staff knows that Heaven's Irish temper rages even hotter when she's on zero sleep, as is the case these days.

"Yes, everything is just fine, Jimmy. Thank you for checking," she says with a smile, looking calmer than I've seen her look in months. It may be forced, but she's doing a good job of convincing him to the point where he nods and gives her a little salute before retreating back to his post.

She lets out a deep sigh and sinks down next to Matteo and Aisling. She smiles and coos at her daughter, taking her into her arms and nuzzling her neck.

The mood swings. Fuck. I don't know how Matty handles it.

Heaven is brutal, even when she's running on a full night's sleep.

And today was tame compared to most other days.

Matteo drops a kiss on the top of her head. "You aren't fat. You're perfect and gorgeous. Stop being so hard on yourself. You just need sleep. And maybe a couple of Valium."

She snickers. "Thanks, babe. And yes, I do need to sleep, so badly. I feel like we're really close this time, but I don't want to jinx anything."

"Really close to what?" I ask, lounging on the side of the pool with my sweaty glass in hand. The ice is all but gone, and I've had it for a grand total of a minute. God, this heat is unreal. I mean, it makes for some pretty nice views of the female guests, but other than that?

There's no benefit.

But Heaven insists on staying. I think being so far away from New York City helps her deal with the fact that she's still estranged from most of her family. Separating herself from them by about five hours makes it easier to deal with than living in the same zip code.

I rub the back of my neck with the cool glass. She doesn't look to be in the mood to talk about her family right now, either. I seriously hope Matteo picks another time to loop her into the Conor shit show. I'm afraid assault might be the least of our concerns if she finds out Conor has been dicking around with the Russians.

"Really close to finding an au pair," she says. "Didn't Matteo tell you we've been interviewing for weeks?"

"He might have mentioned something," I say, a shred of a memory of a conversation making the connection in my mind. "So, what, you hire this au pair thing, and you get to sleep?"

"Sleep and a whole lot more!" Heaven says, excitedly clapping her hands, making Aisling laugh.

"I'm down for the 'whole lot more,'" Matteo says with a grin.

"The girl I've been with for the past hour is really terrific. I think she's a fantastic choice and I brought her up here because I want you to meet her, too. And of course, Aisling needs to meet her," she says to Matteo.

I crane my neck. "I don't see anyone. What happened? She get lost or something? Maybe your au pair needs an au pair herself," I crack.

Heaven rolls her eyes. "She needed to use the ladies' room. I talked her ear off and walked her all over the hotel for the past hour."

"Whatever you need to get you back to normal," I say with a playful smirk as Heaven flips me off. "Real nice mothering, by the way."

Heaven jumps up and waves her hands in the air. "Anya! We're over here!"

Cue the record scratch sound effect.

My eyes travel in the direction Heaven is standing and I feel my chest tighten. I'm suddenly pulled into one of those movie sequences where the sexy-as-fuck girl walks toward her destination in slow motion while every other person stares with their mouths open, her hair flowing behind her, her hips swinging in the most seductive way imaginable.

Anya...the au pair?

No fucking way.

This can't be the same girl I drove to the Bellagio.

She was hot, but this version?

Jesus. She's transformed herself into the exact type of nanny you *don't* want around your husband.

Long, lean legs that were covered by yoga pants are now on full display under a little sundress, probably not the most nanny-ish thing to wear to an interview, but I'm not complaining. Neither is any other man drooling over the sight of her. And the messy ponytail from the airport has been replaced with loose, sexy waves that cascade down her back.

To my brother's credit, he just hands Heaven the baby, nods stiffly, and shakes Anya's hand when Heaven makes the introductions.

Heaven is a definite stunner, but Matty would have to be dead to not notice the girl in front of him.

"Here is our little pumpkin, Aisling," Heaven says, snuggling the baby close as Anya tickles her under the chin, a big, bright smile on her face.

Interesting.

She's got no patience for old ladies, but bring on the babies?

Anya definitely didn't strike me as the 'mommy's helper' type.

I could see her more suited to the 'daddy's fluffer' category.

"And this is my brother-in-law, Dante," Heaven says to Anya, waving her hand toward me.

I watch as recognition seeps into her features, her cheeks a little more pink than they were a few seconds ago. I sweep my eyes over her, from the polished red toenails to the hint of boob peeking out from the neckline of her dress, my lips lifting as she forces a smile at me.

"Nice to see you...again," she says in a tight voice.

I can tell she's wondering whether or not I'm going to tell my brother and sister-in-law that I had my tongue down her throat less than two hours ago.

Not.

Heaven wouldn't be thrilled to know that her au pair's hands were all over me earlier.

I'm not stupid.

I want her to get this job.

My cock *aches* for her to get this job.

So fucking hard.

Forget Brooklyn Red Dress-slash-Death.

This has nothing to do with loose ends needing tying.

This has to do with pure, unadulterated lust.

And, damn, it's choking me right now like a noose wrapped tight around my neck.

I can deal with a little caregiving myself.

I just hope Aisling is a good sharer.

Chapter Eight
ANYA

Oh my God.

Those pecs look more delicious than I ever imagined...and I want to taste.

I stretch out my hand to shake his, making a concerted effort to not sweep my tongue over my lips as I drink in the inferno that evidently is Dante Villani.

He grasps it with a knowing smirk, not at all acknowledging the fact that we were devouring each other outside of the Bellagio a little while ago.

I suddenly stiffen, pulling back my hand like it's just been singed, electricity crackling in the air between us.

Once the thick cloud of desire lifts, the realization smacks me across the face.

Hard enough to leave a mark.

He's one of *them*.

And little do they all know, my job isn't to be the perfect nanny.

It's to take down the people who were involved with Maks's murder.

More specifically, *them*.

And nobody, not even Mr. Dark, Dirty, and Delicious, is going to derail me from my objective.

I plaster a bright smile on my face.

I will get this job.

I will make these people love me.

And then I will destroy them.

"Pleasure to meet you," I say, keeping my voice as even as possible. Interesting. He's not going to out me.

Which means he wants me to get this job.

A smile plays at my lips.

Pretty but so ignorant.

He has no idea what I will do to anyone who had a hand in my brother's murder.

And this job is only the beginning.

I wish my uncle had given me the whole story when we spoke earlier. He was evasive about a lot of the details and it pisses me off to no end when he hides things. It's like he doesn't trust me, and after everything I've done for him over the years, all of the jobs I've completed, he should treat me like an equal and not like one of his freaking soldiers.

But this job is a way for him to build himself back up in the eyes of the bratva, and I'm going to do my part to help him regain his status.

Because as far as I'm concerned, anyone who had a single thing to do with Maks's murder should and will be punished.

Viciously.

And for as gorgeous as this guy is, he is the enemy. Hell, they all are.

So I ignore the tingling in my hand when his skin brushes against mine.

I forget how it felt sliding against my ass, how his fingers drove me over the edge the night before at Velvet Lounge.

Instead, I remember my brother and what we had before it was broken.

He was my only real family.

Uncle Boris plays his part and watches out for me, but I'm not stupid. I know I'm a means to an end for him. He'll use me to get what he wants and I'm not naïve enough to believe he thinks of me as the daughter he never had.

He's self-serving and dark as hell. And yeah, he may have taken us in after we fled the Ukraine, but he worked us both damn hard to keep himself on top.

It wasn't enough.

Because he always fell prey to his own inner demons of greed and rage.

But right now, I can't think about Uncle Boris and his battles with the bratva. I need to be the most convincing and charming girl possible so that I can get him whatever we need for his 'contact'.

I keep my smile plastered across my face as Heaven fires off her ideas about the position, half-listening as I run through scenarios in my mind.

But confusion clouds my mind.

My objective is clear — help my uncle close the deal with his elusive 'contact' so that these Villani people suffer the way we have. I understand why I'm here and what I need to do to avenge my brother's murder.

But what escapes me is the part Dante plays with the bratva...as a hit man.

Because I'm damn sure he was there to kill Vigo last night.

The pieces of this very seedy puzzle are so jagged, I don't know how they'll ever fit together.

The Villanis obviously had dealings with Vigo Kosolov. That's why Dante showed up at Tatiana. He told me as much. But what was he after? Was it really just a debt he wanted to collect?

Or something else?

And how does this 'contact' fit in? Why is he after the Villanis?

My job isn't to ask questions, as my uncle never misses an opportunity to point out. But these thoughts continue to gnaw at my brain, mainly because I feel like some damn big details are missing from this very sketchy picture.

"Anya?"

I blink fast. "Yes."

Heaven grins at me. "I asked if you'd like to hold the baby."

"Of course! She is so precious!" I say with as much enthusiasm as I can muster, even though I want to lash out at every one of these people to find out what they know about the murder. I take Aisling's squirming little body, hugging her tight against me. I have to make a good showing.

I have to find out the truth about my brother's murder.

And these people are going to lead me straight to it.

Hatred for everyone who is responsible for yanking away all that was good in my life bubbles to the surface as I bounce Aisling and watch her family stare at her with adoration.

Family.

It's something I miss every day.

Something I'll never know again.

A pang assaults my heart as a lump forms in the back of my throat.

They shouldn't be happy, not with the things they do, not with the lives they've most certainly taken and ruined.

And yet, while these toxic thoughts run through my mind, I still manage to get Aisling smiling and laughing, and her mother is looking at me like I'm the second coming of Christ right now.

Out of the corner of my eye, I see Dante eyeing at me with a question in his gaze.

"Oh my God, she is so great with you!" Heaven exclaims. "How soon can you start?" she asks excitedly.

"Right now!" I say with forced enthusiasm.

"Fantastic!" Heaven says. "Your references were so impressive, and the service absolutely raved about you!"

"Heaven," Matteo, her husband, says, standing up from his spot next to the pool. "Let's take a little walk, okay?"

Heaven gives Aisling a kiss on the cheek, babbling about details that I only half-hear. My eyes are on Matteo and he is staring at me. Hard. Not in the 'I'd love to fuck you' way, but in the 'I'm very suspicious of you' way.

I swallow hard and give them a little wave. "Take your time! We'll just be getting acquainted out here!" I say in a cheerful voice.

"Dante, behave yourself," Heaven calls over to him with a threatening look on her face. Matteo grabs her arm and pulls her inside of the hotel before she can utter another warning. I don't bother to bite back the grin on my face when I walk over to him and sit down on the pool ledge. I kick off my sandals and step into the cool water, positioning Aisling on my lap.

"So," Dante says, sitting back on his hands. His smooth, bronze skin glistens in the sun and I fight the urge to drag my tongue over his pecs.

I simultaneously fight the temptation to close my hand around his throat until he tells me what the fuck he was doing at Tatiana and what he knows about my brother.

But I restrain myself on both counts, keeping my hands glued to the baby so they don't get any ideas of their own.

"So what?" I ask.

"So, this is the job you came all the way to Vegas to interview for?"

"How ironic that you almost killed me outside the airport and made me miss said interview," I say in a teasing voice. See? I can be charming when I want to be.

He grins. "Thank fuck I hit the brakes when I did."

Thank fuck indeed.

I certainly didn't relish the idea of spending my first moments in Vegas splattered across the pavement.

"Speaking of hitting the brakes..." I look at him from under my eyelashes. "Don't think that what happened at the Bellagio is going to happen again if I get this job. I'm a professional."

"Yeah, I can see that," he says. "I'm just trying to figure out...a professional *what?*"

My mouth drops open. "What's that supposed to mean?"

He leans toward me, his blue eyes blazing with heat that can rival the sweltering air around us. "It means there's a lot about you that doesn't exactly scream nurturing."

"Oh yeah? What does it scream, then?"

His lips curl upward into a wicked smirk. "It scream a lot of things that sure as hell aren't appropriate for a little kid to hear."

I grit my teeth. "I'll have you know that I've been taking care of kids for the past five years now. My references are amazing because *I* am amazing!"

"Looks like I struck a nerve, yeah? You're getting pretty damn defensive about your qualifications. But I'm not the one you need to convince. I don't have a say in this decision, sweetheart."

"Don't call me sweetheart," I snip. "I'm not one of your little gold-digging groupies. And by the way, who are you to judge *me* when it seems like all you do is live off the spoils of your family? What are you, some trust fund baby or something?"

"Ouch," Dante says. "Judge much?"

I take a couple of breaths. I have got to control my temper or he's going to tell his brother I'm some crackerjack who by no means can take care of this baby. "I'm sorry," I mutter. "I'm just a little bit tired. I didn't get much sleep last night."

"Yeah, me either," he murmurs, averting his eyes for a fleeting minute. For a second, my mind trips back to our time at Velvet

Lounge, when his body was pressed against me and his mouth was hot against mine.

Is he thinking about that, too?

"And to answer your question, no. I'm not a trust fund baby. I run my own international business. But my job isn't a typical nine-to-five one. I work on a few big projects a year, travel, take meetings with clients. I set my own schedule so I can be free for my family when they need me."

I narrow my eyes. "If that isn't the most evasive job description I've ever heard. Why didn't you just tell me the truth, that you're a contract killer?"

"Because it might have scared you off," he says without missing a beat. "And Heaven would have kicked my ass if you high-tailed it outta here."

Holy shit...?!

Did he seriously just admit to me that he was at Tatiana to kill Vigo in his own twisted way?

"Gotcha." Then, he laughs, a low rumble that reverberates through me. "Holy shit, your face was priceless." He reaches for Aisling and takes her from me, blowing raspberries on her belly. "This silly girl thinks I'm a hit man," he sing-songs. "So silly! So silly!"

I bite down on my lower lip. Why does he have to be hot as fuck and equally adorable? "Okay, so if that's not your gig, then what is?"

"I invest in real estate for my family," he says. "I travel to different locations, check out properties, meet with clients who are interested in investing. That kind of thing."

I nod, not believing him for a single second, although I pretend to eat up every bullshit word. He doesn't know it was me last night. And that guy was most definitely not a glamorous, globe-trotting real estate investor.

He was a thug.

A killer.

I watched him with that gun.

And now I know it for sure.

A grin plays at my lips as I watch him with Aisling. She grabs hold of his ear and tugs and he lets out a yelp as if he's being stabbed through the eye.

It only makes her laugh harder.

Sweet thing that she is.

I reach for her, helping Dante extract his ear from her death grip.

That's when it happens.

That's when the noxious scent from her diaper assaults my nostrils and my gut knots in response.

I almost gag, it's so horrific.

And I've been around decaying bodies.

"Oh my God," I rasp, holding her straight out as she kicks her legs. "She's kicking. She shouldn't be kicking. What if it leaks?"

Dante lifts an eyebrow at me. "Okay, says the au pair. Don't you deal with this kind of shit all the time...literally?" He snickers at his own joke. "Why don't you just change her?"

"Change her," I repeat. "Well, yes, of course, but I don't have..." I twist left and right. "Equipment..."

"You mean, like diapers?" He stands up and runs a hand through his hair. "You're right. I didn't bring her bag with me. Come on,

I'll show you the nursery."

I furrow my brow. "Just like that? They haven't even hired me."

He shrugs. "Whatever gets me out of doing the dirty deed."

I let out an incredulous giggle. "But you don't even know me!"

"I've heard several times how amazing your references are. That's good enough for me." He pulls on a t-shirt and folds his massive arms over his chest.

"Are you sure your brother and sister-in-law won't be angry that you brought me up without them giving me the okay?"

"Why? Do you really think I'd let anyone hurt my niece?" he says, his gaze darkening. "Because I'd do anything to protect her. *Anything.*"

"That's good to know," I say, forcing a smile and cradling Aisling in my arms, hoping to God the poop stays securely in her diaper until I can get her changed. I had time to watch plenty of *YouTube* videos before I showed up here and exploding poop?

It's a thing.

A fucking heinous, gross, and gravity-defying thing.

Dante wheels the stroller into another hotel entrance, one that leads into a long hallway with a private elevator bank at the very end. "This leads to the private residences. Heaven and Matteo have one on the forty-eighth floor. Actually, they have the whole floor," he says with a snicker.

When the elevator opens on the forty-eighth floor, we are standing right inside of the apartment. It's not the penthouse because there is a fiftieth floor. "Who lives up on the top two floors?" I ask Dante.

"My brother Sergio and his fiancé Jaelyn live on fifty. And Tommy Marcone lives on forty-nine when he's here in town with his wife. He's only here about six months out of the year because he does a lot of traveling. But he's here this week to personally cater Aisling's christening."

My mouth drops open. "Tommy Marcone? The celebrity chef?"

"The one and only. Our families are joint owners of this place and Tommy owns the restaurant downstairs."

My mouth drops open. I've never been much of a cook, but I love watching his show on *The Food Network* because he is sexy as hell and hysterical to boot. "That's amazing. I'm a big fan."

"Maybe you'll get to meet him at the party." Dante winks at me. "You know, *if* you get the job." He brushes against me completely unnecessarily, his eyes glimmering with innuendo. "There are lots of perks."

My skin prickles when his warm breath flutters against my cheek.

Do not betray me, body! I will not stand for it!

"I assure you I have no interest in any of your *perks*," I snap. "I think I made it clear that our relationship will be strictly professional."

"I'm not used to such a blatant rejection," he murmurs, lounging against a marble column.

"Actually, if memory serves, it was two rejections." I lift an eyebrow. "Now why don't you tell me where I can find the nursery?"

My eyes sweep over the expansive space. Floor-to-ceiling windows line the perimeter, and the furniture and décor are minimalist and modern. A mix of creams and whites makes the apartment look airy and bright, and it would be a completely glam look if not for the scattered toys, blankets, and various other baby necessities cluttering up the place.

To be honest, it looks like the nursery is everywhere.

But in addition to the nursery, there must be some kind of office or hiding spot for this information I'm to retrieve. I'll have to investigate more later...when I don't have a baby swimming in poop and babbling in my ear.

Dante struts down a hallway and pushes open a door at the end. The room is drenched in cotton candy pink, black, and white.

Also very glam...for a baby, anyway.

It's probably the most adorable room I've ever seen, though.

My chest tightens.

This little baby sure is a lucky one. She has so many people around her who absolutely cherish her, and I'm sure she can feel that love, even at such a young age.

But one day, she might lose it...everything...just like I did.

It's because of the world we live in and the choices that are made for us.

We don't always have a say in how our lives unfold, but we have to put the shattered pieces together and move forward.

A twinge of sadness deep in my chest jolts me and I find myself squeezing her tight, as if I can protect her from her family's sins.

I can't.

I'm one of the people sent to punish them.

Because they already made choices for their baby girl, choices she never had a say in.

Choices she will be forced to live with when the time comes.

"Hey," Dante says in his low, sexy voice. He snaps his fingers in front of me. "You look a little lost. You want me to show you around the place?"

I pull my lips into a tight line and expel a sharp sigh. "Thanks, but I can find my way around a nursery," I say, taking in the various pieces of furniture. The one in the far corner looks to be the changing table, so I start walking in that direction. I place Aisling down and fumble around next to it for diapers and wipes. Heaven has a whole lot of other stuff piled on the sides of the changing table, but I stick with the basics because that's what my *YouTube* training taught me to use.

Holding Aisling down while pulling open a diaper proves to be more challenging in reality than it did for the mom on YouTube, but I work at it, finally getting it spread out. Seconds later, I have her out of her bikini bottom and am ready to unleash the devastation that is the poop diaper. I take a deep breath and almost gag until I manage to get it out from under her and roll it up. I grab for the wipes, my eyes now watering from the intensity of the stench. My fingers can't work fast enough to pull out wipe after wipe, some of them getting jammed in the stupid container.

Oh my God, I would so much rather impale someone with a hot fire poker than do this...

Dante chuckles behind me as I finally finish wiping every bit of the poop away. I glance next to the baby and bite down on my lower lip. That's a pile of dirty wipes. The mom in the *YouTube* video had *one*.

I scream at her in my mind.

How?!

"Lemme help you out," he says, coming up behind me and reaching for the pile of wipes. He stuffs them into a Ziploc, along with the diaper, and tosses it all into a trash can.

All while he's pressed against my back.

And it's making my fingers tremble as I try to fasten this clean diaper.

I squeeze my eyes shut. This is not ideal at all.

My evident incompetence with babies, my insatiable appetite for *him*...

I'm here to do a job...one with a very murky objective which I hope will become more clear very quickly, but a job nonetheless.

"Trust fund babies would never have done that," he murmurs against my ear. My spine stiffens, heat radiating throughout my body as it did when I was plastered against him last night, and again at the Bellagio only hours earlier.

"Dante?" Heaven calls out. "Are you guys in here?"

"Yep," he replies, reaching over me to tickle Aisling's belly before giving me a long, hard lust-filled look.

Oh, yeah.

I caught that.

Not like he was looking to hide it.

The corners of his lips curl upward.

Oh, no. He definitely wanted his message to be received.

Stat.

And I got it loud and clear.

I suck in a breath as he heads out of the nursery and scoop up the baby who no longer smells like sewage. She blows her own version of a raspberry and despite myself, I smile.

She's pretty freaking adorable. I shouldn't let my deep-seated hatred of her family touch her.

None of this is her fault.

Just like the hell Maks and I experienced after our parents' death wasn't our fault.

The kids are always the victims.

I wrap my arms around her tight. "I know it doesn't look like you're a victim, but trust me, you are. And your parents are selfish assholes for saddling you with that reality," I whisper into her ear. She giggles and grabs hold of my hoop earring.

"Whoa!" I say, peeling her tiny hand off of it. "You're going to pull it right off! Such a strong little girl!" I say in a sing-song voice.

Shit, now I sound just like the rest of them.

"Oh, Anya!" Heaven says, breezing into the nursery. "I was worried when you disappeared from the pool, but I knew Dante was with you, and he...well, he's good to have around in case of a crisis." She winks at me.

Yes, in the case of a crisis where a group of insurgents tried to overtake the pool deck. It would be good to have a professional assassin on my side.

But she doesn't elaborate and I don't ask the question.

No need to, since I already have the answer.

At least to one question.

She takes Aisling and ushers me into the living room where Matteo and Dante are standing against the windows. Dante eyes me like he's a starving man and I'm a slab of raw meat.

Matteo, on the other hand, just eyes me with that curious-slash-suspicious gaze. I'd seen it just before he pulled Heaven away from uttering the job offer that was on the tip of her tongue.

I grit my teeth. He doesn't look to be on board the Anya Welcome Wagon.

Shoot. How the hell am I going to get what Uncle Boris needs if I don't get this job? I mean, am I going to have to seduce Dante to get back up here if they go in a different direction?

Actually...

That sounds pretty damn good to me, and I feel my nipples pebble under my dress as the thought percolates...everything I'd have to do in the name of family loyalty...all of the salacious sacrifices I'd have to make...

Argh! I flash a tight smile at them all, ignoring my inner battle.

This is for Maks, not for me!

How can I even think these things, knowing what I do about these people?

A tiny voice reminds me that I still don't have the full story, but it doesn't matter. I'm convinced that I am surrounded by evil...a worse evil, at the very least.

Okay, well, whatever happens, I will figure out my next steps. I cannot be stopped. I will do what Uncle Boris couldn't and avenge my brother's death.

Somehow.

"Anya," Heaven says, a big smile spreading across her pink cheeks. "We'd like to offer you the job, if you are interested. Matteo and I talked it over, made a few more calls, and we think you'd be a perfect fit for us!"

I gasp. "Oh my gosh, thank you so much! I would love to!"

Heaven looks so happy right now. It's hard not to like her. Like, I really need to focus on killing her with my mind because she's just so...jubilant. Maybe it's because she finally has some help, maybe because she knows a good night's sleep is now within reach...which is something I'm kind of struggling with myself right now.

Regardless, she's sweet and happy and perky.

Like an older sister I never had...

Ugh!

Why am I having these thoughts? This is business! They are not my family, nor will they ever be!

"So I know you're headed to UNLV in the fall, but maybe we can work something out," Heaven says, talking a mile a minute about her future vision for this au pair relationship she's desperate to develop with me.

After only having known me for a grand total of about an hour, give or take.

She seems awfully trusting for a mob boss's wife.

Admittedly, I don't know much about the family dynamics, but it would seem that she should probably be a little more wary of strangers living in her home.

And judging from the exasperated look on Matteo's face, he agrees.

"Heaven," he interrupts in a commanding voice. "Let's figure out the next steps after Anya has gotten situated here. I'm sure she has plans for her college experience, and they probably don't involve cleaning spit up and crap diapers." He lifts an eyebrow at me. "Right?"

I nod, quick to agree with him. He literally wears the pants, but clearly doesn't hold all of the power. He knows it and so do I, but I'll throw him a bone anyway. "Yeah, I mean, I'm definitely open to talking about an extension of my services, but your husband is right. Let's see how things go over the next few weeks."

Heaven's grin widens and she throws up her hands. "You know what, I'm just so blinded by the joy and anticipation of being able to sleep again that I'm getting ahead of myself."

"As usual," Dante pipes in.

She rolls her eyes. "I guess we can start with more immediate things, like the christening."

"Christening?" I ask.

"Yes, it's on Saturday, and there is so much to do before then. I was really afraid we wouldn't be able to find anyone before then, and I am so happy that we did! And that she's so perfect!" Heaven dances around with Aisling. "We have so many people coming to see our beautiful princess, right? Uncle Patty, Aunt Maura, Grandpa Paolo, Uncle Roman…so many people who want to hug and kiss you!"

She must seriously be delirious from lack of sleep.

Still…for as much anger as I feel, I can't help but smile, remembering the tight-knit relationship I had with my own mother before she died. She was always so happy, so cheerful, and so doting on me and my brother. In retrospect, I guess it was her way of shining light on the darkness that loomed over us on a daily basis. She brightened our world to the point that we couldn't see the gloom that would eventually overtake us all.

A pang in my chest jars me when I think of Maks and my jaw tightens.

He was the one reminder of that light that I had left to cling to.

And these people are somehow responsible for extinguishing it.

"Anya, when would you like to start?" Heaven asks.

I force a smile. "I don't have any other obligations, so the sooner the better!"

"Fabulous!" Heaven says. "I already have a room set up for you. Wishful thinking, I guess." She chuckles. "Would you like to see it?"

"Oh, sure," I say. "I'd love to!" I say with false brightness.

Over my shoulder, I catch a glimpse of Dante and Matteo talking, their heads close together. I really wish I was a fly on the wall behind them. I wonder whose murder they're plotting right now.

My gaze lingers on Dante for a second longer than I mean for it to. The muscles in his bicep flex when he runs his hand through his hair, his jaw tense. Despite my knowledge about him and this family, a shiver of desire shuttles through me.

"It's just down this hallway," Heaven says, pointing. I guess she may have said it earlier, but because my gaze was all tangled up in Dante, I missed it.

Dante looks up, his blue eyes narrowing at me. He flashes a half-smirk that makes my knees wobbly and I twist away, my breath hitching.

I really have to get this body of mine under control and in line with my head.

These carnal sensations are very distracting and I need to focus on the task at hand.

My own specialty...destruction.

I hurry out of the room behind Heaven, taking stock of my surroundings. Lots of closed doorways. One of them must be an office, right? Not that I have any idea what I'm looking for or who I need to deliver it to, for that matter.

There is always the possibility that the Villanis don't keep their criminal dealings documented on paper.

That will be a challenge.

It will force me to come up with some other creative way of getting what I need. I could always figure out a way to get Dante spilling some incriminating secrets while he sleeps...

A tingling sensation in my belly accompanies the delicious vision of Dante's hard body tangled up in a stark white bedsheet dancing through my mind.

Oh, for fuck's sake!

How twisted am I?

I need to hate these people!

I need to hate *him*!

Heaven pushes open a door and waves her hand around. "I hope you like it," she says in a soft voice.

My breath catches as I take in the space. It's three times the size of my bedroom back in Brooklyn, decorated in soft creams and blues with gold accents.

Blue is my favorite color.

She could never have known that.

I walk in, running my hand over the plush comforter and throw pillows. Sheer white panels with gold threads weaves into the fabric hanging next to the window overlooking the Strip. The furniture is cream with crystal knobs that glimmer in the overhead light.

It's gorgeous.

And another tiny shred of resolve falters as I turn to say thank you, but I choke on the words before I can get them out, an unexpected gaggle of tears gathering in the back of my throat.

My mother and I decorated my bedroom back in the Ukraine in this exact way. She wanted me to wake up in a place that was as bright and shiny as I was.

Heaven beams at me, her eyes sparkling as bright as the crystals in the ceiling chandelier. "Do you like it?" she asks, biting on her lower lip. "We can change whatever you want. I just want to make sure you're completely comfortable here."

I swallow down the sadness and ignore the sharp pain assaulting my heart at the memory of me and my mother smiling and laughing as we worked, flicking paint at one another as we transformed my space into...well, *this*.

God, I haven't thought about my real home in so long before today.

And now that the wound has been torn open, I want to crumble onto the bed and just let out everything that I've kept bottled up for so long.

Heaven takes a tentative step toward me. "Anya, are you okay? You look a little pale."

I give my head a quick shake and force it all down...the torment, the despair, and the rage.

As usual.

I only allow it to unleash when I'm sitting on top of a victim, ready to impale him with a sharp steel blade.

"I'm fine," I manage to say in a shaky breath. "It's perfect. It reminds me of...of my old bedroom. A long time ago..." My voice trails off. "I love it."

Her face lights up. "Oh, great! I'm so happy to hear that! I picked everything out myself. I tried to think of the exact space

I'd love and this is what I came up with!" She winks at me. "I guess we have the same taste, huh?"

"Seems so." I smile tightly. "Um, I think the only last loose end I have to tie up is bringing over my things from the Bellagio. That's where I'm staying."

She wrinkles her nose. "That place? So twenty years ago," she mutters.

I chuckle "So I've heard. But I guess that doesn't matter anymore, right?"

"Nope!" She grabs my arm and leads me back to the living room. "Dante! I need you to take Anya back to the crappy Bellagio so she can get her things." She hands Aisling to me and practically dances over to Matteo, putting her hands on his shoulders. "And I think you and I have some planning to do. You know, for *later*."

Dante makes a gagging sound and stands up from the couch where he was sitting. "I just threw up in my mouth a little bit there, guys. Can you save your *planning* for after we leave?" He walks over to me, a lazy grin on his face. "In fact, I don't want to poison Aisling's ears with talk of your sordid sex life, so we'll just take her along for the ride. Give her a chance to get to know her new *friend*."

The way he says 'friend' makes the hairs on the back of my neck prickle.

Matteo pulls Heaven onto his lap and tosses Dante a set of keys since we clearly can't take the Ferrari. I pick up the diaper bag and sling it over my shoulder and the three of us head out of the apartment and down to the lobby. I watch as Dante balances Aisling in his left arm, keeping her snuggled against his chest. He's smiling, she's smiling, and I swear I feel the thing I swore I'd never feel...

The ovary thing.

I can't explain away the pang I feel in that area as I walk alongside them and stare, just like all of the other pathetic women I pass.

The two of them just look so precious together. Endorphins are practically oozing from Dante's body, and every single woman in his path seems to get swept away in them. They look at him, practically drooling, licking their lips because not only does he have the face and body of a fucking god, he's carrying a beautiful baby girl.

That's crack to most of the female population.

And evidently, to me as well.

We get outside and one of the valets comes over for the keys. Seconds later, a blacked-out Cadillac Escalade pulls up in front of us and Dante pulls open the back door, fastening Aisling into the car seat facing backward. Then he pulls open my door and winks. "Your chariot."

He *so* doesn't seem like the assassin type.

But then again, maybe that's how he flies under the radar. He's smooth, charming, and cocky with a bad boy glint in his eye — not the brooding, menacing, killer kind of guy.

I step onto the running board to climb inside, but my foot slips forward and I grab onto the door to keep myself from tumbling out of the car.

My arms flail, trying desperately to grip any part of the door that I can, but my fingers slip off the leather. "Ahh!" I yelp, my body plummeting right into Dante's arms before my face kisses the cobblestone driveway.

I breathe deeply, drinking in his masculine scent and letting it awaken the butterflies in my belly.

Before I met Dante, I'd never felt the damn things.

I had no idea they actually existed beyond the romance novels I'd devour.

But in the past twenty or so hours, they've been fluttering and flitting around pretty much nonstop whenever he's in the vicinity.

Jesus.

I don't even know who I am right now!

I feel his heart racing at the same speed as mine as our eyes meet. He holds me for a few seconds longer than necessary before turning me upright and placing my feet on the ground. "You okay? I know those running boards can be tricky." He winks at me and a rush of heat floods my cheeks.

I flip my hair. "Yeah, well, I guess the bottoms of my sandals are a little slippery."

"Or you just wanted an excuse to be back in my arms," he murmurs.

I gasp, pushing him away. "You are such an arrogant ass!" I snap. "I told you that wasn't happening again!"

"Yeah, yeah," he says with a smirk. "I heard what you said. But maybe your body is telling you that it doesn't agree with that mouth of yours, the way it did when I dropped you off at the Bellagio."

I slowly climb back into the truck, holding tight to everything I can. Only when I'm seated do I flash him a death look. "Don't pretend to know what my body wants. And don't flatter yourself into thinking it wants *you*."

He snickers and closes the door once I'm inside. My pulse beats hard against my throat as he jumps into the driver's seat and flips on the satellite radio to some noisy rock station. "You're kinda sensitive, yeah?"

"You're kinda annoying, yeah?" I snort.

"I prefer to think of myself as curious," he says, pulling away from the curb and out onto the Strip headed toward the Bellagio. "Inquisitive. And you're pretty much the opposite. So let's add that to the list. Doesn't like to talk, isn't wild about old women, doesn't have friends, and completely shut down emotionally. What gives? Who made you this way, Anya?"

"Whoa!" I exclaim. "That's a lot of analysis for knowing me barely two hours! And nobody made me this way, thank you very much. We all have pasts that shape us, right? I mean, you obviously have one of your own. Is that what turned you into this egotistical, entitled, whore magnet?"

Oops. I didn't mean for that last one to slip out…

"Whore magnet?" His eyebrows lift. "That's harsh. I'd have thought you could come up with something that sounds a little nicer than that."

"So you're not arguing the other things I said."

"I think you may have unfairly judged me," he says. "But just so you know, I'm adding defensive to my list for you."

I roll my eyes. My God, he has me in such a twist! Why can't I just shut it down, dammit?

Aisling babbles in the backseat as the pounding bass guitar blares through the speakers. "What the heck is this, anyway? And how can you subject the baby to this devil worship music?"

"Okay, first, it's not devil worship music. It's Metallica." He pauses. "Maybe a little devil worship, I don't know. And second, Aisling loves it. She knows all of my favorites — Tool, Ozzy, Black Sabbath."

I shake my head. "You're crazy. You're going to poison her brain with this crap!"

He chuckles as he turns into the long driveway of the Bellagio. "Trust me, with her genes, she's got enough poison running through her veins already. Anyway, don't take my comments as judgments. I'm observant and I listen." He shrugs. "If you're gonna be taking care of my niece, I want to know this stuff. What makes you tick."

"I don't work for *you* so I don't really see how it's any of your concern," I say in a sweet voice.

"True, but because of my work, we'll be together a lot. And inquiring minds wanna know." He steps on the brake as a valet comes over to take his keys.

"Just leave it up here," Dante says with a nod of his head. "We'll only be a little while." Then he slips the guy a twenty-dollar bill as he gets out.

He jogs around to my side and opens my door, holding out a hand. "Wanna just jump?" he asks with a twinkle in his eye. "Or are you gonna let your shoes make that decision for you?"

I let out a little huff, fighting the urge to dive against him and step onto the driveway as he takes Aisling from the car seat. He balances her on his hip and we walk into the hotel, which, after being inside of the Excelsior, does seem a little…dingy.

We walk into the hotel, and out of the corner of my eye, I can see Dante evaluate every last bit of the place. He studies it in a way that makes you believe he's just giving a sweep of a glance, but in reality, he's devouring every single detail.

I know because it's the exact way I take stock of situations.

Being observant is essential in our line of work, even though he still hasn't admitted to me we share a common occupation.

"Well, what the fuck do we have here?" A deep voice comes up behind us as we head toward the elevator and I jump at the intrusion. A beefy, dark-haired guy who looks to be about Dante's age fixes a glare at us and folds his arms over his ample chest. "Since when do you slum it around these parts, Villani?" he snips sarcastically.

Dante chuckles as he turns toward the man. "Petey, when the fuck are you gonna ditch this place and come work for the hottest place on the Strip?"

"Oh, you mean the Hard Rock?"

They both laugh and Aisling chimes in with her own brand of belly laugh.

Petey shrugs. "Jimmy took me back after I got out. It was a no-brainer. You're picking 'em real young these days, huh?" Petey says with a nod at Aisling.

Dante rolls his eyes. "She's my niece, prick."

"Good to know. I thought you mighta knocked up some broad." His eyes flicker in my direction and he tries to bite back his words. "Uh, girl."

"Nah. Nobody's been able to pin me down yet." He looks over at me and winks. "But ya never know when that may change. Shit happens when you least expect it, right?"

"I guess. I mean, that's what happened when I got shipped off. I didn't expect that shit."

Dante laughs, dropping his voice. "Well, when you get caught with a bag full of cash that doesn't belong to you, is it really that much of a shock?"

"I guess I just thought I was better."

"That kind of thinking will get you pinched in a hot second."

"Yup. It sure as hell did. So why the hell are you here? If the boss sees you, he'll exterminate your ass, so if you're running some kind of a scam, do it fast and I'll turn my back on it."

"I appreciate the show of loyalty, but I'm here to pack up my niece's new au pair. She's found greener pastures, away from this tenement."

"Nice. So she's the nanny," he murmurs, giving me an appraising look.

"I am standing right here," I snip. "You don't have to eye me like a freaking beef kabob."

Petey does a double take and Dante smirks. "You never were too smooth about shit like that," he says.

Petey throws his hands in the air. "Eh, sue me. I just got outta the clink, for fuck's sake."

Dante nods. "Yep, smooth as fucking silk." He slaps Petey on the back. "Listen, we're gonna go, but if you ever want a better gig, you know where to find it. I'll make it happen."

"Thanks, Dante." He looks at me again and my skin crawls under his lewd stare. "And good luck, nanny."

"Au pair," I say through gritted teeth.

"Yeah, whatever. Enjoy the diaper part of the job." He gives Dante a little salute and walks around a corner, disappearing into the casino.

"What a fucking tool," I mutter as we walk toward the elevator bank.

"He's okay. You've got to learn not to take yourself so seriously. The guy's a little pent up. He's harmless."

Harmless. Yes, I could split his ass in two without a second's hesitation.

"And how exactly do you know Petey?" I ask as we step into the elevator. I stab the button for my floor and the door closes. "Do you know him through your real estate investment business?" I ask lightly, playing the part of the dumb blonde. I tilt my head to the side, wondering if he buys it.

"He's not an investments kind of guy," Dante says. "But you already know that, don't you?"

I shrug. There is a hell of a lot I don't know, things I'd very much like to know, but nobody seems to be cooperating. Like my uncle, who hasn't answered the text I sent earlier about getting the job.

"He did security work for my family back when we started out here. But he's got sticky fingers. It's why he got pinched in the first place."

"So why'd you dangle a job in front of him?" I ask. "Why would you want to deal with that?"

"Because you never want to alienate someone who can get you something you need. Petey is a thief, but he's got a lot of friends. And everyone needs friends in the casino business. Can never have too many."

"I thought you were in real estate investments."

"My family is in the gaming business. I help them whenever I can."

"So they'd appreciate the help of an ex-con?"

"Jesus, I've been probed before, but this is way more invasive. I won't lie. I kinda like it. Although I'd like it more if it included whips and chains. Really make the interrogation interesting." He chuckles. "By the way, I'm adding judgmental to your list."

I put my hands on my hips. "Is it wrong to call him an ex-con if that's what he is?"

"No, not wrong. But you prickle every time I add something, and I like getting a rise out of you." The elevator dings and we get off, standing face to face in the hallway.

"So where are we going?" he asks. "I'm in your hands."

I snort, twisting away from him and stalking down the hallway. "You'll never be in my hands."

"Never say never. Those shoes of yours have a mind of their own. They crave what you're too stubborn to admit you want."

The tingles that follow those words assault my body, igniting every cell.

It's not that I'm too stubborn.

It's that I feel completely disloyal for even thinking these crazy things about him, for letting myself feel anything for a man who may have had a hand in my brother's death.

He's got darkness in him. Sure, he uses humor and innuendo and that whole fun uncle façade to cover it up, but a person who suffers the same affliction can see right through the mask.

A person like me.

Because for a good portion of my life, I've been consumed by the murk with no hope for even a sliver of light to shine through.

So, no, it's not me being stubborn.

It's me resisting what I secretly want because it's forbidden.

And wrong.

And deadly on so many levels.

For both of us.

Chapter Nine
DANTE

I can't forget that kiss, dammit. No matter how hard I try to erase it from my memory, something about her keeps dragging me back in.

There are plenty of other things I could be doing right now.

Instead, I'm hanging all over her and my niece, and why?

Because I can't accept the fact that she's denying her feelings about the Bellagio kiss.

Okay, fine, I can't accept that she's denying *me*.

It shouldn't matter. I don't get tied up in relationship strings. I like living day to day and on the edge, not answering to anyone, chasing down targets, free as a fucking bird to come and go as I please.

And yet, here I still am.

How excited would Matteo be to know that this girl has me completely inside out right now, to the point where I'd consider hanging around here for longer?

We walk back into the apartment and Aisling is draped over Anya's shoulder, her chubby arms hanging limply at her sides.

The kid is completely starched.

I watch as Anya rubs her back and cradles her as she walks into the nursery to lie her down for a nap. She peeks at me over her shoulder and grins at me before she disappears down the hall. Her ass swings gently from side to side, her leg muscles tightening with every step.

Christ, do I want them wrapped tight around me.

And of course, my balls tingle as a result of the X-rated images now wallpapering my mind.

She doesn't realize that every time she lets me in a little bit, my cock gets more and more excited at the prospect of making her acquaintance.

But she's the au fucking pair.

Off limits.

Besides, she's young. Just a kid. I have no business being around her, with her, on top of her...

Argh!

I push back my hair and grab a beer from the refrigerator, using the granite countertop to pop off the top.

The cool liquid hits my lips and I guzzle it down, mainly to cool off what's igniting deep inside of me.

My cell phone rings and I grab it out of my pocket, stabbing the Accept button.

"Patty," I say. "What's going on?"

"I just came from a meeting," he says, his voice dropping. "And Conor dropped a bombshell on us. Are you ready?"

"When it comes to your fucknut brother, I'm never ready, so just give it to me."

"He's coming with us to Vegas. Says it's time to make amends with Heaven, for the family, for my father, for everyone. He wants to meet his niece, says he's wasted too much time being angry. He wants to unite our families once and for all."

My jaw drops. "Shut the front door."

"It's fucking true, dude. I felt like my head was gonna spin off my body."

"You think your dad or your aunt had something to do with it?"

"I don't know. I mean, Niall and Quinn were always gonna come, but my dad is a stubborn sonofabitch when he wants to be. As much as he misses Heaven, he'll never make the first move."

"And forgive me for being a little suspicious of Conor suddenly wanting to be one big happy gangster family after he almost killed his sister." I take another sip. "You sure he wasn't high?"

Patrick chuckles. "No, I didn't get a chance to check out the toxicity report before the meeting."

"I'm just sayin'..." I shake my head. "Maybe when the shit with the Russians went bad and he fucked over Vigo, he decided he needed more muscle so he decided to use the christening as an excuse to connect."

"I don't know what the reason is, but he seems damn anxious to get out there."

"He's gotta be running from something. And the last thing we need is for whoever or whatever is chasing him to show up on our front door step." Patrick and Conor aren't on the best of terms, but it's still his brother, so I opt against telling him that I will fuck Conor's shit up permanently if he starts trouble out here. I don't need his bad decisions chasing down my family.

My trigger finger itches and damn, I'd love to play target practice with Conor's head.

"Well, listen, give Matteo a heads-up. He needs to be prepared for whatever this will become, you know?"

"Yes, I can't wait to have that conversation since he's so gracious and agreeable when it comes to shit with your family." I roll my eyes. My brother has been on edge for the past months, knowing that the other shoe is about to drop.

And here we go.

We've gotten tangled up in way too much lately, starting with that whole standoff with soldiers from the Volkov Bratva at Roman's place back in Manhattan. Seems like my brothers have this knack for getting involved with women who wear bright red targets on their backs...targets that somehow are transferrable and end up splayed across ours.

In the case of that bratva run-in, Roman's fiancé, Marchella, ended up on their radar because of her idiot brother. He killed the nephew of some guy named Boris after the nephew surprised him during a raid on a drug stockpile.

I get it.

The kid was family and Boris wanted to avenge his death.

So, the Russians came, they saw, they wanted vengeance.

But we didn't let them have it.

Instead, I drove their vodka-soaked asses outta our territory and back to Brooklyn.

They didn't like that much. And Boris always vowed he'd be back to collect on what he was owed.

He hasn't, and it's because he's a low-level pawn with no real authority in the bratva hierarchy. There was no order to kill

Marchella. It was pure bloodlust on Boris's part. He had no backing when he showed up at Roman's, just a grudge.

I rake a hand through my hair.

The last thing we need is to have the Russians up our asses again because of Conor. We already put that to bed. Volkov and Matteo had an unspoken agreement to leave the whole thing in the past, and I'll be damned if it gets resurrected.

And if they came here looking to roast his ass, I'd gladly hand it over.

Vengeance be fucking theirs.

Anya appears in the doorway of the kitchen, one of the straps of her sundress slipping off her shoulder. She casually leans against the doorframe, her long blonde hair cascading down her arm as she eyes me with curiosity.

"Listen, I've gotta go," I mutter, my eyes never leaving her face. "I'll call you after I speak to him." I click the End button and put my phone onto the granite countertop behind me. The neckline of her dress is low enough to give me a peek and my fingertips sizzle with longing. I want to drag them up and down the sides of her slim torso again, feel her body hum under the palms of my hands.

I clear my throat. "Where's, ah, the baby?"

She shrugs. "Our little outing must have been too much excitement for her. I changed her diaper and she never once opened her eyes."

"So I guess that means it's time for your first official break," I say, a teasing smirk playing at my lips.

"I guess so," she says softly, inching toward me. "You know, I'm perfectly capable of occupying myself. *I'm* the au pair. I don't need one myself."

"You're saying you want me to leave?" I ask, her floral scent close enough to taunt my nostrils.

"I'm saying that I don't need a keeper." She runs a hand through her long blonde hair, lazily throwing back her head. Her tits press tight against the fabric, and the deep ache in my balls is back.

Not that it ever really left.

But damn, I'd love for someone to give it some relief.

A little lick, rub, and tug action would make me blow like a fucking volcano, make my head right again.

Anya parts her lips, turning her face up toward mine.

I should be thinking about damage control.

She reaches out, placing her hand on the counter next to me, her hip grazing mine.

I should be thinking about finding Conor and beating him to a bloody pulp.

Instead, I'm thinking of all of the different, creative ways I could be this girl's very naughty, kinky keeper.

I meant it when I said I'd punish her.

I'd fucking make her scream, beg, cry, and wail for more.

I press my body against her, backing her into the stainless steel refrigerator. "I'm saying you do," I growl, reaching behind her and fisting her hair as I crush my lips against hers.

Fuck! No!

Wrong, wrong, wrong!

I plunder her hungry mouth with my tongue, coiling heat raging through every extremity.

But God, it feels so right.

And in that moment, I forget that she's my niece's au pair.

I forget she's a kid herself.

I just get lost in her — all of her.

I dig my fingers into the small of her back and she bucks her hips against me, rubbing herself against me. My cock is so hard, it's ready to explode through my shorts. I slide it against her, making her gasp as I rub my bulge against her pussy. I reach around and knead the flesh of her ass before lifting her into my arms.

She throws her arms around my neck, her teeth tugging at my lower lip as she thrusts into me. And just like that, I'm dry fucking her in my brother's kitchen.

The au pair.

On her first day of work.

I've completely corrupted her.

And basically let her do the same to me, because, let's face it.

This girl is no innocent.

The palms of my hands tingle as I smack the plump globe of her ass. I love the sound…the power I have over her in that instant. Her eyes fly open, her face flushed a deep shade of pink. The feeling of my hand hitting against her flesh sends electric currents directly to my balls, and I can come like a rocket right now if I let myself.

Just from spanking her.

She looks at me, her eyes half-hooded and I grab her by the hair. "You're a dirty girl, aren't you?" I hiss. "You come out here with your dress falling off of you and you expect me to ignore it?

Huh?" I tug her hair harder and a tiny mewl escapes her lips. "Your job is to be a good girl, but you're so fucking bad, aren't you? And you deserve to be punished." I smack her again, bringing one hand around to her pussy and slipping my digits into her wet slit. I drive them into her as she writhes against me. "You're so wet. That tells me you love it, that you want me to punish you, that you like my hand stinging your ass. Is that true, Anya? Tell me!" I grunt, balancing her in one arm as I drag my fingers in and out of her soft pussy.

She whimpers against me, her head resting against the refrigerator. "Yes," she whispers.

"Louder!"

"Yes!" she whisper-shouts. "Oh my God!"

The click of the keycard sliding into the door lock sounds. "Fuck!" I whisper as Anya's feet hit the floor. She hurries to adjust herself, but there's nothing I can do about myself.

No adjustments to be made.

It kind of is what it is.

I wink at her, giving my fingers a quick suck. She grabs the back of my head and kisses me hard on the mouth before jumping back once again.

When Heaven and Matteo walk into the kitchen, at least we're a respectable distance apart from one another.

Shit, if these walls had eyes…or cameras…

I'd be dead, that's for sure.

Heaven beams at us, and I can tell right away from the glint in her eye and the pink tinge in her cheeks that she's finally gotten laid.

Good for them.

And good for me.

"I didn't expect you guys back so quickly," she says, pulling open the refrigerator and grabbing a bottle of Pellegrino sparkling water.

"Yes, well, I didn't have much to move over here," Anya says. "And Aisling was so tuckered out that she fell right asleep."

Heaven gives Matteo a knowing look. "Yeah, well, we know how long that lasts, and it's never enough! I bet she'll be babbling in about ten minutes. I swear, I don't know where her energy comes from."

Anya laughs, her bright white teeth flashing in the late afternoon sunlight streaming into the windows. The gold highlights in her hair shimmer, and I ache to run my fingers through the glossy waves again.

Matteo snaps his finger, and the sound jerks me from my borderline X-rated thoughts about the sexy new hire. I look up and see that his forehead is pinched. He nods toward his office and we back out of the room while the girls keep up a steady stream of chatter about things I can't be bothered to follow right now.

I need to focus, and not just on the memory of Anya's hot body pressed against me. Matteo is not happy right now, and I have a feeling I already know why.

He closes the door behind us and collapses in his chair, holding a hand to his head.

"Matty, you should be relaxed right now. You just fucked your wife. Why isn't that making you smile?"

He slams his fists on the desk. "Because of her fucking family, Dante. Because I just found out that asshole brother of hers is coming for the christening after all of this time not seeing Heaven, not speaking to her, not even texting to ask about

Aisling." He shakes his head. "I swear to Christ, if he ruins this for her, if he dares make her anxious or upset or—"

"We'll all have him, Matty. Don't worry about that."

He rubs the back of his neck. "We need to corner him once he gets here. I wanna hear directly from him what the hell he's doing with the Volkov Bratva. We escaped them once. I don't want to make a habit of it."

I nod. "Patty has nothing."

Matteo rolls his eyes. "Why am I not surprised? He's too *GQ* to be useful."

"Well, if Conor doesn't make a move, Patty can't track it. It's not entirely his fault. It's not like he's missing anything."

Matteo lets out a groan and sits back in his chair. "You know what? I'm calling Roman." I come around behind him and sit on the edge of the desk. He stabs my youngest brother's phone number into his laptop and waits until Roman answers. He's covered in whipped cream and chocolate syrup.

I stifle a laugh but Matteo just glares at him.

"You had to answer the call like that?"

"I thought it might be important and didn't have time to clean up," Roman says with a shrug. I can see his fiancée Marchella in the background giggling and playing with their puppy Bella.

She's also covered in cream.

"I feel like we're interrupting something," I say with a snicker.

Roman licks some cream off his finger. "Well, then get on with it so *I* can get on with it, yeah?"

Matteo's lips stretch into a straight line. "Conor is coming to the christening."

"Shit," Roman says. "Did he call Heaven?"

"No, Aunt Maura sent me a text. He fucking couldn't have even sent it himself, that pansy ass prick!" He fists his hair. "Guys, I seriously wanna kill the bastard. Like 'drag a fork down the front of his chest and then gouge out his eyes' kill him."

"Easy," Roman says. "Do we know why, all of a sudden, he wants to be included in family shit again?"

"I have a feeling it's because he's done something stupid and needs us to bail him out. He's got nobody else because everyone else on the planet wants him dead more than we do," Matteo grunts. "But there's a problem. He's gotten himself involved with the Volkov Bratva. You remember them, right, Romo?"

Roman groans and rolls his eyes, spraying some whipped cream directly into his mouth. "Those fuckers. I thought we were rid of that bullshit. How'd Conor get mixed up with them?"

"None of us know," I say. "But Patty and I went to that place in Brooklyn to investigate while I was in New York and ask one of the top guys some questions."

"And? How'd that go?" Roman asks.

"Not great. He was already dead." An image of Red Death flashes before my eyes and my cock thickens. Fuck, where the hell did that come from? A tiny twinge of guilt takes hold because I had my tongue down Anya's throat and my dick pressed against her only a few minutes ago.

Besides, the assassin blew me off before I could get anything else from her.

She's gone.

Over.

Vanished into thin air.

I'm envious. I used to be so damn good at that, too, pulling the whole disappearing act thing after a hit.

Christ, I need my life back!

"You think Conor did it?"

I sigh. "I think there's a lot we need to find out. And Patty's been tailing him, but no luck. He hasn't seen anything suspicious. Then the travel plans came out and the puzzle pieces are falling together. It all points to some fallout with the Volkov Bratva. I'd stake my life on it. He's coming to us for salvation because if they catch him first, they'll incinerate his ass."

"Okay, so what do you need from me? You want me to go to Hell's Kitchen and dislocate every limb on his body and put him in traction so he can't fuck around with the outside world for the near future?" Roman asks. "Done and done."

"No, just keep an eye on him, Romo. Ask around, go in the back door."

He flashes a wicked grin. "Fuck yeah, bro. That's my plan. Right after we get off the phone."

I roll my eyes. "Just use your network and figure out what the hell the Russians have on him. And how much money he owes them since it's gonna become our debt to pay."

"The hell it will!" Matteo says. "I'd rather let them pull the skin from his bones before I give them a goddamn penny!"

"If it's gonna keep Heaven and Aisling safe, you'll pay," I say with a pointed look.

He lets out a sigh and collapses back against the chair. "I know. But I might have his dick cut off anyway. Just because of everything he's done to screw us over. You know he's angry that I shut down every deal he's managed to make since nobody is gonna pick Conor over me as a business associate."

"Yeah, that's gotta be pissing him off big time. No wonder he went to find the Russians in Brooklyn. Except now he's screwed them over too."

"Romo, we need to keep his black cloud away from us. Make it happen, yeah?" Matteo snaps.

"You've got it." He looks down at himself. "Can I go now? I'd really like to fuck my fiancée."

Matteo doesn't reply. He just hits the End button and shakes his head at me. "The future of the family, huh?" he grumbles.

"Hey, be thankful it's only whipped cream. Things could be worse. At least we don't have a Conor."

"Yeah, thank fuck for that," Matteo mutters. "There's no way I'm letting him anywhere near Heaven and the baby, by the way. You make sure that you have a target on him at all times and you pull the trigger if he so much as picks his nose and it looks suspicious." He shakes his head. "I don't trust him for shit, and if he's coming here for money, that's all he's getting. I will put a knife in his eye if he makes one false move."

"Don't worry. I'll be right behind you to twist it when you do."

Chapter Ten
ANYA

"Have an amazing time!" I say with false cheeriness, waving at Heaven and Matteo as they leave the apartment for their first night out in what seems to be a long time. I pick up Aisling's hand and shake it at her parents, and Heaven comes back for one more big kiss before Matteo drags her out the door. "Anya, you have all of the phone numbers, and Dante will be back soon with dinner, okay? We'll be back around one."

I nod. "Not a problem! She will be absolutely fine, no worries at all!"

"Have a good night," Matteo says curtly. My eyebrows furrow as the door closes, and I make a funny face at Aisling. "Daddy doesn't seem to like me very much," I croon. "What do you think, baby girl? Do you like me?"

Aisling giggles and stuffs my finger into her mouth.

"That's what I thought," I say, pulling my phone out of my pocket again. Still nothing from Uncle Boris.

Tiny alarm bells go off in my mind. He still doesn't even know I got the job! How the heck am I supposed to be an investigator if I don't even know what I'm looking for?

But more than that, I'm getting nervous about the radio silence. I step through the events at Tatiana in my head, trying to recall if I made eye contact with anyone who might be able to pin his murder on me.

Dante sure as hell doesn't know it was me, but someone else who might have inside knowledge about the bad blood shared by Vigo and my uncle might see something different.

And if they couldn't find me, they'd look for him next.

A shiver ripples through me and I dial his number again. This time, I let it ring about twenty times before giving up.

I say a silent prayer that his ringer is off. Or that he accidentally left his phone somewhere. Or that his phone is out of battery.

Anything other than the horrible alternative of him lying facedown in a ditch somewhere, paying for a crime he didn't commit.

But if any eyewitnesses could pin the actual murder on me, they'd also know he called in the hit.

Volkov wouldn't think twice about slicing his head off, no matter what kind of deal he was promised.

And I'd definitely be next on his hit list.

I wander out to the balcony and sink down onto one of the chaise lounges. There are firepits on the two far corners. Obviously for ambiance because there is absolutely no need for heat out here in the desert.

In the sweltering summertime, no less.

I sit back against the cushion and cuddle Aisling against me, staring up at the dusky blueish-purple sky. "How could I let him touch me like that?" I ask the baby. "I walked right into it and climbed him like a freaking tree! But, oh my God, did he taste good. And he smelled amazing...like cloves and spice and sex. Oh, yes, sex. So much sex..." I give my head a good shake. "What the heck is wrong with me, little girl? Huh? I am a hot mess and a half over your uncle."

Tears spring to my eyes and I let out a shuddering breath. "What am I even doing here? I'm out here, by myself, on my own with no direction at all, doing a job I have no clue how to do. And what's worse is that I'm falling for a guy who was part of something that hurt me so deeply, I will never, ever heal from the wound."

"Babababababab!" Aisling says, her voice muffled as she continues gnawing at my finger.

I shake my hand, letting out a deep sigh. "I can't get in touch with my uncle, I'm living in the same place as people who had a hand in killing my brother, which I can't even confirm because my uncle has fallen off the face of the Earth!" I let out a huff. "It would be so much easier if we switched places right now, you know? I could be a cute little baby and you could deal with the adult stuff. Sound good?"

I smooth the top of her head. It's so soft and she smells so amazing.

She's also not sticky at all.

Of course, that's in part because I keep wiping her down after she eats or drinks anything at all. Jesus, I've wiped her down so much, I've probably worn away her top layer of skin. I rise to a seated position and balance her on my lap. "I have an idea. Why don't we go and check out Daddy's office? We have to hurry before Uncle Dante comes back, though." I stand up and set her on one hip, walking back inside. I have no idea when he'll be back, and I don't want to get caught so we have to work fast looking for something. Don't ask me what, though. Because I can't tell you!" I sing-song. "Because I don't know! But maybe it'll just jump out at me, right? I mean, that could happen. I'm sure I could pick out shady paperwork."

Sure, I can. With all of my shady paperwork training.

I roll my eyes as we walk down the hall together in the direction of Matteo's office. I saw him pull Dante in their earlier, and I can only hope he didn't lock the door when he left.

I twist the handle and the door opens.

Bingo!

He obviously forgot to lock it, which is really strange since he clearly doesn't trust me for shit.

His brain must have partially melted from the quickie afternoon sex they had because there's no way he'd have just left the gates to the kingdom open like that. His mind was evidently in other places.

Works for me, though.

I creep into the room and head for his desk. The top is immaculate. Polished. Shiny. Not a single fingerprint or a stray piece of paper. I frown. He's the head of a big-time mafia family. He wouldn't leave illicit business dealings documented and out in the open for anyone to see and steal.

Dammit!

I try to pull open one of the drawers.

Sonofabitch!

Locked.

Every single one of them.

Nothing incriminating at all that I can see.

But I'll bet behind those locks, there's a very different story waiting to be told.

And I desperately need to read it!

I back away from the desk and meander around the room, checking out books and photos and assorted knick-knacks. There's some signed Yankee memorabilia scattered around the place, mixed in with some signed jerseys and pictures of the Italian national football team. There's even a soccer ball stashed in a corner. I smile down at Aisling. "Was Daddy hoping for a boy?" I murmur.

Then my eyes fall on the family photos.

Interestingly, there aren't any professional wedding photos of Matteo and Heaven. Knowing what I do of Heaven and her taste so far, I'd have expected at least one. Instead, I just see what looks to be a selfie at a restaurant. It's the two of them, a little flushed but smiling big for the camera. Matteo's arm is outstretched, so I can tell he took it himself.

A happy and private moment for the newlywed couple.

But no other photos posing in front of fancy cars with lots of flowers and bridesmaids and champagne.

I guess they decided to eliminate the bullshit.

That photo is real, not staged.

The corners of my lips lift.

It's exactly what I would want, not that pure happiness is something I've come to expect in my life. In fact, it's something that keeps getting yanked away, so I think it's best not to even bother chasing it.

I walk over to another bookshelf and let out a low chuckle. They clearly didn't go the same route with Aisling. She's only five months old, and by the looks of it, has had more photo shoots than a lot of models.

They clearly adore her and each other.

I feel a sharp pang in my chest.

Perfect little family.

I want to hate them. I have to hate them.

But I can't fight the emotions bubbling in my chest when I watch Heaven with Aisling and Matteo, when I see the light in Matteo's eyes as he looks at his wife and plays with his daughter.

I've been here for less than a day with no real objective in sight other than focus on the hate.

But the human in me is fighting really hard against my vicious alter ego and again, the thought crosses my mind about the twinge of remorse I always feel when I pull a trigger...no matter what, no matter who.

It always takes me a second to block out the fact that there may be some redeeming quality that I'm about to snuff out.

I've seen a lot of redeeming qualities today.

And have gotten zero confirmation of the non-redeeming ones.

Motherfucker!

I hate that I'm waffling like this, that I'm concerned about this baby, that I'm drowning in pent-up desire for Dante, that I actually like Heaven and Matteo.

I was supposed to come here protected by a wall of pain and anger, and it's just crumbling like a stale cookie around me?

After mere hours?

I am on this quest for revenge, and I need to remember that.

I'm a heartless bitch. It's why I'm so good at my job. I am cold, unfeeling, and brutal, dammit!

"Babababababa!" Aisling says, jerking me from my self-pep talk.

I nuzzle her neck and make a funny sound with my mouth that has her chuckling loudly.

Oh, for Pete's sake!

I'm not an au pair!

No, I am a freaking hot mess, though.

In the distance, I hear the keycard sound and I dart out of the office, pulling the door closed quietly behind me. I jog into the living room, my bare feet pattering against the cool, polished floor tiles, just in time to see Dante push open the door. His arms are laden with bags, and scents wafting from whatever is inside tease my nostrils, making my stomach rumble.

I wasn't even hungry a minute ago, but whatever he's carrying makes my mouth water.

He grins at me. "I have a surprise for you."

I settle Aisling in her Pack and Play and walk into the kitchen for plates, napkins, and utensils. Since I'm not sure where anything is stored, I just keep opening and closing cabinet doors until I find what I'm looking for.

"You know, while I appreciate the hand-holding, I can actually manage to do some things on my own." I peek at him through the half-wall leading into the living room. "You don't have to babysit *me*, Dante."

But even though I try to keep my tone light, the gravity of my words makes his brow furrow. "You know what? That really hurts, Anya. And after I brought you a whole meal prepared by your culinary idol, Tommy Marcone." He shakes his head and picks up the bags he'd just started unloading. "I guess I can find my brother Sergio and eat with him and his fiancée. I'd hate for all this food to go to waste on someone who doesn't appreciate my chivalrous efforts."

And as if on cue, my belly growls at me. I hear the message loud and clear.

Don't you dare let him leave with that food, you bitch!

I sigh. "Dante, wait. I'm sorry."

He shakes his head, still packing things into the bags again. "Nope, now you're just saying it because you want my food. Uh-uh."

"It's not because of the food!" I screech. "I'm sorry for saying that stuff."

"I don't believe you," he says, narrowing his eyes at me.

"Then, don't believe me!" I say, throwing my hands in the air. "I just..." You just what, Anya? You just happen to find yourself in the tangled web of a man who may have played a role in one of the most devastating experiences of your life and you don't know how to handle it? "I just am not used to being waited on like this." Okay, it's weak, but it's better than the alternative admission.

Part of me wants to throw him down on the couch, hold a knife to his throat, and demand he tell me everything he knows.

The other part of me wants to throw him down on the couch and ride him like a thoroughbred in pursuit of the Triple Crown.

In this moment, it really is a toss-up between the two.

"I'm supposed to be the caretaker," I say, my voice quivering a little as the words tumble from my lips. "I've always played that role and I guess I just don't know how to handle it when someone takes over for me." It's not entirely bullshit, either. As I got older and Maks became more and more unhinged, it was up to me to keep things on an even keel back in Brooklyn. I did what I could to make sure he was clean, fed, and clothed since he lost all desire for anything other than vengeance. I was always more calculated and methodical in my actions, which made me more of an asset to the organization. Conversely, Maks acted purely on emotion, always ready to unleash the fury stored deep within him. Hell, it's part of the reason I went with him the night he was killed. I figured with me in the car, he wouldn't pull any of his crazy ass stunts.

I had no idea that the tables would flip as they did.

Uncle Boris's words float back into my mind.

Maks was weak. He let his feelings rule his actions! Do you want to end up like him, Anya?

I swallow down the anger, trying desperately to keep myself calm. A few deep breaths settles my racing heart.

Dante folds his arms over his chest and stares at me. "You know that's the most you've told me about yourself since I almost ran you over this morning."

I manage a smile. "Oh yeah? So I bet you're going to add more to your list about me now. I don't have friends, don't like to talk, have no patience for old people...and what else?"

"Damaged," he says, his eyes boring into me. "There's a reason why you do this, why you wanted this job, and something tells me it's not because you love babies." He steps toward me and my breath hitches. "You're so closed off. Is it because you failed in this role before? Is that why you're trying to make up for it with strangers?"

My jaw drops. He got all of that from what I said?

He's too goddamn pretty to be that perceptive!

I swallow hard. "I'm not damaged," I say, trying to keep my voice even.

"We're all damaged, Anya. In some way or another. We're all looking for redemption."

"I don't need redemption! Spare me the dollar-store psychobabble," I snap. My jaw tightens, palms sweaty as they rub against my legs.

Dante circles me like a lion eyeing his prey. "So mysterious. So shut down. But so in need of carnal pleasure," he muses. "Even if you don't want to admit it to yourself. You're looking for something you either haven't found or had taken away. Admit it."

I roll my eyes. "That's your insightful analysis, huh? Because I got caught up in the moment—"

"A moment you created, if memory serves." He smirks. "Remember, rubbing up against me, touching my arm, giving me that fuck-me-now look?"

I throw my hands into the air. "Fine! I created it. Twice. I admit it!"

"So now are you going to admit the other thing?"

"What other thing?"

"That you're damaged."

"Jesus Christ!"

"Language," he says with a quirk of his brow.

I let out a snort. "You know what? I've lost my appetite. So thanks for that!" I turn on my heel, ready to stalk toward my room when I stop short.

Aisling.

I turn back around, scoop her up, and head back down the hallway. My stomach gurgles and clenches as my pulse throbs against my neck.

Fuck him for seeing all of that!

And how, by the way? I basically told him nothing and he managed to pull all of that from the minimal words I uttered.

I sink into the plush leather recliner in the corner of the room that overlooks the bright lights of the Las Vegas Strip. I stare into the night sky, at all of the stars twinkling against the blackness. I never saw that many stars in Brooklyn. The dark, ominous cloud of a hopeless future always hung low overhead, blocking any slivers of light from shining through.

But here, it feels like the cloud has lifted, albeit temporarily.

I had no idea what wounds would be torn open by being out here in Vegas. All of the things I resisted for so long, thrown in my face, taunting me because I'll never have them myself.

I made choices. A lot of choices.

And they defined my path.

It's not glamorous by any stretch, but it's been set.

I have to deliver for my uncle, for our livelihood, for our future... the future Maks will never get to experience.

Deliver what, though?

That's the hundred-million-dollar question.

My stomach rumbles again and Aisling's even breathing tells me that she's dozed off.

I wonder what was in those bags...

Tommy Marcone? *Really?*

There was so much scrumptiousness just beyond my fingertips and I screwed it up.

What's worse than shutting down is cutting someone off when they peg you exactly right.

And damn, did he peg me.

I also am not stupid. It's clear that he's hanging around at the request of Matteo. The guy doesn't trust me at all. I get it. He's got a lot at stake on a daily basis, and bringing a virtual stranger into his home doesn't give him a warm and fuzzy.

Rightly so, considering Uncle Boris had some in at the agency and was able to pull strings to get my bullshit resume sent directly to the Villanis. That's why Dante is here. He's watching me, making sure I don't act out of line. I'm actually shocked they left me here alone with the baby when Dante was getting dinner. It also makes me wonder who else is watching...and from where.

I already know what Dante would do to protect Aisling. He basically told me he has no limits when it comes to his family.

I dip my head down and inhale deeply, letting Aisling's sweet scent fill my lungs. It's weird, but it calms me. Makes me feel like I'm in the right place...for all of the wrong reasons, of course.

I rock her for a few more minutes, fuzzy fantasies about what kind of feast I missed out on looping through my mind. I haven't eaten a damn thing today, and this was my big chance to sink my teeth into a gourmet meal made by my cooking idol.

But I blew it because I couldn't handle that someone else could see my truth.

As my eyes drift closed, one final thought takes hold of my sleepy brain, refusing to let go.

Where the fuck is Uncle Boris?

Chapter Eleven
ANYA

Crack! Bang! Pop!

My throat is so tight, I can barely breathe as I stare at the man splayed across the dirty tile floor.

Three shots, right to the chest.

I sneak a look up at my uncle and he glares at me. Instead of giving me the approval I so desperately crave, he grimaces. "You hesitated," he says in a cold voice. "You gave him the opportunity to grab his gun and shoot you in the fucking head!"

I bristle at his tone. What the hell does he expect from me? I'm an eighteen-year-old kid! I should be hanging out with friends, reading books, watching silly movies, and dating boys — not killing gross and disgusting men like the one at my feet.

All because he double-crossed my uncle.

I mean, yeah, I owe my uncle a lot.

Everything, actually.

But when do I get a say in how the rest of my life is going to unfold?

Will I ever?

"I did," I say, my voice unwavering. "I can't help it. I keep seeing my parents' faces right before I pull the trigger."

"Change what you see in that moment," he seethes, narrowing his glassy blue eyes at me and backing me against the wall. "Imagine the faces of the fucking men who killed your parents!" he bellows. "That should make you furious and anxious to squeeze the trigger! Revenge, Anya! It's always about revenge!"

His words pelt me like sharp rocks that slice into my flesh. My pulse throbs against my neck, my breaths growing more and more labored as the tension-filled seconds tick by. I try to suck down oxygen, but an icy noose loops around my neck, making it impossible to fill my lungs.

"Uncle Boris, lay off," Maks grunts as he walks into the room and surveys the scene. "She got him, didn't she?"

Uncle Boris spins around, his eyes spitting white-hot flames at my brother. "So, you're good with her being sloppy in her actions? Good with her taking after you, Maks?"

Maks rolls his eyes. "Give her a break. She just started—"

Uncle Boris pokes Maks in the chest with his finger. "Don't give her any advice, Maks. I'm trying to keep her alive!"

"What the hell does that mean?" he says. I clench my fists at my side, silently willing my brother to shut his big mouth. He never knows when to back down and it's going to turn out very badly for him one day.

"It means you don't ever listen when I give you an order. You do what you want when you want because you're driven by the toxic bullshit eating you alive from the inside out. It clouds your judgment. The only reason you're still alive is because of me! It's the only reason why both of you are alive!"

"Oh, so that makes you uncle of the year, huh?" Maks shouts. "You saved our asses and now we owe you ours? Fuck that!"

Uncle Boris grabs Maks by the jacket and throws him against the wall. "You wanna leave, Maks? You think you can survive for a single second on your own?"

A momentary look of panic flits across Maks's face and then disappears as he grits his teeth. "I think I can protect us both without having to kill people for a living!"

Uncle Boris lets out a low, growly laugh. Shivers slither across my skin, the sound assaulting my ears. I cringe as it gets louder and more harsh.

"You walk out of here without me and you die," he hisses. "Plain and simple. And if you don't believe me, just try. Watch what happens to your precious sister before you suffer the same fate. They're just waiting for you to make your move, Maks."

My eyes fly open and I let out a gasp, perspiration pebbling on the back of my neck as I'm jolted awake by the nightmare. My uncle has always been a controlling bastard, and he'd say things like that all the time to keep us in line and focused. The threat of the unknown always loomed over us like a noxious black cloud.

It's one of the reasons why I'm here right now, why I still can't seem to break free.

And why I'm still letting him pull the strings.

Because deep down, I'm still that scared little girl whose parents were brutally slaughtered in their house, their family haven of safety and comfort.

It takes me a few minutes to remember that I'm no longer in that dingy bar in Brighton Beach, that I'm somewhere else.

Somewhere safe and warm.

Wait, where the is that, again?

I blink fast, my eyes adjusting to the darkness. I'm suddenly very aware of a warm bundle sitting on my chest, and I thank God that my harsh return to the real world didn't seem to wake her at all.

My face feels so greasy. Jesus, I need a shower desperately.

And some food.

In that order.

I carefully rise from the recliner, a crick in my neck shooting sharply down the side of my body as I turn my head. The gorgeous bed Heaven made up for me looks so inviting, and I make a silent promise to try it out just as soon as I wash the airplane grime off of my body.

I tiptoe over to the crib next to my bed and carefully lie Aisling on the mattress. I guess Heaven wanted to make sure I definitely did not miss the baby's cries in the middle of the night.

No worries there since I haven't had a restful night's sleep since before the night Maks was killed.

I'm actually the ideal candidate for an au pair, in that regard.

How freaking ironic.

I stare down at the baby. She looks so peaceful and angelic lying there. My gut clenches. So much love. So much happiness. So much hope.

I had all of that once, too, kid...

I scrub a hand down the front of my face and set up the baby monitor next to the crib, taking the portable walkie-talkie thing with me into the adjoining bathroom. I really hope the shower spray doesn't wake her up. She didn't nap too much today, but I've always heard that babies have this sixth sense...like they know when you're comfortable or sleeping or in the middle of something and pick exactly that time to start wailing.

I take a few, exaggerated steps toward the massive white granite and marble bathroom, looking up and around in awe. I think I'll take the risk...

There is an enormous soaking tub in one corner of the room, sleek mirrors hung over the 'his and hers' sinks, and rich, dark wood cabinets that pop against all of the white. A modern crystal chandelier hangs from the ceiling with matching wall sconces on either side of the room.

It is the most gorgeous bathroom I've ever had the pleasure of showering in.

And speaking of the shower...it has jets...on every wall.

That's a lot of shower power.

I turn on the spray and look around for toiletries in the drawers and closets. I find toothbrushes, toothpaste, disposable razors, deodorant, shower caps, and a whole assortment of other things that I can't get to back in the bedroom because I don't want to wake Aisling.

I quickly brush my teeth and pull on a shower cap before stepping under the hot spray. I stand there for a few minutes, just letting the water run over me. My eyes are squeezed shut and I don't move a bit, letting the heat relax my tense muscles. My senses are enveloped in the steam which smells like lavender...how?

My God, this au pair life, for as long as it lasts, is going to be a hell of a lot more luxurious than my own personal reality.

I can definitely deal with dirty diapers and spit up and screaming babies for a week in these digs.

I finally drag myself out of the shower after indulging in a host of L'Occitane shower products to the point where I am hella pruney.

But I haven't felt this relaxed and loose in a long time, even with the knowledge that I am pretty much on my own flying blind right now.

I guess it's good when the noose loosens a little bit.

You can actually breathe easy since there isn't a toxic haze hovering in the air around you.

I towel off with a thick, fluffy bath sheet and wrap it around me, cursing myself for not bringing in a change of clothes. Now I'm going to have to drag one of my bags out into the hallway because I'm certain the rustling sounds will wake Aisling. I slather myself with rich-scented moisturizer and pull a brush through my hair before grabbing one of Heaven's perfume bottles and dousing myself with it.

I stare at my reflection in the mirror, running a finger over the five-pointed star on my left breast. I wasn't careful about hiding it at Tatiana and Dante's mouth was definitely feasting on my boob. I can't let him see it now. The secrecy combined with the symbol of my mafia life would not be a good thing for him to discover. I got lucky last night when my dress was hanging off my body and he didn't spot it. I can't take that chance again. I rummage in one of the drawers and pull out a small Band-Aid. The tattoo is small and perfectly concealed once I place the adhesive over it.

I let out a deep, shuddering breath.

It doesn't seem possible that only twenty-four hours ago I was plunging a knife into the throat of Vigo Kosolov, and now I'm in charge of a tiny baby on the opposite side of the country.

But here I am.

Still starving, by the way.

I grab the baby monitor and shut off the bathroom light before I head back into my bedroom. I hold the towel tight around myself and pick up one of my bags, hoping it's the one that has my pajamas in it.

I make it into the hallway and let out the breath I'd been holding. You can hear a pin drop, it's so quiet. Instead of unzipping the bag right outside of my door, I carry it to the front of the apartment, as far away from her as possible and dig around my things. Dante must have turned off the lights because the only shred of light illuminating the place is courtesy of the Strip below.

My fingers close around a pair of flimsy pajamas and I grab them, dropping the towel and pulling them on quickly. I take a deep breath, the scent of food still lingering in the air.

I rub my belly. "Easy, girl," I whisper. "Let's see if we can find any leftovers for you."

I place the monitor on the kitchen island and open the refrigerator door, peering inside when a heavy feeling comes over me. My pulse throbs inexplicably and a chill slithers down my spine.

Someone's eyes are on me.

I slowly close the refrigerator and take a tentative step backward.

Have I been compromised?

What if my uncle really was taken? Tortured? Killed?

Would he have given me up?

Was this whole thing a setup?

My mind is going a mile a minute with all of the possible scenarios...

For all I know, Dante could have gone out on the town, leaving me alone with Aisling. It's not like we left on good terms before I stormed off, leaving him with that feast...

I swallow hard, the glimmer of a steep blade catching my eye. In a flash, I grab the knife and spin around, ready to attack. A strong hand grabs my wrist, slamming it back against the refrigerator as he slaps his other hand over my mouth.

Cool blue eyes glitter back at me and I bite down hard on Dante's thick fingers. He lets out a silent yell and pulls his hand away from me.

"You fucking asshole!" I hiss. "Are you trying to give me a heart attack?"

"I was trying not to scare you," he growls.

"Oh, good plan!" I whisper. "I could have killed you! I might still!"

He rolls his eyes, letting out a little chuckle. "Your instincts are pretty good. Not good enough, though."

I gasp. "Screw you! It's pitch black and the middle of the night!"

He lifts an eyebrow. "You got any other excuses?"

I grit my teeth. He's right. He totally had me right then. That knife was absolutely useless in my hand while he had it pinned to the refrigerator. If it had been a real break-in, a real assailant, what the hell would I have done? How would I have protected myself?

And Aisling?

"What the hell are you doing?" I hiss.

"Well, I was trying to get your attention without you screaming your pretty head off."

"And that's the best you could come up with?"

He shrugs. "I figured if I called out to you while I was on the couch watching you change, you might have screamed."

My eyes widen to the point where they might just pop out of my skull. "You watched me change? You sick fuck!"

"You know, your language is really not appropriate for tiny ears," he murmurs. "I think we might need to work on that."

"*We* don't have anything to work on!" I push past him, not intending to give him the satisfaction of eating a single morsel of his food after that stunt. "Now, if you'll please fuck off, I'm going back to bed!"

He captures my waist with his thick, muscled arm, pulling me backward. "Why? You're afraid I might expose you?"

My heart stills. "What in the fresh hell is that supposed to mean?"

His breath is hot against my ear. "You're afraid I'll let my brother and sister-in-law know that you like to drop your clothes in front of windows? That you pretend to be horrified when you find out you were watched but that you secretly love knowing someone's eyes are on you, caressing every curve of your body?"

Oh God...

Tingles shoot through my core as his grip on me tightens.

"You felt me," he whispers. "You know you did."

I nod. "Yes," I rasp.

"What would you have done if you saw me watching you, Anya? Would you have climbed on top of me? Rubbed that pussy against my hard cock?" His hand travels up my back, his fingers tangling in my hair.

What kind of assassin gets sidetracked by cock? Huh?

Well, evidently, this one does.

I let out a tiny whimper as he tugs my hair, forcing my head backward.

"Now why don't you tell me what you're really hungry for?" he grunts, spinning me around and lifting my body into his strong arms. "Because you may have thought it was food you wanted, but..." He pushes aside my panties and slides his fingers into my pussy, balancing me in one arm. "Your body tells me it had something else in mind. Something hot, something dirty, and something very fucking bad."

"What about the...the baby?" I squeak out. "She's going to wake up soon. She's been sleeping for a while..."

"Well, then, I'd advise you not to scream too loud," he says, a devilish smirk on his face. He backs me against the window and lets me down, my feet hitting the cold tile as I slide down the front of his body. He drops to his knees, pushing my shorts and panties down to my ankles and forcing my legs open. When his tongue dips into my pussy, a gasp escapes my lips. My ass presses against the clear glass as his mouth executes a delicious assault on me. Demanding fingertips dig hard into my flesh as he plunders me with his tongue, taunting my clit with gentle nips of his teeth. I fist his hair, my head falling back against the glass as I thrust my hips into his hungry mouth. Every nerve sizzles under the erotic spell he's cast on my body, blood rushing between my ears as the orgasm tears through me, leaving me breathless and starved for more.

Ripples of ecstasy cascade over me as his tongue makes a path for my mouth. He lifts the hem of my shirt and slips it over my head, letting it flutter to the floor. Then he continues massaging my flesh with his devious tongue...until he gets to my Band-Aid.

And I swear for a split second, he knows.

He runs his finger over it and I can't bear to open my eyes because he'll see the truth in them if I do.

Instead, I let out a tiny mewl and a soft giggle. "Are you trying to torture me?" I whisper, dragging my fingernails down his back.

"No..." he says slowly. "What happened here?"

"Oh, Aisling scratched me," I murmur, running my hands down either side of his torso. "Her nails are so sharp! I need to ask Heaven where the nail clipper is tomorr—"

He doesn't even let me finish my sentence before he crushes his lips against mine, tugging at my lower lip with his teeth. His demanding hands grip my hips tight, sliding around to my ass and clenching the flesh to the point I squeal, partially out of pleasure, and partially because I can't compute how he just morphed into this animalistic alter ego.

And it's a little disturbing, quite frankly.

He can't know, can he?

I played it off.

He'd have called me out if he didn't buy my excuse.

Then again, he expects me to have a bunch of them stored up...

I try to ignore all of these annoying voices in my head, totally cockblocking me right now.

He doesn't know, okay!

So all of you just shut the fuck up!

I push his shorts to the floor, and grasp his long, hard shaft in my hand, pulling away slightly to bring the palm of my hand to my mouth. I lick it and grasp his cock, rubbing harder and faster as he attacks my mouth with the same voracity he did last night.

The kind that makes my entire body shudder.

The kind that makes my skin sizzle under his fingertips.

The kind that makes me so wet, so lustful, and so ready to feel him inside of me.

He closes his hand around mine, positioning the tip at my entrance, dragging it up and down and pressing it against my clit.

"Fuck me, Dante," I breathe. "Fuck me against this window!"

He lets out a low groan and pushes inside of me, my walls stretching around him. I gasp, it burns. Oh, God, it fucking burns, but in a good way.

The best way, actually.

He thrusts deep inside of me, slow at first. Then, he lifts my leg and leans it against his hip, just like he did the other night.

And holy fuck, I want to scream because the pleasure coursing through me is so intense, I almost forget who I am and why I'm here.

Occupational hazard.

He drives his hips into me, pounding me harder and harder and I pant for breath. His lips crash into mine, his hands fisting my hair as he fucks me against the glass for the entire Las Vegas Strip to see.

Then, he lifts my other leg and balances me in his arms, his cock throbbing, pressing deeper and deeper as he angles my legs. Sparks in my belly ignite, shooting out to the tips of my fingers and toes. Our bodies slap together, the scent of sex and sweat intermingling in the air around us. I throw my head back, hitting it hard against the glass.

"Fuck," I moan. "Oh my God, that feels so incredible. Make me come, Dante. Come with me now!"

"I'm not wearing a—"

"I don't care!" I pant, choking on my labored breaths. "I'm on the pill!"

A guttural roar erupts from his throat and his movements speed up. I dig my teeth into his shoulder to stifle the scream that threatens to escape, a flash of bright white light exploding across my eyes with the same intensity as the explosive force that shatters me from the inside out.

Dante thrusts a couple of more times before tremors rock his body and he collapses against me, both of us struggling for breath. He collapses against me, his chest heaving.

"Fuck me," he murmurs.

"Yeah, I just did," I say, huffing and puffing myself. "And it was amazing."

"It was..." he says, staring into my eyes with an intensity that makes the hairs on my skin prickle. "Different...but not..."

I furrow my brow, letting out a breathless chuckle. "You're not making much sense right now. Did the orgasm fry your brain?"

"Maybe," he mutters, dragging a finger back down over my Band-Aid. "You should put something on that so it doesn't get infected."

I swallow hard and nod. "Okay, I'll check in the bathroom. I'm sure there's something in there."

In a strange kind of daze, he bends down to pick up my pajamas and I put them back on quickly, running a hand through my hair. "I wonder what time Matteo and Heaven will be home," I say, desperately trying to fill the silence.

Dante stares out the window at the bright lights below. "They aren't used to being out this late. Matteo is probably falling asleep in his dessert right now."

My stomach growls at the mention of food and I rub a hand over it. "Speaking of dessert...is there any chance you didn't finish all of that food before?"

He looks at me, those blue eyes lancing me with unanswered questions and unconfirmed suspicions. But he doesn't ask anything.

He just stares.

And that is way more torturous, in my opinion.

So looking at me all day long didn't give away my identity, but fucking me did?

I'll never understand men.

But knowing where his head is at right now means I have to be even more careful.

"There's still some in the fridge. Come on, I'll heat it up for you." He flashes a half-smile. "Tommy is very specific with the instructions for re-heating his food. If you fuck it up, you'll ruin the flavors or some shit. I don't know. I guess if I were a culinary wizard I'd care more, but when I'm hungry..." A wicked glimmer in his eyes makes goosebumps shoot up my legs and down my arms. "I'm just gonna take it, however I can get it."

I nod, forcing a smile. "I'm starving, so I promise I won't be picky."

I follow Dante into the kitchen, watching the moonlight bounce off of his muscled back, his smooth, bronze skin glistening. I long to run my fingers over it again, to feel his biceps tense as I rub my hands down his thick arms. I want to trace the outline of his pecs with my tongue. I want to—

"You allergic to anything?" Dante asks, interrupting my delicious fantasy as he walks into the kitchen.

"Not that I know of," I murmur, patting down the front of my pajama shirt where it hits my Band-Aid.

He turns to give me a long look, drinking me in from head to toe. But there's conflict in his eyes.

I can see the hunger, the longing, and the lust.

But I can also feel the suspicion. It's heavy in the air around us, picking away at his desire like a fingernail scratching a scab.

He wants me but doesn't know exactly who I am.

I feel the same inner conflict and it's tearing me apart.

I want him but know I can never…will never…have him.

Especially after I complete my objective and bring his whole family to its knees.

The fantasy of a happy and perfect future for me will always be just out of reach.

It's the life I chose, not that there was much choice in the matter.

If I wanted to live, I had to go down a path.

Now I'm in so deep, there is no way out.

I'm trapped in my life like a rat in a dirty, dark maze.

I wander, I hunt, and I avenge.

Period.

There's no happily ever after for me.

I'm not like those romance novel heroines at all.

Damaged? Check.

Broken. Check.

Redeemable? Fuck no!

And girls who can't be redeemed never find their true loves.

That's their punishment, I guess. Their lot in life.

Their curse.

I busy myself by taking the food packages out of the refrigerator as Dante heats up the oven. He's muttering something about temperatures to himself and I sneak a peek at him as he fiddles with the buttons on the oven.

What the hell is his story?

Because for as many lies choking me, I'm two-hundred percent sure that he's burying just as many.

He doesn't really know who I am, but he keeps himself pretty guarded, too.

And even though I know I should leave it alone, I can't.

I want to know the truth.

I want to know exactly who I'm falling for…the first person who's turned me inside out like this in so long, I can't even remember the last time it happened.

If ever.

I lean against the counter next to him, watching him load the tin containers onto the racks. "I'm kind of surprised you didn't devour it all," I say.

He turns his head toward me. "I guess I lost my appetite, too," he says gruffly.

"Sorry," I say softly.

He shrugs. "Hey, everyone deals with things in their own way. I don't criticize. I have my own shit to handle and I know I screw it up plenty." He chuckles. "But I screw up less than my other brothers, so there's that."

"Yeah…" I murmur, a faraway smile tugging at my lips.

"So what are you planning to study at UNLV?" he asks, completely knocking me off my game and catching me tangled in my salacious highlight reel.

"Oh," I say, tucking a strand of hair behind my ear. "Business."

Dante nods, closing the oven door and taking a seat at the kitchen island. "Seems like a smart choice."

I shrug. "I figure it'll help me get set up for a job."

"What do you wanna do when you graduate?"

Heat flares in my cheeks as I try to come up with a response. Nobody has ever asked me this question before because my 'job' is already kind of set in stone as far as anyone knows.

And since I barely finished high school and have zero plans to get a legitimate job, I'm completely caught off-guard. Finally, I just force a laugh and shrug. "Does anyone really know what they want to do once they graduate?"

He quirks an eyebrow. "I think people generally know what kind of skills they have and how they can put them to the best use. And make the most money from them. You have any specific skills, Anya?"

"You mean, other than childcare?" I say, snickering.

"Yeah, that's exactly what I mean," he says, his eyes darkening. "I have a feeling that there's a lot more to you than meets the eye."

"Sorry to disappoint you," I say, struggling to keep my voice even. "But I'm definitely a 'what you see is what you get' kind of girl. I love kids, reading romance novels, and warm weather."

"So there is more to add to my list," he says.

"You know, you keep digging into me but…" I say, picking up the knife from the kitchen counter and twirling it around my fingers. "You were awfully skilled with that little knife trick earlier. You know, the one where you managed to get it away from me before I had a chance to slit your throat? You grab that one from your own bag of tricks?"

"I wouldn't call it a trick. I just know how to defend myself."

"I think that's more than just defending yourself," I say quietly. "And definitely not something I'd expect from a real estate investor. I'd imagine you don't have to defend yourself against too many knife-wielding sellers, yeah?"

"I don't know about that. I'm a pretty tough negotiator."

We stand there, dissecting each other's words as the delicious scents from the oven waft in the air around us.

"I can imagine."

Dante gets up from the stool, walking over to the oven but then diverting in my direction. He backs me against the refrigerator and laces his fingers with the hand still holding the knife, sending it clattering to the floor. My pulse throbs against my neck as he presses himself against me. "Tell me what you were going to do with that knife, Anya," he murmurs.

"I was going to protect myself," I whisper. "And Aisling."

"How did you know I was there?" he mutters, his forehead almost pressed against mine.

"I just…I felt something. And I didn't know if you'd gone out. We were alone as far as I knew. Someone could have broken in…"

"Is that what you were expecting?"

"What?" I rasp.

"Waaaaah!"

I jump, Aisling's shrill cry shattering the air through the baby monitor. I push Dante away from me, my gut clenching as I hurry down the hallway toward my room. I run inside and pick her up from the crib, settling her against my racing heart.

Jesus! I knew that knife stunt tipped him off!

He is totally onto me.

I walk the baby around until her cries turn into soft whimpers. I know I need to feed her, but I also need to get my head screwed on straight. I have to give him something…anything…to get him to trust me, at least until I get in touch with my uncle.

I let out a shallow breath and walk back toward the kitchen. Dante already has a bottle ready for her. He must have mixed it when I went to my room. He reaches out and she jumps into his arms, clawing at his hands until the nipple is secured between her lips.

"Thank you," I say. "You know, um, one of the reasons why I became an au pair is because I spent a lot of time volunteering with orphan babies back in New York." I don't even know where that came from, but it sounds good. And it is kind of an extension of a truth. I guess maybe he needs to hear it.

It also sounds like I'm grasping at straws, but I'll take the risk.

He clearly doesn't trust me, so why am I making up some stupid bullshit story to throw him off? To ingratiate myself with him?

So I can sleep with him again?

He sinks onto the couch as Aisling nestles into his embrace. "Volunteering, huh?"

"Yes," I say, walking into the living room. "I started doing it when I was a teenager. My neighborhood in the city had an orphanage and I used to make clothes for the kids." This is all true. Part of my seamstress therapy with Olga.

But I never had a desire to get close to the kids.

He narrows his eyes at me. "Interesting."

I shrug. "I just wanted to do something to help."

"Why?"

A lump forms in my throat. "Because I knew what it was like to not have parents," I whisper, my voice quivering slightly. I didn't mean for that to slip out.

I didn't intend to give him any insight into my past.

But it does feel good to say the words, to open up and speak my truth.

It is one-hundred percent true, too.

"What happened to your parents?" he asks.

I swallow hard past the lump. "There was a break-in at my house. They were both killed. I was only thirteen."

"That's horrible. I'm really sorry," he says. "I lost my mother. I know how hard that is. Can't imagine losing both of my parents."

I nod. "Thanks. And I'm sorry for your loss, too."

An uncomfortable silence permeates the room. I'd intended to quell his curiosity with my tale of woe, but instead, I poured a cup of salt in my now-open wound.

Because I *am* very much alone, and that fact is more glaring than ever, considering my one lifeline is still MIA.

"Do you have any brothers or sisters?" Dante asks.

"A brother," I say. "But I don't see him anymore."

"That's rough," he says. "My brothers and I can go at it pretty hard, but we're really tight."

"Sounds nice," I say softly.

"You should reach out to him. Figure out a way to make things better. It's family for life, you know?"

Tears spring to my eyes and I blink them away. " Yes. You're right. Maybe I should try."

"Good." He nods toward the table. "You still hungry?"

"Ravenous," I say with a shaky laugh.

His lips curl upward into a wicked grin. "I'd love to feast on something other than that porterhouse."

"I'd love that, too," I murmur.

"Eat. I'll hold the baby," he says, nodding at the food.

"Are you sure?" I ask.

"Just as sure as you were when you said you'd never kiss me again." He winks. "Don't devour it all, okay?"

I sit down as he quietly sings a song to Aisling in Italian. The picture of him bent over her, smiling and crooning into her ear actually makes my nipples hard.

It's beautiful.

Powerful.

And...really fucking sad, if I'm being honest.

This baby...she's a precious angel who will be just as corrupted, if not worse than, as the rest of her family. Hardened, damaged, and tormented by things she could never change.

The orphaned babies back in Brooklyn...same thing. Maybe they'll find decent parents, but more likely, they'll end up living like me.

Committing murders to survive in all senses of the word.

Lying, stealing, doing unspeakable things all in the name of loyalty, expectation, and obligation.

I'm sure Maks never intended that I'd turn out the way I did, but deep down, I bet he knew I'd need skills to live on my own, that he was on borrowed time because of all the missteps he'd made.

So he made sure I learned them and used them.

Me, the orphaned babies, Aisling...we're all the same.

I'm older, of course. Somewhat free to make my own choices now. But at one time, I, too, had been protected from my family's mistakes, safe from their poor judgment.

And then I was plunged into a deep, dark hell that I can't seem to escape.

Part of me wants to fling myself at Dante, to scream at him, to pound my fist into his beautifully chiseled jaw because how dare he contribute to this existence for his niece?

How dare he turn her life upside down?

How dare any of them hurt her?

Because it is inevitable.

I manage to choke down the delectable morsels of food, but my gut is so damn twisted at the poisonous thoughts looping through my mind, I miss it all.

I suddenly feel ultra-protective of her, like I'm the only one who can save her from the evils that lurk everywhere.

How ironic is that? Me, of all people, looking to save someone else.

Before the night my parents were killed, I never thought people were watching us and plotting against us, waiting for an opportunity to strip us of everything we held dear.

I never imagined we'd lose the most important people in our lives so brutally.

"Here, let me take her," I say, wiping my mouth with a napkin and standing up from the table. "Eat before it gets too cold." I take her into my arms and settle into the couch cushion. Aisling doesn't miss a beat. Hell, I don't even know if she realizes I've just stepped in for her adoring uncle.

Her adoring uncle who will never admit who he really is...what he really is.

I should detest him...all of them.

But instead, I just keep drawing parallels.

Finding similarities and connections.

I swallow a groan.

Dammit, they are the enemy!

Or, are they?

Because right now, I don't have confirmation of anything — no instruction, no clarity, no direction at all.

I'm just caught here in this glamourous alternate reality where I'm perpetually on diaper and spit-up duty, lusting after the forbidden.

Somehow that seems like it can be even more deadly than any alternative.

Chapter Twelve
DANTE

I don't know how much time has passed since Anya dozed off.

Seconds…minutes…hours?

Feels like I've been sitting in this spot forever, just watching her.

I stand up from the couch and fold my arms over my chest, staring as her body gently quakes with calm breaths.

Who are you really, Anya?

Her face is relaxed, angelic even. Her mouth is slightly open, hair splayed over the back of the couch.

I'd like to say she's so exhausted because of what I did to her earlier.

But something tells me there's a much bigger burden weighing on her, a façade she's desperately trying to keep in place.

It's familiar to me because it reminds me of myself, closed off from everything that can possibly compromise me and my ability to do my job.

We're so damn alike. Maybe that's why I'm so tangled up in her net. I couldn't pull away if I tried.

She gave me more than I'd ever thought she would when she told me about her family.

But I want more.

Hell, I want everything.

I raise my arms to the back of my head, stretching out my limbs as I pace around the room, Anya and Aisling completely oblivious to my angst.

What happened between her and her brother? Why is she on her own out here?

I scrub a hand down the front of my face.

She obviously knows how to defend herself.

Anya went for that knife in the kitchen before, held it like she knew exactly what to do with it.

And she didn't like that I overpowered her. Not one bit.

Didn't stop her from climbing me like a tree afterward, though.

Naked.

See, this is the problem with being on the bench for too long. I'm thinking too much, losing my damn edge. I'm a hit man, for fuck's sake. Not a glorified babysitter.

Handling Miguel Rivas was a good respite, but not nearly enough to sustain me.

This little 'vacation' is fucking draining the life outta me.

Or at least it was until yesterday.

Anya has my head in a million places and I don't like that a single fucking bit.

Before she showed up on the scene, I was ready to bolt the hell outta Vegas and get back to my life, the one where I get in, pop my target, and get out.

No thinking.

No strategizing.

It's simple because I'm an action kinda guy.

But this pull Anya has on me…it's making me second guess everything I thought I wanted.

I can't even count how many times over the past few months Matteo has tried to convince me to stop running, to stay and find something more stable out here.

I shot him down every time.

How can this girl, someone I literally just met, make me second guess myself?

I know I need to leave Vegas once this Conor shit is handled.

But she makes me want to stay.

After months of insisting I'm better on my own, she's given me a reason to explore a different path.

A kid, for fuck's sake.

I fist my hair.

I can't be that guy.

If I stop running, I'll never be free from the demons. They hunt me relentlessly and won't ever stop.

If I stay, they'll catch me.

And I can't live with that guilt roped tight around my neck.

It's why I started on this path in the first place.

A groan threatens to slip from my lips, and I hear the key card click in the door lock.

Thank fuck!

I need to get out of my damn head.

Getting laid is supposed to clear your mind, not clog it up even more than it already was.

Heaven and Matteo step into the apartment, their heads bent together as they whisper and chuckle softly.

Anya, on the other hand, doesn't move.

She's completely starched.

As is Aisling.

Heaven slips off her shoes and comes over to the couch, not making a sound when she sees me slap my index finger over my mouth. She takes Aisling and cradles her against her body as she walks into her bedroom.

I place a blanket over Anya and she snuggles deeper into the couch with a contented sigh.

My fingertips graze her soft skin for a second longer than necessary and I yank it away, gritting my teeth.

I need a drink. Or ten.

I follow Matteo into his office and sit in one of the chairs.

He pours me a shot of whiskey and I gulp it down.

"What's the matter, Dante?" he asks.

"I don't know," I mutter. "Just preoccupied with this Conor thing. When are you gonna tell Heaven?"

He sighs. "I have to tell her before he shows up here. I just don't want it to ruin the day for her. She's so excited, and even though all of that shit with her family is always on the back burner, she's in a good place right now. Especially with Anya being here. I don't want to mess around with that and put her in a dark place again."

"I get it." I let out a deep sigh and scrub a hand down the front of my face. "You know this shit will never go away, don't you?"

Matteo furrows his brow and laces his fingers together, but no words are spoken.

I lean forward. "There will always be threats. You know that. Look at all of the enemies we've dealt with over the past few years. And we only inherited more when we joined the Red Ladro syndicate." Red Ladro is a tight knit group of families – ours, the Severinovs, and the Marcones. We work closely together to run various organizations and operations throughout the country and make a shit ton of cash in the process.

"You think we should have passed on the opportunity to join?" He waves his hands around him. "Dante, this place is a goldmine. Do you know how much we can do out here? How much we *will* do because of these associations?"

"Look, Matty, I'm not telling you how to run the family businesses. I'm just saying that the life we lead is full of risk and danger. You've done everything you can to shield everyone you love, but you're always gonna have tiny holes that can't be plugged. It's just the way things are. Someone will always try to get close, to hurt you, to sabotage what we've built."

"Jesus Christ, Dante. Your glass isn't half-empty. It's fucking invisible!" He narrows his eyes. "Why don't you say what you really want to say instead of giving me a lesson in mob life, huh?"

"You know exactly what I'm saying," I grumble. "I have to get out."

His nostrils flare as he seethes his next words. "You know, you think running away is the answer. You've believed that for years, ever since Emilia was killed. You've blamed yourself. Hell, you've *tormented* yourself, going into every shithole corner of the world to hunt down the same kind of scumbags who did that to her."

"What's so wrong with wanting to exterminate those bastards?"

"Nothing," he says. "But it's not a job to you. It's a personal mission. You believe that the more kills you rack up, the closer you get to redemption. But it wasn't your fault. It was her idiot brother Vito who opened the door to that hell."

"I was the one who was supposed to be watching over her," I grunt. "She was my responsibility!"

"And what was his responsibility? Huh? Going out, partying with the wrong fucking people, racking up debts that he'd never be able to pay. You weren't her keeper, Dante. You went above and beyond to keep them both safe. You could never have predicted that Emilia would have gone out looking for him that night while you were sleeping. This is all on Vito. When are you going to accept that?"

I press my fingertips to my temples to prevent the splintered memories from that night from consuming my mind, but it's too late.

"As soon as I woke up, I went after her. I knew exactly what she did and why she did it. She was always so worried about him, and he didn't give a damn about her or the danger he invited in when he got caught up with those assholes." I shake my head. "And it wasn't enough that they killed Vito. What they did to her..." A lump forms in the back of my throat. "I can't forget that. I can't just ignore the fact that I had a part in that whole thing. I should have known what she was going to do and stopped her. Such a goddamn waste..." I mutter.

"You did everything you could." Matteo sits back in his chair. "You have to let it go. Because you put yourself in a shit ton of danger every time you take one of those jobs. You think we have cracks in the foundation? Lemme tell you, you're just as much at risk on your own."

I roll my eyes. "Come on. I'm like a ninja. Nobody can touch me."

"Until they do." He glowers at me. "So pardon me for wanting to keep you away from the jaws of the huge ass lion snapping at your heels."

"Did you ever think that I actually like what I do? I consider it a community service-type gig, ya know?" I wink at him. "I'm doing my part to keep the world free of those sick and twisted bastards."

"And I'm sure the world appreciates it."

"I'm no good to you if I go soft, Matty."

"I have no doubt that you'll find any way to keep yourself sharp and lethal." He smirks. "Just think about it. If you started your own security firm here, you'd have plenty of clients with enemies that you could tear apart, limb by limb."

"Great." I snort.

Matteo lifts an eyebrow. "Besides, there's plenty going on here in Vegas that can keep you edgy. Just like Miguel Rivas."

I flash a half-smirk. "I was wondering what took you so long to bring him up. How'd you know?"

He shrugs. "I know most things. I just choose not to divulge them until I need to."

"Okay, enough about me and my plans. Let's get back to the immediate problem." I place my glass on the table. "Since you're all-seeing and all-knowing, do you really think the Volkov Bratva would go after us, knowing we're associated with the Severinovs?" I shake my head. "I mean, Alek will torpedo their asses back to the fucking Ukraine or wherever they crawled out from under if they make any moves against us."

"He would do what he could, but this isn't syndicate business. We're partners with the Severinovs, but they're not our muscle. They'll fight alongside us but they won't overstep. They have their own demons to deal with." Matteo gets up and places a strong hand on my shoulder, his jaw tightening. "If there is a threat, if the Volkovs are watching and waiting, if Conor really is on their hit list...we need a plan of attack. That sonofabitch has put us through too much already. If he's coming here to bring the fight to us, we have to be ready for it, whether or not it's ours to finish."

Chapter Thirteen
ANYA

"I have the perfect dress for you!" Heaven squeals, clapping her hands together as she stands in front of her monstrous closet a couple of days later. It's early in the morning, but she's definitely on a mission. I've been so busy with the baby and running errands with Heaven for the christening that I've barely seen Dante.

Or maybe he's just been avoiding me since the fogged-up window episode.

He hasn't been around, and I figured with us living in the same apartment, we'd still see each other, even in passing. I guess Heaven and Matteo decided I'm not some psychopath and its okay to leave me alone with the Aisling after all.

Maybe they decided *I* don't need a babysitter anymore.

Or maybe he's just out doing "family business."

Either way, I miss seeing him.

I miss his teasing voice and his mischievous gaze.

And…much as I hate to admit it…I miss how I feel when I'm around him.

I bounce Aisling on my hip, watching Heaven dive into the racks of dresses, shoes, and handbags.

"Ohh," I breathe as she holds it out to me. "It's gorgeous." I narrow my eyes at the tag.

Versace.

Really?

For the au pair who's burping and changing Aisling pretty much every hour on the hour?

"Heaven, the dress will be destroyed if I wear it," I say, handing it back to her. "I can just wear one of my sundresses."

Heaven lets out a snort. "The hell you will. I want you to show off that beautiful figure. And I've got shoes to match!"

I shake my head. "You're really being too generous—"

She waves a hand in the air. "Stop. It isn't like I can fit into it anymore," she says with a hint of glumness lacing her words.

"You just had a baby!" I exclaim. "Of course you'll get back into that dress. You'll be back in fighting shape so soon!"

She rolls her eyes. "Not unless I can find a calorie-free substitute for chocolate soft serve ice cream with butterscotch sauce."

I smirk. "We all have vices. I get it."

She takes the baby and sits down on a white leather recliner, nodding toward the closet. "Anya, I am your boss and I demand you put that dress on. And I want to see the shoes with it, too! Go!"

I bite down on my lower lip. This is so incredibly bizarre.

Heaven is like the big sister I always wanted. Someone to gossip with, to try on clothes with, to cook with, to laugh with.

I had that relationship with my mother and then she was gone.

I never got it back.

It's part of the reason why I was so envious of Dottie and *The Golden Girls* from the airport. To nurture that kind of relationship over so many years, growing up together, experiencing life together — I missed out on all of that. Nothing about my life has been normal for as long as I can remember.

And here I am, trying on dresses deep in the enemy's closet.

Forget irony.

This has to be some alternate universe.

I pull off my tank top and start to unbutton my shorts when my phone buzzes in my back pocket. I grab it, my heart thudding so loud, it almost drowns out the sound of the familiar, guttural voice.

"Uncle Boris," I whisper. "Where have you been? It's been days! I've been calling and texting—"

"I know, Anya. And I am sorry I didn't get back to you. But I have been busy working on something very important for our cause."

"I'm sorry," I say in a hushed tone so that Heaven can't hear me. "But what could be more important than the well-being of your niece? You know, the one you order around but never bother to check in on?" It's been days and I am pissed off at him for leaving me hanging like this.

I don't give a damn what kind of plans he's putting together.

I could be dead for all he knows or cares!

Anger bubbles in my veins.

He's never been the father figure I need, but he's the only one I have.

I press my lips together, my eyes darting at my half-naked reflection in the floor-length mirror.

Like it or not.

He's been using me as his personal weapon for years, why should I be shocked that he's pulling this shit again?

You have nothing else, Anya. Nothing, nobody...

I bite back a scream.

Don't I fucking know it?!

"You could have called back to check on me. You're the one person on the planet who's actually supposed to give a damn," I mutter.

"You're right," he says in a flippant tone. "But there were things that had to happen back here, to prepare for our work in Vegas."

"What work?" I ask, holding my hand around my mouth the muffle my voice. I manage to unzip my shorts and slide them to the carpet as I balance the phone against my ear. "And what do you mean 'our'?"

"We will discuss all of the details tonight when I arrive."

"Wait, you're coming *here*? I thought the plan was for me to get the information your contact needs. Since when do you need to be here?"

"Since the plans have changed," he snips. "My contact would like to acquire the information himself."

"That's a good thing since I've basically heard nothing that could possibly be useful to you. I haven't met any of these other elusive brothers you mentioned, and Matteo's office is locked up like Fort Knox!" I say in a frustrated whisper.

"You don't have to worry about it anymore," he says gruffly.

"Well, then, what the hell do you need me for?" I demand. "This is ridiculous! I've been living with strangers for days and changing shit diapers for what?"

"Having you there gives us access, Anya. Your work is not in vain. And soon enough, we will have plenty of money and even more power. Ivan Volkov will be eating out of our hands, I can promise you that."

I roll my eyes. I've heard it all before. Uncle Boris has delusions of grandeur. It's why we're in this shitty position to begin with, the one where we're scrounging around for any job that can make us a windfall.

And I question that this is it.

Who the hell knows who his contact is, and who's to say the contact won't kill him once he gets what he wants?

Unless my uncle has a different idea about how to deal with the contact…one that involves me killing him first.

"I don't know if I'll be able to get away tonight. The baby's christening is tomorrow and I'm not sure—"

"You're the au pair, not the full-time nanny. Set hours means you get time off to meet your dear old uncle who flew in for a special dinner and to take a tour of UNLV, where you are so excited to go in the fall."

I bite down on my lower lip. "Okay, I might be able to get away for a little while."

"I will text you the details tomorrow once I land."

"Okay, Uncle," I say, slipping off my flip flops and stepping into the high-heels Heaven left for me. "Have a safe—"

Click.

"Flight," I grumble, stabbing the End button. He really is a huge prick more often than not. I totally understand why so many people want to either kick his ass or just flat-out kill him. And yeah, I feel a tiny bit guilty thinking that since he took us in, brought us to Brooklyn, gave us a roof over our heads, and food to eat.

But he's not my dad. Not even close.

They were estranged, and the only reason we found him was because Maks had gotten a birthday card from him not too long before the attack. It was the only address we had for him, and thankfully, it led us straight to him with only the clothes on our backs.

He put up with raising two teenagers because he realized very fast what we could do for him and how we could make him money. He didn't care what kind of danger we'd walk into as long as we walked out with cash, drugs, or stolen goods he could turn around and sell. And then Maks died and I graduated to hired killer.

And now he really is all I have.

Sometimes I wonder if I'd be better off with nobody.

My heart aches as I gaze at myself in the mirror, the tight, white dress clinging to my every curve.

Fresh, bright, white — on the outside, anyway.

I just hope all of the red staining my ledger doesn't seep into the fabric. I'd hate for the devil inside to tear through and ruin the angelic effect.

Even though it's a total façade.

I smooth down the front of the dress and can't help the smile that lifts my lips.

God, this feels so incredibly surreal...

I try to enjoy the moment until my gut knots, my mind trying to process what in the hell plans my uncle has concocted. A strange sensation floods my insides when I think about Aisling. Whatever happens, she can't be involved.

Hurt.

Or worse.

I feel so oddly protective of her, maybe because of the fact that we're kind of kindred spirits. What will become of her? She's young, so however this plays out, it won't torment her emotionally the way it did me when my parents were killed.

Blood rushes between my ears.

How it plays out...I still have no clue.

He still hasn't told me a single detail...about anything.

And the biting question continues to feed on my brain...how much can I really trust him?

If push comes to shove, deep down, I know he'll pick money and power over me.

I've tried to deny that to myself over the years, but after Maks, it was a hard realization to not bury. Everything unraveled faster than a cheap rug after that and Uncle Boris just spiraled.

He never really stopped.

Just changed his manic direction.

The only thing that keeps me on course here is the fact that these people need to pay for taking away something so precious from me. I don't care if they weren't the ones who pulled that trigger. Anyone who wanted to hurt my family like that, anyone who made the decision to carry out the murder — they're all guilty as far as I'm concerned.

I take a few deep breaths.

I just have to stay on course for a little while longer.

But being immersed in this life makes it so damn hard.

Part of me just wants to scream and cry and beg them to just tell me why!

The other part knows it's too dangerous.

Just like my feelings for Dante.

Exposing either would be disastrous.

Tiny hairs on the back of my neck prickle as Heaven's voice carries into the depths of the closet. "Are you ever coming out of there?"

I walk out to the bedroom, balancing carefully on the carpet. The skinny heels make me teeter slightly with each step I take into the thick carpet. I stick my hands on my hips and do a little half-twirl. "What do you think?"

Heaven's green eyes sparkle. "It's perfect. Just like I knew it would be. You look beautiful, Anya."

"Hey, Heaven, what time are—?"

I look toward the door to find Dante's blue eyes glued to me as his question dissipates in the air around us.

My breath hitches, and when our gazes tussle, my mind trips back to the last time I saw him. I still can't look at that window without feeling those delicious tingles assault my body.

He's definitely been avoiding me. That much is clear.

And it has to be because he doesn't trust me.

Smart guy.

But my God, as the days pass, I find myself fantasizing more and more about reliving those stolen moments. If I had to guess, it's because I crave human contact. It has to be why I'm so attached to Heaven and Aisling, and why radio silence from my uncle really didn't bother me much.

Deep down, I want to live this fantasy life for just a little while longer.

I feel wanted, needed, and cared for.

I haven't felt that in a damn long time...not for the right reasons, anyway.

Whenever I've had time to myself over the past couple of days, I either sit out by the hotel pool or hole up in my room to read one of my romance novels or I go for a run.

And all I think about is *him*.

Part of me is glad he's been MIA.

Dante saw too much of what I've been trying to bury, and that made me retreat into myself.

I already told him more than I should have.

Even though it was liberating to let some of that poison seep out of me, I can't give him anything else.

It would make me too vulnerable, too exposed, too emotional.

And it might dilute my hate and kill my resolve.

Bad, bad, bad!

I catch Heaven look from Dante to me and then back again, a tiny smile lifting her lips. "What time what?" she asks, a glimmer of mischief in her eyes.

She obviously sees something.

And I *feel* it again, way down to the tips of my toes and all the way up to the ends of my hair.

Wanted.

Desired.

Craved.

A shiver shimmies down my spine and my shoulders shudder in response.

"What time…" Dante repeats, as if he can't even remember his question. Wow, am I really that much of a sight?

Or is he just sidetracked by the fantasy of fucking me against a window overlooking the entire Las Vegas Strip?

Heaven makes a point of looking at her diamond-encrusted Rolex and lifts a perfectly sculpted eyebrow. "Any day now, Dante. Can't you see we're a little bit busy here?"

He blinks fast, dragging his gaze off of me. "What time are Patty and Maura flying in?" he finally asks.

"They'll be in at eleven," she says.

He nods. "Okay. I'll take care of it."

"Thanks. Don't tell anyone else, but you're the best brother-in-law ever!" she squeals.

"Whoa! What in the ever-loving fuck is that supposed to mean?" a booming voice demands from out in the hallway. "You cheatin' on me, sis?"

A tall, dark, and delicious version of Matteo and Dante pops his head into the room. "We made an agreement, remember? Nobody but me gets that title!"

Heaven's cheeks turn bright pink and she claps a hand to her mouth to stifle a giggle.

"Busted!" Dante says with a snicker.

The new guy gives me a long, appraising look. "Here I am, coming up to welcome the new nanny, and I find you feathering Dante's ass. What kind of shit is that?"

He walks into the room and sticks out a hand to me. "Sergio. I run this place."

"Anya," I reply. "And well done. It's beautiful."

Sergio nods, a smirk lifting his lips. "Dante said you were staying at the Bellagio before my sis hired you." He shakes his head. "You don't wanna be caught dead in that shithole, sweetie."

"So I've heard," I say with a snicker. "Jeez, it's like you guys all rehearse from the same script," I murmur.

Dante shrugs. "Maybe we all just share the same brain."

"Scary!" Heaven squeals. "I refuse to admit I think like a Villani man!" She waves her hand around. "Okay, boys, hit the road! We're still beautifying in here!"

I sneak a quick glance at Dante. My breath hitches when I see his eyes darken with lust, the same lust flooding my insides right now.

Oh my God, why do you have to be so goddamn irresistible?

I need to hate you, not constantly want to mount you!

Dante pushes Sergio out of the room. "Come on, let's go." He gives me a long look that makes goosebumps pebble my arms and legs before he pulls the door closed.

Heaven crosses her arms over her chest. "Care to tell me what those googly-eyes were all about?"

I recoil. Shit, she's observant. "I don't think he was—"

"Not his," she says with a grin. "Yours."

A hot flush creeps up the sides of my neck, and my cheeks flame as I sputter an intelligible response. It's not exactly professional to be caught pining for your employer's brother-in-law. "No, I don't...he's not...I mean, I'm not interested in Dante." I wave my hand around. "Like, at *all*."

She nods. "Okay. And you're sticking with that story?"

"It's not a story!" I say. "Honestly."

Heaven shrugs. "I really want him to find a nice girl, someone other than the usual hoes, you know what I mean? The ones who are all about what he can do for them, socially, financially. I want him to find someone he can really care about and settle down with. He's a good guy. Takes care of his family. Great with babies," she says with a pointed look at Aisling.

"He's, um, really nice," I stammer. "He doesn't have a girlfriend?"

"Not in the entire time I've known him," Heaven says, getting up from the bed to unzip me. I hold an arm over the top of the dress in case someone else, like maybe Matteo, decides to barge in here next. "I just want him to be happy. Sergio and their other brother Roman are both engaged. Dante needs someone. His job is..." Her voice trails off and my ears perk up.

"What about his job?" I ask.

She shrugs. "I don't know. It keeps him moving around too much. He can't put down roots, you know?"

"I guess that's what it takes to be a successful real estate investor, right?"

Her brow furrows slightly before she plasters on a big, bright smile. "That's right! Always putting his career first, that guy."

Yep. *So* not a real estate investor.

"How'd you and Matteo meet?" I ask, popping back into the closet to do a quick change.

She lets out a dry laugh. "It wasn't exactly love at first sight, that's for sure. We'd never get 'proposal of the year' votes for our story, either."

"What do you mean?" I pull back my hair and adjust the straps of my tank top as I come back out of the closet.

"I didn't have much choice in marrying Matteo," Heaven says. "I did it for my family, not for love."

"Wait, so you were arranged?" My mouth drops open, my words soaked in disbelief. "Like, no dating? Had you even seen him before you married him?"

"Oh yeah," she says. "I went to live with him the night he proposed. But we weren't on the best terms at that point. Actually," she muses. "I hated him. Hard."

"Wow," I murmur. "I can't believe it. An arranged marriage? What century is it?" I giggle.

"I know. It sounds so incredibly old-world. But both families had something to gain, so we did it." She shrugs. "And even though I swore it would never happen, we fell in love. Crazy, powerful, forever kind of love."

"That's unbelievable." I shake my head. "I'd have never guessed you hated him based on the way you guys are always falling all over each other."

"He's a tough one. Doesn't show much emotion. Having Aisling kind of changed the guy he shows to the world."

"Yeah, I still see the emotionless guy," I quip.

"He's very protective," Heaven says. "And he doesn't trust easily."

"I get that. He's got a lot to lose."

Heaven nods. "We both do."

I swallow hard, feeling like a complete shit heel for even entertaining this dialogue with her. I need to change the subject. I can't listen to any more of her gushing when I know I'm about to choke her with it.

"So, Patty and Maura — who are they?" I ask, trying to steer the subject away from the blissfully married bubble they live in.

Her face brightens. "My brother and my aunt. I'm so excited to see them! It's been so long since we left Manhattan."

"Dante said you've been out here for a while."

"Yeah, it wasn't a hard call to make after everything happened," Heaven says darkly, lifting Aisling and sniffing her butt. She scrunches up her nose and holds her up. "Eww!" she sing-songs. "Somebody needs a diaper change!" Heaven starts to take her over to the changing table but I stop her.

"Here, let me," I say, taking the baby from her.

She sinks back on the bed. "Thanks."

"So what about the rest of your family?" I ask. "Are they coming to the christening, too?"

Her jaw tightens. "No."

"Why not?"

"I don't speak to them," she says abruptly.

"Oh, I'm sorry," I say, biting the inside of my mouth.

"Yeah, it's been awhile." She shrugs. "Difference of opinion, I guess. My father screwed me over and promoted my oldest brother Conor over me. Family business." She presses a hand to her forehead. "My brother is an idiot and an asshole. A huge liability for my father and his business. But he promoted him anyway." She rolls her eyes. "A lot more happened, but that was the straw that broke the camel's back. And we haven't spoken since."

"I can't imagine," I say, a lump forming in my throat. What I wouldn't give to have my brother back for even a few minutes, to feel him gather me in a huge bear hug, to tell him once more how much I love him and appreciated everything he did for me. "And there's no way to fix things?"

"No," she says with finality. "He's dangerous, and I don't trust him. I don't want to be anywhere near his sinking ship. And I definitely don't want him near my daughter."

Hmm, I'm kind of feeling her right now, since I'm having those very same thoughts about my uncle.

Talk about the utter betrayal.

Siding with the enemy and saying 'fuck it' to family loyalty.

"It's really terrible," I say, treading lightly with my words since nobody likes big mouth opinions about their own family crap.

I know I don't.

"Thanks," she says, taking Aisling from me and hugging her tight. "My father hasn't even met his granddaughter," she says. "I mean, I fully expected Conor to be dead by the time she was born, but color me shocked. He's still causing plenty of trouble back home."

I manage to force out a nervous chuckle but really, I don't want to be involved in this. I've heard too much, seen way more than that.

And done?

Well, damn.

I've done every single thing I know I'm not supposed to in this situation, including Dante.

Although...I don't regret it at all.

I will live vicariously through those memories for the rest of my days.

Which may be few in number if I screw this up and my uncle has anything to say about it.

"Well, he's definitely missing out. They all are," I say with a smile.

She nods, dropping a kiss on Aisling's forehead. "Yes. Yes, they are," she whispers to her daughter.

And there's that damn pang again.

The one that tells me I want more than I'm willing to admit.

Jesus, I need some distance!

"Hey, um, Heaven," I say, twisting my hair around my finger. "I know it's not great timing, but I was wondering if I could take off tonight to meet my uncle. He's coming into town to check out the UNLV campus with me, and then we'd planned on having dinner."

She nods but I can see she's very far away from me and this conversation. "Tonight," she repeats with a blank stare on her face.

"Yes. I'll only be gone a few hours so I can help with the baby when I get back."

And with a start, she snaps out of her reverie. "No, don't worry about it. We'll be fine. You have a great time with your uncle."

"You're sure? Anything you need for the christening, I can do with you—"

"Anya, seriously. It's fine. I have plenty of help. And you've barely taken any time to yourself since you started." Heaven smiles but it doesn't reach her big bright eyes as it normally does. "You have fun. We'll have a great day tomorrow." She winks at me. "And you'll shine like a star in that dress." With a quick, affectionate squeeze, she walks out of the room and I follow, marveling over that conversation. I didn't expect any of what I just heard. Looks like there is no shortage of more parents making shitty life decisions that will forever impact their children.

I don't know anything about Heaven's family other than what she just told me but if I could, I would tell them just what total and complete assholes they are for disowning her and Aisling the way they did over some bullshit business decision.

They have time to fix their mistake, unlike others who never got the chance.

How strange.

Here I was, thinking Aisling and I were the kindred spirits.

Who would have thought that it would be Heaven and me instead?

Chapter Fourteen
DANTE

"So the nanny..." Sergio waggles his eyebrows at me as we stand outside next to the balcony infinity pool. "She's fucking hot. You nail her yet?"

"She's not a nanny, she's an au pair." I toss a glance over my shoulder, watching Anya follow Heaven into the kitchen.

"Oh, she's definitely got a pair." Sergio snickers and gulps down the rest of his water. "But you didn't answer my question."

I roll my eyes. "I don't kiss and tell."

"And I didn't ask if you kissed her." A wicked glint makes his blue eyes twinkle.

"Just drop it, okay?"

"Fine. Why are you so sensitive, anyway? You getting tired of playing bodyguard?"

"It's been months, Serge." I sink onto one of the chaise lounges and lean back with a deep sigh. "I wanna help. I really do. But this isn't me. It's not who I am, who I want to be."

"You sure about that? Because you look pretty damn cozy here every time I see you. Getting in time with the baby, now you have a new plaything." Sergio holds up his hands. "Hey, I'm just saying. She's smokin' hot and yours for the taking. What the hell is wrong with that life, D?"

I rub the back of my neck. "Nothing, for a while. Until I get itchy and need that adrenaline rush again."

"I don't know. It sounds like a good plan to me. You get to unwind for once in your life. Why not enjoy it?"

Jesus, it does sound good, in theory. For someone else.

But my head is just in a million places right now, especially with Anya around. Part of me is afraid that if I stay too long, I won't be able to keep myself from falling back under her net. That's why I've been avoiding her. It's dangerous. She makes me lose focus and I can't figure out why. I can't help protect anyone if my head isn't in the game.

Of course, avoiding her means I'm not around to protect anyone, so that plan doesn't exactly work, either.

And my head has us back in Heaven's bedroom, peeling her out of that hot-as-fuck dress.

Right now, I feel just like the trust fund baby she thought I was when we first met.

Useless. Entitled. Vacuous.

I need purpose.

"You talk to Matteo about this?"

"Yeah. He thinks I'm using my job as an excuse to find redemption."

"Are you?" Sergio lifts an eyebrow.

I shrug. "Maybe."

"You think you're ever gonna get it?"

"Nope," I say. "But does that mean I should stop trying?"

"I think if you stick around here for a little while, you'll see that you can figure out how to build a future instead of trying to fix the past."

"Did Matteo feed you that line?" I snort. "Jesus, you guys sound like you're reading from the same script."

"He's worried about you. So am I. You've been dicking around for long enough. It's time to set yourself up for the long term." He shrugs. "You can't be a hit man forever."

"It's what I'm good at."

"Maybe it's time to figure out what else you might be good at."

"This place has nothing for me." I fling an arm over my eyes to shade them from the sun. "I like my job. Love it, actually. I'm fucking awesome at it, too. I get paid a lot of money to handle shit other people can't. That's how I always contributed to the family. I took care of anyone who was a risk to our empire." I sit up and squint. "But here? There aren't any threats. There's just a really fucking paranoid boss who wants constant surveillance on his wife and kid. I agreed to do it for a few months but now…I don't know. I love them to pieces, Serge. But I don't wanna be stuck out here forever. Matteo keeps telling me to open my own personal security firm out here for the whales who need protection for their cash and drugs and whatever the hell else."

"Sounds like easy money to me," Sergio says.

"Too easy, it's boring," I grumble.

"I don't know about that. Anya seems like she can add plenty of spice to your days here, bro. Nights, too." He chuckles.

And there it is. That pull is back, just at the mere mention of her name.

But I don't do normal. I don't do relationships. And I definitely don't do long term.

How the hell would that even work?

I've got enough of my own baggage, and Anya clearly has a staggering amount of her own.

The sex would be incredible for as long as it lasted, but I'd eventually jump ship like always because it's who I am.

Forget the fact that Matteo would murder me for laying a finger on her.

Besides, I have a calling and it's to kill the bad guys.

Well, *worse* guys since I guess technically I am one of the bad ones.

At least I have somewhat of a moral compass, though. It doesn't always point due north, but I use it.

Sometimes.

"*Dante!*"

Oh, shit. That doesn't sound good.

A door slams and Matteo storms out of the apartment, his eyes blazing and damn, those flames are fucking scorching.

I force a smirk. "You rang?"

He stalks over to where I'm sitting and stabs me in the chest with one of his fingers. "You fucking jerkoff! I can't believe you!"

"Don't poke me like that, Matty. I'll kick your ass! What the hell is wrong with you?" I ask, smacking away his finger.

"Heaven set up cameras all over the goddamn place when she hired Anya," Matteo seethes "She can see every inch of this place. It's a good fucking thing she missed your midnight fuck-fest, right against that window!" he bellows. "I had my coffee against that window this morning, Jesus Christ!"

Uh-oh.

"Cameras? Really? I've been here pretty much the whole damn time!"

"Are you going to explain yourself?" Matteo hisses.

"I told you I needed some action," I say, shrugging.

Matteo fists his hair. "I want to choke you right now," he seethes. "Her job is to take care of Aisling, not you! She's just a kid, for Christ's sake! And you nailed her anyway!"

"I wasn't thinking," I say.

"Oh, you were thinking, just with the wrong head," Sergio quips.

"Shut the hell up," Matteo growls at him. "Don't you have a hotel to run?"

"I just came up here to check things out and meet the new girl." Sergio winks at me. "Score, dude."

"Get out of here," Matteo demands. "Or I'll kick your ass next!"

Sergio puts up his hands. "Okay, okay. You know I'm only up a couple of floors if you need me." He disappears inside the apartment and Matteo glares at me, his forehead pinched. "How can your head be so far up your ass, Dante? We have so much crap to deal with right now and you just forgot about all of it? Just to get off? You lost focus!"

"Hey," I say, pointing a finger at him. "You knew I wasn't happy, that I haven't been happy. I've been your little bitch for months now, just skulking around and waiting for someone to attack. But nobody has and I don't want to be here forever, Matteo. I get that you're nervous but you've got a solid network out here. You don't need me hovering like a damn helicopter."

He rubs the back of his neck. "So you won't even consider the security firm?"

"I don't want to be a fucking chauffeur to these arrogant asshole millionaires! I want my life back."

But even as I say it, a small part of me resists the words.

Same way it did when I told Sergio I wanted out.

Because that tiny part is intrigued at what my life could become if I stayed.

Damn.

Where the hell did that come from?

I convinced myself it was time to move on.

And the mere mention of what happened between me and Anya has me conflicted.

"Dante," Matteo says. I can see he's struggling to keep himself under control right now. "I can't keep tabs on you when you're buried in some obscure corner of the world doing a hit. You're good. Very fucking good. But what happens when one day, someone is better?" He shakes his head. "I have a responsibility to the family, to Papa. It's to protect you all however I can. You haven't been in the same spot for longer than a couple of months for the past ten years!"

"I know. And it's made me very fucking rich," I say with a smirk.

"You can't take it with you, Dante," he says. "You also can't do this forever. I want you to play a bigger role with the family businesses. We're growing fast out here and I need you to be onboard with our direction."

I let out a deep sigh and lean back against the lounge chair. "I like my life, Matteo. I miss it."

"We have a lot of enemies, Dante. Someday, you'll get a message with instructions for someone you need to 'handle' and that someone is going to be you."

"Jesus, that's morbid."

Matteo shrugs. "It's the way things go. Nobody gets away with murder forever. And you've fucked a lot of people over for your career. Unforgiving people. Vengeful people. And your sniper rifle will only get you so far."

"It's been a rough year," I muse. "Can't argue with that. But you can't make me change who I am."

"I think you're full of shit. I see the way you are with Aisling. I think you want that yourself."

"Pulling out the big guns now, huh? Why do I need my own kid when I have her?" I say with a snicker. "I get to give her back for the gross stuff."

He sighs. "Look, all I'm saying is that it may be time to do something different. Find a different way to get your kicks." His expression darkens. "And I'm not talking about Anya."

"I'll consider it."

"Don't even think about laying another finger on her. I need you on top of your game." Matteo's gaze darkens. "Because those cameras picked up a lot more than just your fucking," he growls.

Chapter Fifteen
ANYA

I stick my key card into the lock and pull open the door to the apartment later that afternoon, careful not to make any noise. Heaven mentioned something about going to lunch with her family once they get in from the airport, so I guess they haven't gotten back yet. I took Aisling for a walk after her afternoon feeding, and she fell asleep almost as soon as the stroller hit the hot desert air.

I won't lie.

I like people stopping to admire her chubby cheeks and big bright eyes. I like when they tell me what a beautiful daughter I have. I always thank them for the compliment, never once bothering to correct anyone.

It feels nice.

It allows me to step out of my own shell and be someone else... someone, much as I deny it to myself, that I aspire to become.

Over the past few days of being out here in Vegas, while I've been trying hard to conjure up all of the hatred for people who stole my happiness, I've realized that harboring all of the emotions is actually preventing me from achieving what it is I really want.

And the longer I suppress the negative emotions — the anger, the resentment, and the disdain — the further away I get from anything remotely resembling a happy ending.

The truth is, the more I get to know these people, the more I wonder about who they really are and what they actually have done.

If anything.

Uncle Boris wants me out here for some reason, but he won't tell me exactly what it is. He's being purposely evasive, which he knows I hate. He admitted to completely ignoring me for days on end because something else took priority over his own niece's well-being.

All of that contributes to my redirected anger.

He doesn't respect me enough to give me direction.

He never has.

I'm just expected to jump when he says how high.

Makes me think that I'm missing a lot of the dots that have yet to be connected and question everything he's told me.

I should have started questioning a long time ago.

Because he's manipulative as hell and uses whoever her can to achieve his goals, which are usually blood-soaked.

So when I see him tonight, I want answers.

I will demand the answers!

And if I don't like what I hear, I will handle things my own way. I'm not going to be his puppet for a single second more.

If he doesn't like it, he'll just have to kill me.

There's no happy ending to *that* story. Not for him.

I lean down and scoop Aisling into my arms, carrying her into the nursery. There's an odor wafting up from her diaper, but there's no way I'm going to disturb her sleep by changing her diaper. It can wait. I doubled her up, in anticipation of this very circumstance.

No poop will be able to escape my master diaper job.

I turn on the monitor and grab the handheld before backing out of the room.

I pad into the kitchen and grab a bottle of water from the fridge, a tiny moan slipping from my lips. This place, this job, this whole existence — it's like an alternate reality and I'm caught in the middle of it with no desire to escape.

My job requires me to leave once I've delivered on the requirements, whatever the hell they may be.

But I don't want to go.

I want to stay.

I like the Villanis.

I'm totally hot for Dante.

And I'm smitten with that baby.

Why can't I have this life?

The question startles me because I've always pushed it out of my mind when it so much as threatens to surface.

But now that it's out there, on the front burner after I've pushed it to the back for days on end, it demands an answer.

And I still don't have one.

All I have are more burning questions...

I mean, why can't I be a student at UNLV? I've always wanted to go into fashion design and merchandising. I love sewing, something I've really missed while being away from Brooklyn.

Why can't I have a tight-knit friendship? Someone to confide in, to laugh with, and to do fun, girlie things with?

Why can't I find true love? A guy who looks at me like I light up his entire universe just the way Matteo looks at Heaven? Someone who never loses a chance to tell me how much he loves me, just like Papa did with Mama before they died?

Why, why, why?

I've never realized, before I hopped on that flight out of JFK International Airport, how much I crave normalcy, happiness, and purpose.

My purpose has never been my own, not since I was a thirteen-year-old orphan.

My purpose has always been the means for someone else to achieve his purpose.

I don't want that life anymore.

I'm not going to be defined by someone else's choices.

It's time I started making my own, not just allowing myself to be victimized by other people's expectations of me.

I take a long gulp of the water, feeling more and more empowered as the ideas percolate.

What I'm proposing to myself is dangerous.

The job of bratva assassin is pretty much a lifelong position.

Kill or be killed.

Those are pretty much your only options.

But I'm tired of living by someone else's rules.

I'm ready to live according to my own.

And good thing I have some lethal, badass bitch skills to help set me up in this big, bad world.

A smile plays at my lips.

I have a list of demands for my life.

And I want to tick off the boxes.

Starting today.

The door clicks and I peek my head around a column to see Heaven and an older woman come into the apartment, their arms laden with bags. I put down my water and hurry over to them to help.

Heaven flashes a grateful smile and hands me some of the packages. "Anya, this is my Aunt Maura. Auntie, this is Anya. Our savior!"

Aunt Maura grins at me, her blue eyes sparkling. "Pleasure to meet you, dear. Heaven has told me such great things about how you've been helping with Aisling." She puts down her bags and clasps her hands together. "I cannot wait to see the little darling! Is she in the nursery?"

"Yes,' I say in a hushed voice. "But she's sleeping." I look at Heaven. "We just got back from a walk and she was exhausted by the heat, I think. She conked out before we even made it back up here."

"Thank you, Anya," Heaven says with a big smile.

It never ceases to amaze me that she let me go outside today with Aisling by myself. I figured for sure Dante would be tagging along, but I'm also not naïve enough to think that she would let me take her baby out of the apartment and not have me tracked by at least a handful of security guards who would have this place locked down in a hot second if I so much as made one false move.

Dante...

Where has he been hiding?

Seeing him this morning made me think he'd come back around because he felt the same things I did.

Do.

But then he disappeared again.

Could I have imagined everything that happened between us? The intensity, the chemistry...my God, it was electric.

How could he *not* have felt it all?

"Why don't you take a break? You've already put in your eight hours since Aisling got up so early this morning. I don't want to violate the terms of the au pair contract," she says with a chuckle. "I need you here!"

"Oh, you've definitely got me," I say. "And I'd love a little break. Maybe I'll go for a run." I take a deep breath. "Hey, do you know where Dante is? He said he'd give me some of the best jogging routes around here."

Aunt Maura busies herself with the bags and Heaven folds her arms over her chest, a knowing smile on her face. "Actually, no, I haven't. He might have gone out for a run himself." She sighs. "He hasn't been his normal self lately. I know he feels like something is missing."

Missing?

"He seems good to me." Understatement of the century if I ever heard one.

She shakes her head. "He isn't happy out here. He wants to get back to his real job, but Matteo wants him to stick around. You know, to help out at the hotel and our nightclubs and things like that..." she trails off evasively.

"He doesn't want to stay?" I squeak out as an icy feeling clenches my heart.

"No. I wish he would, though. Maybe he just needs a good enough reason to stay," she says, giving me a pointed look. "I bet you could convince him."

I swallow hard. Holy crap, are my thoughts that transparent?

"Well, if he doesn't want to stay, I don't think a virtual stranger can't convince him." I force a smile. "He knows what's best for himself, I'm sure."

"I don't think so," Heaven says. "He needs to settle down and have a real life with roots. He can't be gallivanting all around the world the way he does. He needs stability."

"My, my, how your tune has changed in the past year," Aunt Maura quips from the kitchen. "Couldn't hold you down with a roll of duct tape, rope, and chains before Matteo walked into Molly's Pub that first night."

Heaven shrugs. "It only took a forced marriage for me to see the writing on the wall." With a snicker, she nudges me. "Everyone needs their own type of jolt. I hope Dante gets his, sooner than later. And you might be just the one to deliver it."

Ha!

Little does she know, that's the plan.

Chapter Sixteen
ANYA

The whoosh of arid air hits me like someone took a massive hair dryer, pointed it directly at my face, and flipped the switch.

It's fucking brutal.

But I need to clear my very cluttered head because I just heard a bunch of things that have my gut knotted like a pretzel.

I stretch out my quads, Heaven's words clanging between my ears like clashing cymbals.

"...hasn't been himself lately...he isn't happy...wants to get back to his real job..."

I grit my teeth and do a couple of side stretches before windmilling my arms.

So everything between us...it's all been bullshit?

A huff escapes my lips as I start jogging lightly down the driveway and onto the Strip. Sweat pebbles over my skin almost instantly, and tiny drizzles of perspiration slip down my spine. Moisture wicking clothing, my ass.

It's not wicking anything!

I'm slowly melting down — my body, my mind, my heart.

And it is goddamn agonizing.

For the first time in forever, I let my guard down for a guy, a guy I've developed feelings for, despite all of my efforts to self-protect.

I guess that's irony for you.

Dante is just like me. He's doing what I've always done because it's the only way to keep focus.

You don't allow yourself to feel because it's dangerous.

You don't let emotions grab you by the throat because they make you do stupid shit.

And you don't let anyone get in the way of your work.

Always keep focus, no matter what.

Those are the rules I've lived by and because of him, I've shoved them all into the dark recesses of my mind because being around him...with him...makes me happy.

Goddammit!

Have we not already established that happiness is not in my cards?

I pick up speed as I sidestep a group of drunk guys slugging down their yard-long, bright red and blue cocktails as they stagger down the sidewalk.

"This is ridiculous!" I huff. "I have a job to do. So, we had sex. Hot sex," I mutter as my sneakers pound on the pavement, my leg muscles aching at the sudden increase in speed. "It's over now. He's leaving and I'm not his little plaything. He can't use me and then throw me away!" I grunt. "I'm not going to be his little distraction, someone to occupy his time with until he gets itchy and needs to bolt."

I stop in front of a street lamp post, leaning against the scalding hot metal, but feeling too fired up with anger that I don't even notice it searing the backs of my legs. I pant for a few minutes, watching cars zoom past, lost in my own pity party.

Because the reality is, I don't want to be a distraction.

I want to be the center of somebody's world.

Forget the fact that this whole thing is twisted as hell because of the circumstances, but I can't ignore the memory of his body buried deep inside of mine, the sensations that course through me whenever he's near, his sultry, manly scent, his heated gaze, and the ass that just doesn't quit.

I feel too much and I've lost control of my heart as a result.

How could I have let this happen?

I should be calling the shots and instead, I'm reduced to a pile of emotional Jell-O because the guy electrifies my insides with an erotic charge that can rival the power grid of Las Vegas.

I cover my face with my hands and let out a muffled yell. "Fuck him!"

But it comes out sounding more like "Mnuhphhimm!"

"Muffin? Fuck yeah, that sounds good."

"Oh my God!" I jump, clutching a hand to my chest as I twist around. My heart rate skyrockets when I see Dante smirking at me, his massive arms folded over his chest. His shirt is stuffed into the pocket of his basketball shorts and he's got a Yankees baseball cap on backwards. Ray-Bans complete his sexy-as-fuck look, and I bite down hard on my lower lip because I am a tiny bit afraid if I don't, my tongue will jut out and do all sorts of unspeakable things, right here in the open.

It's Vegas, so I doubt anyone would even notice.

Although, since it's Vegas, they might join in.

"Did I scare you?" he asks, that shit-eating grin making my knees wobble.

"Not even close," I hiss.

"Good, so how about a snack?" He winks at me. "You, know, since you mentioned *muffins*."

I press my lips together. No more distractions! "I don't have time. Aisling is probably up from her nap and Heaven—"

"Heaven has her aunt." He stretches his arms overhead and I watch his biceps flex, the sun glistening on his bronze skin. I can feel my tongue sweep over my lips and his smirk widens.

Dammit.

Just another instance of my body betraying me!

I fix my ponytail and give him a quick wave. "I'll see you later." I start to jog back toward the Excelsior, berating myself for allowing his gorgeousness to once again shatter me. I am a badass bitch. I don't let guys unravel me like this. Nobody has that privilege!

Not even a minute later, I hear a second pair of sneakers thumping along the sidewalk next to me.

"I don't know why you're following me," I grumble.

"We're going to the same place, yeah?"

"I'm not really sure," I snap. "I mean, it's not like you've been hanging around the apartment. You kind of pulled a disappearing act after what happened the other night."

"Yeah, I've been...busy."

"Busy trying to figure out how quickly you can get out of Vegas?" I say, silently chiding myself for sounding so bitter. Argh! My head and my heart are not on separate pages. They're immersed in two very different books. On two different planets. In two different galaxies!

He slows down. "What are you talking about?"

My lungs are ready to revolt right about now as my run comes to a stuttering halt. I turn to look at him, quirking an eyebrow. "Heaven said you're on your way out." I shrug. "That's cool. I'm sure there are lots of real estate opportunities waiting for you. I get that you want to move on with your life."

I do, too. Just in a different direction.

"She told you that?"

I shrug. "Yeah, she said you're not happy or whatever. That you're not yourself. That you want to leave."

He adjusts his cap, averting his eyes for a long second. "Yeah. It's true. I did."

"So what's stopping you? If you want to leave, just go." I glare at him, shielding my eyes from the sun.

With a shake of his head, he pulls off his sunglasses so I can see the confusion in his eyes. "Why do you even care?"

"I don't!" I let out a deep sigh. "Look, Dante, it's hot as balls out here, and I hate to sweat, so I'm just going to head back, okay? If you don't take off before tomorrow, I guess I'll just see you at the christening." I start to run again but he grabs my wrist and pulls me back, but my foot skids along a patch of gravel and I collide with his chest.

My mouth waters.

I want to lick.

I need to taste!

Ugh!

I put my hands on his perfect pecs and shove away from them. "What do you want with me, Dante?" I ask.

"I'm still trying to figure that out," he says, his voice low and thick with conflict.

"Well, let me make it easy for you. I know you're leaving, so whatever this is? It's done. I need to keep my focus...on the baby and my...my school plans. I don't need any distractions, okay? We had a fun night and it's done. So just let it go."

"What if I don't want to?"

I narrow my eyes and stick my hands on my hips. "What the hell is that supposed to mean?"

He lets out a sigh. "Anya, Heaven was right...kind of. I have been wanting to leave Vegas for a while. But over the past few days, I've been feeling differently. A lot differently. Like maybe what I thought I wanted isn't what I want now, because of you. And it doesn't make any sense to me because it's been such a short amount of time and I barely know you. But I can't get you out of my head. It's why I pulled away for a little while. I needed to make sure what I was feeling...and who I was feeling it about... was real."

My mouth drops open. "About me?" I whisper. "You're feeling this stuff about *me*?"

"Is that so hard to believe?"

And just like that, my heart races faster than it did while I was running.

I could come up with so many reasons why it shouldn't be possible.

But I know how I feel about him and that renders all of those reasons meaningless.

I swallow hard. "Are you sure?"

He nods, caressing the side of my face. "There's something about you, Anya. Something that makes me feel like we're more alike than we both know. Something that tells me this is crazy but right. I don't know much about you, but I know a ton, if that makes any sense."

Breathless. I am absolutely breathless right now, and I'm standing perfectly still.

"And it really all started when you ran in front of my car at the airport." His lips curl into a mischievous grin.

"Hey, wait, I didn't run in front of your car!" I screech, throwing my hands in the air. "You were driving like a lunatic and I was minding my own business, just crossing—"

He doesn't let me finish, though. All of a sudden, his strong hands grip my waist and gently pull me toward him. His mouth smothers mine, silencing my voice and devouring me voraciously for all to see. His tongue juts between my lips, coiling heat radiating throughout my core. I press my fingertips into his back, letting him infuse my entire being with pure, wanton lust.

He wraps me tight in his embrace and my body molds against his, fitting perfectly into my spot.

My spot...

I never thought I'd ever use those words in relation to a guy.

When he pulls away, we're both breathless. "What I was trying to say is that maybe I want to stick around."

"I don't want to be the reason why you stay," I murmur. "I don't want you to resent me if it doesn't work out. Besides, it would get weird, you know all of us living with your brother and sister-in-law. Kind of crowded, don't you think? And that whole sex against the window thing couldn't be a regular occurrence because, you know," I shrug. "It'd be like we were living with parents. I mean, they are parents. Not ours, but still." I give my head a quick shake to keep from rambling anymore. "I don't know. It's complicated. Maybe that's just the bottom line," I finally rasp.

Dante grins. "Okay, breathe, Anya. Jesus, I think that's the most you've ever said to me at once, do you know that?"

I laugh and clap a hand over my mouth. "That's probably why I try to limit my words. When they get away from me, they just keep coming, like a sea of bullets."

Yikes. Bullets. How incredibly apropos.

"Lemme just address one of your concerns, okay? I don't live with Heaven and Matteo. I know you have this whole useless but pretty trust fund baby perception of me, but it's not true. I've got my own place. I'm not a freeloader." He smirks. "I mean, I don't pay for it, but I've got my own space. With plenty of windows," he says with a wink.

"Mm-hm," I say. "All of that sounds really good. The only thing I don't remember saying is 'useless but pretty.' I think that's just you projecting."

He smacks my ass and then squeezes it, making me squeal.

"Oh, you like that, huh?" He draws me near, his lips brushing against my ear. "Why don't I take you to my place and show you how use*ful* I actually am? And then I'm going to make you scream so hard, you'll never say shit like that again."

"Or maybe I'll like it so much, I'll keep saying it." I waggle my eyebrows. "Now, are you going to take me to your place, or are you going to fuck me against this street post?" I shrug. "It *is* Vegas, after all."

"Tempting, but no." He grins at me. "The things I'm gonna do to you have to be behind closed doors or I'll get arrested. And that whole pretty thing will be very bad for me in the clink." With a chuckle, he nods toward the hotel. "Race ya back?"

"A competition. Nice." I wiggle my fingers in a little wave and take off like a shot. He's on my heels but challenge accepted. No way do I lose.

Of course, by the time I get to the hotel entrance, I can't breathe, my face is purple, and my eyes are bugging out of my head.

But hey, I won.

We catch our breath for a minute, the unspoken promise of what awaits us upstairs hanging in the stagnant air between us. Finally, when I don't feel completely wilted, Dante laces his fingers with mine and pulls me into the revolving glass door next to him. I can't stop staring up at him and smiling. I want to pull my eyes away, I want to feel as if I have some sliver of self-control left, but there's nothing.

I am hopelessly consumed in all that is him.

He's staying...because of me.

Shut the front fucking door.

I never expected to hear those words, even though deep down I yearned to hear them tumble from his bitable lips.

"Anya!"

That definitely jars me. I turn around to see who could possibly be calling my—

And then it hits me.

Dottie and *The Golden Girls* said they were staying at the Excelsior.

A smile tugs at my lips. How happy they look in their brightly colored, button-down shirts and white pants...what is it with older women and their white pants? It's like a uniform! And how do they keep them so freaking clean?

Maybe it's a secret that gets uncovered as you age.

Dottie trots over to me and throws her arms around my neck, not caring at all that I am a sweaty mess. "I didn't think we'd see you again!"

I smile. "Well, I got that job I told you about."

Dottie furrows her brow. "Job? I don't recall—"

"It's fine," I say, knowing full well why she doesn't recall. It's because she never let me get a word in edgewise. Anything I said got completely drowned out by her yapping.

Still, she's cute and excited and obviously having a grand time.

"And this young man is the one who brought you here!" she exclaims.

Memory like an elephant. Maybe she's more observant than I gave her credit for being.

"Is he your boyfriend?" One of the others pipes in and a hot flush creeps into my cheeks. I sneak a look up at him and he grins down at me.

Then he looks at Dottie and flashes those bright white teeth before answering. "Nah, we're just having sex."

I bite down on my lower lip to keep from laughing when I see the shocked expression on her face. And then to her credit, a second later, she winks at me. "Ride it while you can, dear. You never know when the horse is going to give out."

"I'll remember that," I say, giving her shoulder a squeeze. "It was great running into you. I hope you have an amazing time with your friends. It looks like you're having so much fun."

"Then you should experience it for yourself. Maybe later? We'll be here!" Her friends let out a collective yell and fist the air.

"That sounds nice. I'll look for you." I give Dottie a quick hug since I'm still learning this affection thing for virtual strangers. And I'm actually not full of shit, either. Maybe I could use a little girl time. I have the night off, and something tells me I'll need a few laughs and drinks after my dinner with Uncle Boris.

She nods, slowly looking between me and Dante with a knowing smile on her face. "In the meantime, you two enjoy!"

And on cue, the girls all hoot and holler as we walk toward the private elevator bank that leads to the residences.

"Look at you, making friends, being chatty." he says, leaning against the wall while we wait for the elevator to arrive. "I might have to make some adjustments to my list."

"I'm hoping you find some new ones to add," I say in a husky voice, discreetly sliding my hand up the leg of his shorts, grazing his half-hard cock.

A sharp ding sounds and the elevator doors open. I push Dante inside, backing him against the back wall, not even bothering to wait for the doors to close again before I crush my lips against his. Our hands and legs entwine as we drink each other in like we've just been running outside in the blistering heat with no water.

Because we have.

And water is seemingly the last thing either of us wants right now.

The elevator hasn't moved, so he pulls away slightly to stab the button for the forty-seventh floor before devouring me once again.

As intoxicated as I am by him, I can still see that we are moving out of the elevator now that it's landed on the floor where Dante's apartment is obviously situated. He backs me down a short corridor and then shoves a keycard into the lock, all while keeping his delicious lips pressed against mine. We stumble into the foyer, and in my periphery I can see it's a carbon copy of Heaven and Matteo's place.

With plenty of windows, just like Dante promised.

"I need to take a quick shower," I murmur against his mouth, raising my arms overhead so he can pull off my tank top.

"I don't understand why it needs to be quick," he says, pulling off my shirt and shoving my shorts and panties to my ankles. I kick them off and step toward him. With a quick flick of his fingers, he has my sports bra fluttering to the floor next to the rest of my clothes.

I loop my fingers into the waistband of his shorts and slither down his calves, holding onto the material until it pools at his feet. He pulls me up to a standing position, his fingers slipping the rubber band out of my hair so that it falls gently down my back.

His eyes drop and he runs his fingers over my Band-Aid again.

Every time he examines it, my belly clenches and the butterflies stop dead in their fluttery tracks. "Any better?" he asks.

I shrug. "Yeah, but I just keep it covered in case she gets the same spot again. I don't want it to get infected."

And how much longer do you think you can get away with keeping that part of your life hidden from him, Anya?

I sure hope it stands up to the shower spray. I'm not ready for the explanation that comes along with the tattoo if the Band-Aid happens to fall off.

I give the palm of my hand a long, seductive lick and grasp his thick cock, sliding my hand up and down his throbbing shaft. He lets out a loud moan, and I know the scratch is already forgotten.

He scoops me into his arms and carries me into his massive, white marble bathroom. His fingers dig into my prickled flesh, grasping my hips, my ass, my tits. His insatiable appetite has turned him into a ravenous predator and I am his prey.

His extremely aroused prey.

He pulls away from me long enough to turn on the shower spray. The enclosure has one glass panel and jets spraying steamy water from each wall. I watch him stand in the center of the mosaic-style mother of pearl tiles, my breath hitching as the water rushes over him, streaming down his god-like form.

He runs a hand through his dark hair, a seductive smirk curling his lips upward. With a crook of his finger, he has me moving toward him as if captured by the most carnal spell imaginable. I step onto the marble tile floor and run my hands down the sides of his torso. His muscles ripple under the pads of my fingertips, his cock grazing my slit. My eyes flutter closed and his lips seize mine, unrelenting and unwilling to let them go.

I wrap my arms around him, trailing my hands up and down his back as he leads me to the far wall and guides me down onto the bench that lines the perimeter. He pushes open my legs, stepping onto the bench with one foot as he positions himself at my entrance. His hand reaches around, forcing my hips to jut toward him as his cock dips inside of me, slowly stretching my walls with the same sweet torture I remember from our last romp. The burning sensation makes me cringe, but in the best way possible.

I lean back against the wall, thrusting my hips against him as he plunders my core. Water rushes over us as our movements become more desperate and frenzied over the next few blissful minutes. I lock my legs around Dante's waist as he drives deeper, fucking me with long, slow strokes that have me clinging to the edge of my sanity.

He thrusts faster and faster as my cries pierce the air. I dig my fingernails into his back, slicing at his flesh like I'm some kind of female version of Wolverine. My pussy clenches tight around him like a glove, beckoning him to connect with me on every level possible. I squeeze my eyes shut, ignoring the water streaming down my face. I don't care that I can't see. I don't care that I can barely breathe.

I just care that I'm exactly where I want to be right now.

Where, crazily enough, I feel as if I'm meant to be...

Dante lifts one of my legs and lays it on his hip to give him leverage as he continues his luscious assault on my body. He plunders me to the point where my brain cells no longer have the power to fire. I pant and huff and moan as he slides against my clit with every push and pull motion.

And then he hits it.

The spot. My spot. Oh holy fuck, it's amazing and beautiful and fucking earth-shattering all at the same time.

My body trembles uncontrollably against him as the sparks blast out of my core, shooting out to every extremity. The euphoric sensations ripple through me, and I come undone in his arms, begging for the release only he can provide.

He pulls me on top of him as he swings around and collapses onto the bench. "Fuck," he breathes.

"I know," I whisper, nipping at his ear. "So good."

He stares at me from under his half-hooded gaze and pushes a wet strand of hair out of my eyes. "I think we should get you nice and clean now." He smirks. "So I can get you really filthy again."

"I like that kind of loop," I say. "I could get very used to that kind of shower treatment."

"Well, then, consider this our little playtime activity," he murmurs. "Forget naps. I'll just fuck you instead," he says with a wicked glimmer in his eyes.

I laugh breathlessly and he stands up, letting me down so that he can grab the soap and a washcloth. We spend the next few minutes soaping up each other's bodies. The lemony scent of the bath soap makes my nose tingle as I rub it up and down Dante's sculpted chest.

When we finally make it out of the spray, our fingers are shriveled like prunes. He wraps a thick white towel around me and then hooks one around his waist. I pull a hairbrush through my tangled hair, my knees buckling as he trails kisses down the back of my neck. I have to grab onto the white marble countertop to keep from face-planting on the floor.

"You hungry?" he asks.

"Yes," I say in a teasing voice. "I guess I didn't get my fill before."

His head whips in my direction. "Then we're gonna have to correct that. Immediately, if not sooner."

I cock my head to the side. "Oh? You're ready to go again? So soon?"

He pushes me against the wall and unclasps my towel, watching as it falls to the floor. "This body already has me hard again." He kneads my breasts, flicking the nipples and making me squeal. "So fucking beautiful," he mutters. "I never knew what the hell I was missing before..."

I swallow hard.

I know exactly how he feels.

And then the realization hits me like a hammer to the temple.

There are so many lies between us.

So much unsaid.

So many questions that can't be answered.

This whole thing between us is a complete fantasy because none of it is real.

The feelings we have for each other...we don't even know who the other is!

The hell with what we feel!

How can this work?

How can we possibly think that this chemistry between us won't ignite and explode like an experiment gone very wrong?

My pulse throbs against my neck as I fall to my knees and take his hard dick deep into my mouth.

I don't want to think about any of those things right now.

I just want to be here in this moment with him where none of the bullshit can touch us.

We can just exist in this blissfully ignorant little bubble for the foreseeable future, right?

I slide my tongue down the length of his cock, kneading his balls as he tangles his fingers into my hair. I tease his slit with my tongue, tugging and pulling his dick with my lips. I suck and I rub until he gasps, yanking my hair as he thrusts against my mouth. The top of his cock hits the back of my throat, and my gag reflex is about to kick in. I squeeze my eyes shut, focusing only on making him feel as amazing as I did when he tongue-fucked me the other night.

And then he pushes me away, gently, but still. I look up at him, confusion in my gaze. "Didn't you like that?" I whisper.

"I loved it. But I don't want to come without you." He takes my hands and pulls me to my feet. "I want to feel your soft pussy wrapped tight around my cock again. I want to feel you come all over me again. I want you to scream my name, Anya. I want you to tell me that you've never been fucked so good in your life, do you understand?"

My nipples stiffen as chills slither down my spine.

I nod. "Yes."

"Good girl," he growls. "Now, let's get that hot ass into the bedroom."

"Is this the part where you unleash your deviance?" I ask. "Because I am very amenable to that."

The corners of his lips lift. "Oh, hell yes." He reaches for me and captures me in his arms, carrying me to the bedroom.

"Was I moving too slowly?" I ask.

"Yeah. And you were talking too much. I need to give you something else to do with that mouth."

I let out a moan as he gathers me close. I drag my fingernails down the slope of his back, lodging them into his hips as he walks. I rotate my hips slightly against him, making him move even faster. My pussy tingles as the head of his cock teases my slit, and I don't know how much longer I can wait to feel him inside of me again.

He lays me on the bed, pulling me toward the edge. He dips his head between my legs and plunges his tongue into my pussy, his thumb and forefinger flicking my clit. My body trembles under his erotic spell, my belly clenching tight as ripples of pleasure rush over me.

"Please fuck me again, Dante," I moan. "Oh my God, please do it now. Don't make me wait! You're making me so crazy!"

His hot tongue changes course almost immediately at my request. With one arm snaked around me, he uses the other to lift one of my legs. He slowly thrusts his thick cock into me, long, hard, and so deep, I cry out, lancing his flesh with my nails as he drives me into the cloud of euphoric bliss I so crave.

A gasp slips from my lips as he presses into me, my breathing ragged as he thrusts harder and faster with each passing second.

I clench tight around him, our bodies slick with sweat as we slide against each other.

"You scream for me, baby," he grunts. "I wanna hear it!"

And that's all the invitation I need. And I hope nobody else is living on this floor because it's possible that these sounds may wake the dead.

He flips onto his back, pulling me on top of him and bouncing me on his cock as I scream for God the Father, the Son, the Holy Spirit, and anyone else who can hear me.

A deliciously tormenting ache rumbles deep in my core, sparks igniting and firing into every extremity, making my fingers tingle and my toes curl. Sensations that I've never felt course through me like a raging inferno. I roll my hips over him one last time, squeezing my eyes shut and letting the orgasm tear through me with a force that shreds my insides in its wake.

Seriously shredded.

That's exactly how I feel.

Well, shredded and zapped of all ability to think or speak.

I can only feel right now, and my God, it's amazing.

I collapse onto the mattress next to him.

I can't breathe. I can't speak. I can't even hear.

And everything tingles, right down to my toes.

Holy shit...

Fucking amazing is an understatement.

I don't know how much time passes before my mouth finds words, how much time before I can stop panting.

I don't even care.

I can stay like this forever.

And then I remember...I really can't.

Chapter Seventeen
ANYA

My eyes fly open sometime later and I sit up with a gasp, very well aware of my nakedness.

I look down at Dante and trace a path over the ripped muscles of his back.

He's naked, too.

And my God, if I could, I'd choose to live out the rest of my days stark naked and under this man.

Under him, on top of him, cuddled into him...I'm not picky.

There are plenty of positions I'd be very happy to occupy for eternity.

I swallow a groan and rub a hand over my face.

I am just violating so many rules today.

But the biggest issues hanging between us — the huge-ass elephant in the room *and* the elephant's twin — is my true identity and reason for being here in Vegas.

Yeah, that will be an interesting one to hash out.

Because for as much of a liar as he might be, I guarantee I'm taking that title.

He opens his eyes a crack as I gently kiss his lips. "Hey," he murmurs in a sleepy voice.

"Hey," I say, dragging my fingers down the side of his arm. "So I was wondering...how do you think this is going to go over with Heaven and Matteo?"

"This thing?" He furrows his brow.

I roll my eyes. "Yes, with us!"

He snickers. "I think Heaven will be just fine with it."

"And your brother?" I bite my lower lip. "I don't think he's a big fan of mine, to be honest. Just a feeling I get."

"You have to know Matteo," he says. "He's a pretty overprotective guy. And now with the baby, he's even worse."

I nod. "I get that he doesn't want anything to hurt them. Or anyone."

"There's always gonna be someone lurking," he mumbles, flinging an arm over his eye.

I take a deep breath. "Who are you protecting them from, Dante?" I ask in a soft voice, pulling at a thread from the comforter.

He moves the arm so that it's no longer shielding his eyes. "Too many people to count, Anya. But that's how things work when you're the king. There are always people waiting to knock you off your throne."

"King of what, exactly?"

He levels me with a stare. "He's a very powerful guy with a lot of cash-soaked businesses under his control. And there are a lot of people who want a piece. Hell, they want it all." He shrugs. "I'm here to make sure that doesn't happen."

"But you don't want to be here. At least, before me, you didn't. Why?"

He sits up and runs a hand through his tousled hair. "You ask a lot of questions, you know that?"

"If this thing between us is going to work, we have to be straight with each other, right?" I shrug. "And I'm just curious because, you know, you're a real estate investor, not a bodyguard. I'm trying to connect the dots, to understand you better."

He lets out a sigh and falls back onto the pillow. "Anya, I think we both know I'm not a real estate investor."

I lie on the mattress next to him. "So who are you then?"

"I'm the guy who always makes sure the people I care about are safe," he says. "And I'll do whatever it takes to get the job done."

"Good work ethic," I murmur with a smile.

"It's complicated."

"Isn't it always?" I muse.

"More complicated than you think." He averts his now-troubled gaze and scrubs a hand down the front of his face. "Family means everything to me. And I let down a family member once. I can't do it again. I won't." He looks back at me. "I guess I've been trying to prove that to myself and everyone else ever since."

"What happened?"

"I was watching over my younger cousin, Emilia, while her brother was out getting caught up with the wrong fucking crowd. He was a troublemaker and he managed to get on the radar of some really bad guys. So after I'd fallen asleep, she sneaked out and went after him because she was worried. They were both killed. But what they did to her before that..." His voice trails off and he shakes his head. "Brutal. Fucking animalistic."

"That's terrible," I whisper. "I'm sorry."

"It's why I take my responsibilities to my family so seriously. I feel like I owe them...all of them. So whenever someone who can hurt any of them crosses my path, I handle it."

Shit, we really *are* the same.

"My brother is dead," I blurt out.

Dante's eyebrows furrow. "I thought you said—"

I shake my head, tears springing to my eyes. "He was killed. Shot to death. I was with him but out of sight. He was my best friend," I swipe at my eyes.

"Shit, Anya. I'm sorry," he says, pulling me into his chest.

"I only have my uncle now," I whisper. "And it's so hard knowing I'm pretty much on my own."

"How are things with your uncle?"

"He's an ass," I say with a sniffle. "But he's all I have left."

Dante shakes his head. "No, he's not. You've got a new life out here. You can write your own ticket."

I let out a dry laugh. "Like you said before, it's complicated. But I just don't..." I swallow hard. "I don't want that life anymore. I want to start over."

"Isn't that why you're here?"

I blink fast, the real reason for my stay in Vegas breaking through the cloud of bliss, comfort, and ripped muscle currently cocooning me. "Yeah," I say softly. "It is."

"So you don't have to go back to it. You can make that choice." He smiles. "Isn't that what life's all about?"

"I just know I've made a lot of bad ones," I say. "I want to start making good ones."

"Me too," he murmurs, stroking the back of my head. "Starting now."

I pull away and look up at him. "Is this totally insane?" I say it more to myself than to him. But really, it's a rhetorical question. I already know the answer.

"Completely," he says, a smirk tugging at his lips. "But I'm all in." He lifts an eyebrow. "You?"

So many thoughts loop through my mind in that instant. My uncle has expectations of me. He's done so much and never loses a chance to rub it in my face. I have obligations to him and to my brother, and my livelihood will hang in the balance if I walk away. Uncle Boris has already promised me that.

Can I just disappear and start over?

Will I be able to pull myself out of his death grip on me?

I have to try.

No, I have to succeed.

I used to think finding my brother's killers would make me whole.

But killing in cold blood only makes me feel more and more empty, a broken shell of who I used to be.

I'm tired of being manipulated by him, of him calling all the shots because I'm afraid of the repercussions, because I feel guilty about him stepping in to take care of us.

I mean, I've been out here flying blind with no direction from him at all, and the reality is, he's just driven by money promised from this illusory 'contact'.

I've trusted him and he's taken advantage of that trust for years. For all I know, this job he sent me to do has nothing to do with Maks, and everything to do with my uncle's plans to reinvent himself for the bratva.

It wasn't until he called off my reconnaissance that the thought even entered my mind.

But now that it's there, it festers like a sore that just won't heal.

I really want to make the good choices. I have to reclaim my life.

And it's going to start tonight.

I glance at the clock.

More specifically, in a couple of hours.

A smile spreads across my face and I lean toward Dante's face, grazing his lips with my own. "Yeah, me too."

He flashes a knowing grin. "So you wanna go again? To seal the deal?"

I clutch my belly, the butterflies fluttering fast and furious now. "I'd love more but I have to go."

"Go? What do you mean? I thought Heaven gave you the night off."

"She did, but I'm meeting my uncle for dinner. He just flew into town today and he also wants to check out UNLV, so..." My voice trails off, mainly because my throat tightens, choking me with all of the lies. "He's an ass but I guess he's making an effort by coming out here." Not like I can tell him the truth.

Yet, anyway.

Once I walk away for good, I'll come clean with everything because these lies are slowly and torturously choking the life out of me.

"I'm kinda shocked she gave you the time off with the christening tomorrow. She's a little neurotic about stuff like that," he says.

"Well, she has her aunt. I guess she figured that was enough backup." I force a smile as I toss my legs over the side of the bed, but he grabs my arm.

"Wait. Let me come with you."

My jaw drops open. "What? Are you insane? How would I...he wouldn't under...I can't just bring you with me!"

"Why not? If I decided to stay here in Vegas because of you, I think that should earn me access to your family, yeah?" He drops a hand onto my thigh and squeezes. "I bet he'd like to see you're being taken care of." With a waggle of his eyebrows, he snickers at my stricken look. "Relax. Not that way, get your dirty mind off my cock."

"He's kind of old-fashioned about this kind of stuff. I really don't think it's a good idea. Yet. But I promise next time he's out, okay?"

I can only imagine how *that* introduction would go.

"Hey, Uncle Boris, I'd like to introduce you to Dante Villani, one of the people you sent me here to destroy. We just had mind-numbing, toe-curling, earth-shattering sex, and I plan to do it again. Like, at least ten times a day if he doesn't kill me for completely duping him and his family first."

I jump out of the bed and wander out of the room in search of my gym clothes. The last time I saw them they were on the floor in the foyer.

I grab them and pull them on quickly, catching a glimpse of the time out of the corner of my eye.

We've been sleeping for two hours!

I know I needed it. Sleep has been evading me over the past few days since I've been getting up with Aisling.

I hop around, tugging at my shorts and crashing into a wall when I lose my balance. I fall backward onto the floor next to my sneakers so I slide my feet into them and tie the laces. Dante pads across the floor, covered only by a pair of black boxer briefs.

I gaze up at him, my body still humming deliciously from the aftershocks of our salacious afternoon delight. He holds out his hands to me and pulls me to my feet, his hands running over my ass and squeezing. "Until later," he says with a wicked grin.

"Until later," I rasp.

It only dawns on me in this very second that 'later' is when I'll have my actual assignment, the one Uncle Boris insists on keeping quiet until we see each other at the restaurant.

Good God, what's it going to be?

What the hell will I need to do?

And is there any way I make it out of this whole?

After everything I just told Dante?

Is being whole a real possibility for me? With the life I've led?

The lies, the secrets, the deception, the devastation — that's who I am.

Is it ridiculous to think I could be anyone else?

Or have anything else?

I swallow hard, past the golf ball-sized lump growing in my throat. I guess that'll be up to me to decide. "Thanks for a great afternoon," I murmur.

"Sounds so final." He winks at me.

Yeah, I'm suddenly afraid that's because it is...

Chapter Eighteen
DANTE

"I need you to get up here," Matteo grunts into the phone. "We have a problem."

"Okay, give me a few," I say, dropping my hand onto the mattress after my brother hangs up on me. He sounds pissed off, but then again, that's kind of his normal tone of voice. And everything with him is a fire drill.

The guy is a ticking time bomb, and it sounds like he's on the verge of explosion.

Maybe it's something about the christening. I'm his bitch, so it goes without saying that he'd need me to run some last-minute errands.

And because I'm such an easygoing guy, I might agree to do it.

I push back my hair, my cock half-hard at the thought of me fucking Anya in the shower earlier. Soaping up her porn-star body, sliding my dick in and out of her tight, wet pussy...argh. I don't want to do anything right now except visit that erotic highlight reel over and over and over...

I finally pull myself to a sitting position and pull on a t-shirt and a pair of shorts. Ever since she left, I've been counting the hours until I can get her back here…on her back, on her stomach, hell, on her fucking head if we can make it work.

I'm an experimental kind of guy.

I slip my feet into my sneakers, and less than ten minutes later, I'm about to knock on Matteo's door. But before my fist even makes contact, he flings open the door. "Office," he hisses. "Now!"

A deep sigh shudders my shoulders and I follow him down the hallway. "Where's Heaven?"

"Out with her aunt. Thank fuck."

"Why? What's up?" I roll my eyes. "Tell me it's not more about Anya being in here the other night."

Matteo's eyes narrow. "She was trying to get into my drawers!" he exclaims. "I don't understand why you trust her so much! Are you that pussy-whipped?"

I throw my hands into the air. "Maybe she's just curious. You're a mysterious kind of guy. Maybe she wanted to find out more about you."

"I don't like that she was in here. If I had anything incriminating out—"

"Which you never would," I interrupt. "So there's no problem."

"I could have," he grunts.

I roll my eyes. "Is that why you dragged me down here? To tell me again that the nanny was wandering around your office?"

"No. There's more." Matteo sweeps a hand through his hair. "Conor called," he growls. "He's here. Wants to meet before the christening to talk."

"What's he want to talk about?" I snicker. "Is he gonna tell you how much money he needs to pay off the Russians?"

Matteo's jaw tightens. "I'm not giving him a damn penny."

"Would Heaven agree? I mean, won't she be pissed off that you make a call that can hurt a lot of people she cares about, including Aisling?" I shake my head. "You can't fuck with the life of your kid, Matty. I know you're angry, but—"

"He tried to kill my wife!" Matteo roars. "If I give him anything, I'll never be rid of him! And I don't want him anywhere near my family! Let the Russians kill him. It'll be less work for me since I won't be the one to drive a stake into his fucking heart!"

"What did you tell him? I mean, is he coming here?" I rub the back of my neck. "That would be a total shit show, just saying. With everyone here for the christening tomorrow?" I let out a low whistle. "Motherfucker has great timing, that's for sure."

"I told him to fuck off." Matteo looks at me like I have three dicks sticking out of my forehead. "What the hell else do you think I would have said?"

"And then what?"

"I hung up on the asshole!" Matteo thunders. "You're acting like you don't know me at all!"

"Relax, I know you plenty." I smirk. "What'd Heaven say?"

"I didn't tell her."

"What do you mean, you didn't tell her? It's her brother and her family. You need to tell her, Matty. He's in Vegas. If you think he's not gonna make an appearance, you're crazy. And do you really wanna risk that he won't bring a guest or two to the church tomorrow?" My eyes widen with alarm. "Fuck," I mutter. "Yeah, you need to tell Heaven, bro."

"Tell Heaven what?"

On cue, my sister-in-law bounces into the room, walking behind the desk and putting her arms around Matteo's neck. "What's up, babe? And please tell me it's not about the caterers. I told Tommy I wanted a very specific menu and not to screw around with his little special twists." She lets out a groan. "Why does it always have to be so difficult working with him? I mean, I get he's a creative, but still!"

Matteo sighs. "Conor called."

Heaven stops her rant mid sentence, her green eyes narrowing. "I'm sorry, did I just hear that right? My asshole brother Conor called you?"

"There's more. He's here."

"Here," she repeats.

"Yeah, in Vegas."

"In Vegas?" she shrieks.

Matteo scrubs a hand down the front of his face. "Are we really doing the whole parrot thing again?"

"Sorry," she snaps. "But I'm having a hard time wrapping my head around the fact that my estranged brother called my husband to chat while he just happens to be here in the city where we live, the day before our daughter's christening! *What the fuck?*"

"I know the timing is bad."

"Bad?" she yells at him. "This is fucking horrendous! What does he want? Money? Drugs? Safe fucking harbor?"

I stand up from the chair and back away from them. Heaven is bordering on psycho bitch, for good reason yes, but I still want to get outta the line of fire. Because the flame torch is most definitely coming.

"He wants to see you. To talk."

"Well, I don't want to talk to *him*!" she bellows, stalking past me and heading to the kitchen. She slams some cabinets and grabs a bottle of whiskey from one of them. Then she screws off the top and slugs from the bottle before glowering at Matteo again. "He's not here out of the goodness of his heart because he doesn't have one! So why do you think he's here?"

Matteo looks at me. "It might be because he's gotten tangled up with the Russians that Dante and Roman kicked out of Manhattan a few months ago."

Heaven furrows her brow. "Kicked out of Manhattan?"

"Yeah, well, they were in our territory looking for trouble. And they didn't like being asked to leave," I say.

"For fuck's sake! He's with *them*?" She guzzles more of the whiskey and grimaces at us. "Anything else I need to know, guys? I mean, please, by all means, keep fucking piling on!"

"Dante fucked Anya," Matteo says, stroking his chin.

Heaven whirls in my direction, clutching the neck of the bottle. I brace myself, ready to take the full impact of the bottle assault that I know is coming.

But instead of hurling it at my head, she smiles. "We're going to come back to that later when I don't want to throw my husband through a wall. But well done!"

"Well done," Matteo scoffs. "Right against that damn window!" he exclaims.

Heaven shrugs. "Kinky but really, TMI."

"Sex with the nanny is fine, but me trying to protect you from that lunatic is bad?" Matteo snaps.

Heaven stares him down. "You should have told me! We're supposed to be a team!"

"He's a psychopath!"

"I know!"

They stand toe to toe, glaring at each other when Aunt Maura wheels Aisling's stroller into the foyer. "I'm just going to take her out for a little walk around the hotel and give you some space, okay?" She makes a dash for the door and I'm right on her heels.

"Guys, I'm getting the hell out of here because I'm honestly a little afraid for my life right now and there is lots of window fucking in my future. Aunt Maura has the right idea." I smirk. "Don't kill each other and leave the kid orphaned."

Chapter Nineteen
ANYA

I thank my Uber driver, Frank, and push open the door of his Toyota Prius, stepping onto the sidewalk. I narrow my eyes at the sign hanging to the right of the restaurant, take a deep breath, and pull open the door.

Artiste.

It's new, exclusive, and right smack in the center of all the action on the Strip. There's a rooftop bar with a separate entrance around the side of the building, and the line is around the corner.

This isn't Uncle Boris's type of place. He'd never plan a meeting at a hot spot like this. Too many curious eyes and ears all over the place. We've always kept a low profile. Being caught in the middle of the party means you have no ability to make a quick getaway.

And in our line of work, you need an escape route.

But if he picked this place, there must be a reason why. I nod at the tall, beefy bouncer standing right inside the doorway. His eyes barely acknowledge me in return and I shake my head.

Places like this always seem to employ such condescending assholes, and I laugh at that because, hello! You're a fucking *bouncer*!

I sigh as I walk toward the hostesses huddled over an iPad screen.

That was mean.

I bet outside of this place he's a nice guy.

The hostesses look up at me with evident disgust when I approach, and I have to stop myself from digging into my handbag for a pen to gouge out their overly made-up raccoon eyes.

I force a fake smile. "Boris Antonov," I say in a sickeningly sweet voice.

And as quickly as the judgment assaults me, it recedes along with the witch-bitch attitudes of these girls.

In fact, they can't move fast enough to get me to a table tucked into a back corner of the restaurant.

At least he's being somewhat discreet.

But I do have to wonder why I got such a reception from the hostesses.

Uncle Boris doesn't exactly have sway or swagger. I mean, yes, he looks like a badass.

Tattooed, menacing, scarred.

But that doesn't equate to power. Especially not in this town.

And it's not like he has any name recognition. Vigo, on the other hand, if he were alive? He'd have people kissing his ass for sure.

But Boris Antonov is a soldier. A peon. A nobody in the organization.

So the hostesses' reactions begs the question…

Who the fuck is the 'somebody' who obviously has them scurrying around like cockroaches?

Because I'd stake my life on the fact that it is *not* my uncle.

He stands up when he sees me walk toward the table and pulls out the chair next to him for me. I look at the setup.

Three places are set.

I quirk an eyebrow and take a quick look around, but we're pretty much alone in this somewhat quiet and secluded corner.

The place to see and be seen has a spot to avoid being seen.

What in the hell are we even doing here?

I sit down and Uncle Boris pushes in my chair. A waiter appears almost instantly with a tray stocked with highball glasses of a clear liquid garnished with lime.

I smile.

Thank God because I really need a drink right about now.

Maybe that will help me figure out how to navigate this whole shit show.

"Anya," he says, returning to his seat. "It is good to see you."

I purse my lips, the sniggering little voice deep inside the recesses of my brain reminding me that I am a mere tool to him. I disregarded it for far too long, but this? Leaving me out here on my own with no direction, floundering around with no knowledge of what I'm supposed to do? Ignoring me for days on end because 'business opportunities' got in the way?

I killed a *brigadier* of the Volkov Bratva, dammit! For him! No questions asked!

I have done so much for him and I'm tired of being a doormat.

And somehow the flicker of hope inside of me for a clear future, not one stained bright red, force out my next words like the catharsis I so desperately need.

Because I'm just tired of choking them down.

"Uncle," I say without bothering to respond to his comment. I take a breath, still pissed as hell but struggling to keep my voice even. "How could you just leave me out here like this? You sent me into their home, into their lives, with absolutely no idea of what to do."

He frowns at me. "You are challenging me again, Anya? You think I didn't send you out here with a plan? I knew Volkov would be suspicious, so I wanted to protect you."

"Protect me?" I let out a dry laugh. "By leaving me in Vegas alone, thinking you were dead because you never bothered to take a second to text me back?"

"I told you, I was focused on this deal. You made it possible when you took care of Vigo."

"Do you realize that I have done everything that you've ever asked of me?" I hiss. "And I've barely gotten a 'thank you' for any of it. I've risked my life more times than I can count for you and never asked for anything in return. I just wanted you to give a shit about me, your only family."

He lets out a dry laugh. "Family," he scoffs. "You want to know how I feel about family? Let me tell you. Your father promised me a windfall if something happened to him and your mother. He swore I'd be taken care of for life if I took you and Maks to America. Well, guess what?" he sneers. "I didn't get shit. I got two pain in the ass kids and not a fucking cent. I had to figure out how to take care of you and then how to teach you to take care of yourselves. I wasn't in this for the love of family or for loyalty, Anya. This is business. It always has been. My brother made empty promises that fucked with my livelihood. *Our* livelihoods. So you need to wrap your head around that and give up on these ridiculous emotions. They're part of the reason your parents were killed in the first place. They let feelings cloud their judgment and that exposed their vulnerability — you and your brother. And you know what happened to Maks." There's an edge, almost a warning in his voice that grabs me by the throat and squeezes. Tears sting my eyes but I blink them back because...weakness.

"It's always been about the money with you," I seethe, clenching my fists. "You never gave a damn about us!"

"I did what I had to do." He glares at me. "I taught you life skills, Anya. I showed you how to get exactly what you want."

"You've shown me what a piece of shit uncle I have." I press my fingertips to my temples. All of the losses I've suffered come rushing back like an all-consuming wave, ready to swallow me whole. Wounds that have been patched up with bandages and bubble gum are torn open, exposing my pent-up grief and anger.

"Don't you dare disrespect me like that," he growls. "Did I avoid my responsibilities? No! I did what I had to do — always! I may not believe in that warm and fuzzy family shit, but when it comes down to it, I take care of my own!" He leans closer, his blue eyes flashing with rage. "That's why I went to Manhattan that night to avenge Maks's death! I went after his killer, Frankie Amante, and I was ready to take them all down as punishment — him, his sister, and his father! But your new bosses, the Villanis, stopped me from fulfilling my orders. The threatened me with a war if I came back for the others. *They're* the reason why Ivan Volkov demoted me, why we've been passed over for jobs. They prevented me from getting the revenge I needed, and I didn't deliver for Volkov. I didn't make us whole."

"So you sent me here as part of a plot to destroy people who didn't actually have anything to do with my brother's murder?" I ask, slowly connecting dots I didn't even know existed. My gut clenches. "How long ago did this happen?"

Uncle Boris presses his lips together, averting his eyes because he got fired up and said way too much.

Although for me, it was just enough to confirm what I already suspected.

I really have nobody.

He is a fucking liar.

And he doesn't give a shit about me.

"Six months ago. Give or take," he mumbles.

"Why didn't you ever tell me about this? How could you keep it from me?" I shake my head. "You told me they played a part in my brother's murder, but that wasn't true! You lied to me after that meeting with Vigo at Tatiana and told me the Villanis were involved with the murder. You made me hate people who did nothing to me — all for your own gain!"

"They are the reason why I was forced to claw my way back up to the top of the organization," he grunts. "That was all you needed to know."

"No! It's not!" I say, my voice rising. Fury bubbles in my chest and I shove back my chair, popping out of it. "I am tired of being used by you. I am finished with your plans and your plots. I'm not a chess piece, Uncle. I am your niece. Your blood. And if you can't treat me that way, with honesty and respect, then I am done with you and your fucking games. And this whole plan? Finished! I won't hurt innocent people on your behalf! I'm done with it! Done with everything!"

Uncle Boris captures my wrist and gives it a tug. "You will sit down now and attend this meeting. You will do what is asked of you and I will make sure you have everything you want when it is all over."

"Didn't you hear what I said?" I ask through clenched teeth? "We have nothing left to discuss!"

"Oh, but you do," a smooth, deep voice trills into my ear from behind. "So sit your ass back down. *Now.*"

I spin around, my breath hitching as I stare into a pair of ice blue eyes glaring at me so hard I actually feel a chill of trepidation sweep over me. "Who the hell are you?"

His thin pink lips lift into a threatening smirk. "I'm the guy who's gonna get you everything you want."

Chapter Twenty
DANTE

I pull up to the valet and drop my keys in the outstretched hand of the young guy who races over to hop in the front seat of my car. I crane my neck but the line out the door goes on for longer than I can see. Throngs of people loop around one of the hottest new places on the Strip, Artiste.

The guy at the door pulls it open for me and nods at me and Patrick, letting us through while the people waiting on line let out a collective groan that they aren't low-key illicit celebrities like us.

"I'm glad you were around," I say to Patrick once we get inside. "I've been wanting to try this place, and I needed to get the hell away from Matteo and Heaven. That apartment is ground zero, and I didn't want to be anywhere near it once your sister really got going. Matteo has his work cut out for him tonight, that's for sure."

Patrick snickers. "Sounds like they'll be having some hot makeup sex later."

I groan. "I don't need that mental image burned into my memory, thanks very fucking much."

"Then let's work on creating a different one, yeah?" He claps me on the shoulder and walks over to the bar where he finds an open spot between two bleached blondes who vaguely resemble Playboy bunnies.

But there's only one blonde on my mind right now, contorted into a number of positions that make my dick tingle with anticipation.

Patrick waves over the bartender, a tall brunette with tits that are spilling out of the top of her shirt — much like most of the women in here tonight.

I guess it's a 'when in Vegas' thing.

"What can I get for you tonight?" she asks, flashing perfect white teeth at us.

"Macallan, neat," I respond.

Patrick nods. "Same for me, thanks."

She gives us a wink and heads off to the glass shelf where the best whiskey is housed. A minute later, she places the crystal highball glasses on the lacquered bar in front of us.

"Feels a little like déjà vu, yeah?" Patrick says, taking a long gulp of his.

"Yeah, I'd really like to forget that fucking night at Tatiana ever happened," I grumble. "Although, having your idiot brother here in town makes that hard."

"I haven't seen him in the past week," Patrick says. "And neither have Quinn and Niall."

"I'd hope that would mean he's dead, but I know that's not the case."

"So what's the plan, Dante?" Patrick looks at me with a lifted eyebrow. "He's the one keeping this wedge between our families.

It's killing my father, even though he'd never admit it because he's a stubborn ass. Niall and Quinn are thawing and it pisses Conor off. I think he's on the brink of doing something really stupid to secure his place as boss of our family."

"There's no shortage of stupid when it comes to Conor," I grunt, draining the rest of my glass. "I don't know what Matteo and Heaven are going to do if he just shows up tomorrow. If it were me, I'd shoot him on sight to keep him away from my family."

"But the Russians will still collect, whether or not he's out of the picture," Patrick says.

"They have their own beef with us." I shake my head. "If Conor really did pile on and screw them over, they'll come for us. All of us. Nobody will be safe. That's what has Heaven and Matteo so crazy. They know it. And there's no guarantee that we get rid of the Russians once we pay, either. They like to leave their own big, red marks, you know what I'm saying? We need another plan."

"Yeah, so us killing Conor doesn't do a damn thing to help any of us." He rolls his eyes heavenward. "This is so damn twisted, Dante. My mother is probably rolling in her grave over this whole thing."

"Well, find peace in the fact that he tried to kill Heaven, and he'd do the same to you if he had the chance."

"True." He smirks. "Fuck him." The bartender puts down two more highballs of whiskey in front of us.

She nods toward the opposite end of the bar, and two brunettes raise their glasses and flash their best come-hither looks at us.

"Come on, let's go down there and say thank you," Patrick says, picking up his glass. "It's been a stressful week. I need to unwind."

"In that case, you can have both of them. I'm good."

"Seriously, man?" He furrows his brow. "Who *are* you?"

I shrug. "I may have something going with the nanny."

Patrick laughs. "You kinky fucker. Isn't she a kid? Heaven says she's young."

"She's not that young. No younger than those girls who sent over the drinks," I say. "And I'm not that old, dick."

"I thought you were on your way outta here after the christening. Back to the love affair you have with your sniper rifle."

"Yeah, well, my plans kind of changed recently."

"Like when you started fucking the nanny?"

I smirk and take a sip of the whiskey. "Maybe."

"Well, it looks like both of us are gonna get laid tonight." His eyes take on a wicked glimmer and he picks up his glass. "You sure you don't want to sample the buffet?"

"Nah, I'm good with my a la carte selection. You get your fill, though."

"Don't have to tell me twice." He laughs. "Funny, you know, 'cause there are two of them."

"You're hysterical, Patty." I roll my eyes and twist away from him, checking out the rest of the dining room when a flash of blonde hair falls into my line of sight...in a dress I've seen before.

Unfortunately, that's not the only thing I've seen before.

Boris, the Russian guy who works for the Volkov Bratva, is sitting in the back corner of the dining room.

And his dinner guest is none other than Anya.

My Anya.

I blink fast to see if it's really them, or if the whiskey is making me hallucinate.

It isn't.

I clutch the glass tight in my fist.

Her uncle.

Her fucking *uncle*?

He's the bastard who vowed revenge on my family, on behalf of the Volkov Bratva.

A chill settles deep in my bones.

Vigo worked for the Volkov Bratva, too...

Blood rushes between my ears and the tiny hairs on the back of my neck stand on end.

The Band-Aid.

The five-pointed star.

The familiar way she tasted and felt pressed against me.

It can't be a coincidence.

I tried to push those things to the back burner, tried to ignore them, but those inklings still festered deep in my mind.

Now they manifest into huge questions that only Anya can answer.

Will she, though? How far is she willing to go to keep me from the truth?

And the biggest question remains — what in the hell does she want from my family?

Only seconds later, I get the exact answer I was looking for.

Conor Mulligan strolls in from a side door and comes up behind Anya. I can see her body stiffen as he hisses into her ear.

I wanna know what he said.

I wanna shoot him fucking *dead*.

With a rocketing pulse, I watch as Boris gets up from the table and leaves the dining area. Anya and Conor are left alone, and the tension between them is so thick, I can see it hovering in the black cloud above them.

They're working together.

Against us.

And now I know the truth.

The question is, what am I going to do with it?

I glare at their table, clenching my fists.

Welcome to Vegas, Conor.

Are you feeling lucky tonight?

Because I sure am.

Chapter Twenty-One
ANYA

Uncle Boris nods at the man. "Anya, this is my partner. Conor Mulligan."

My brow furrows and Conor flashes bright white teeth at me. He looks like an evil doppelgänger of a young Brad Pitt. Hot but ominous.

At least, that's what the expression on his face tells me.

"I believe you know my sister, Heaven."

I suck in a breath. Oh my God... "You," I gasp.

He holds up a hand. "Now, don't tell me you're one of those girls who believes everything they hear without getting all sides of a story."

"There are obviously reasons why they won't let you near them," I say, narrowing my eyes. "I heard enough from Heaven. And seeing you here now tells me those reasons are pretty damn valid."

Conor gives Uncle Boris a look. "Give us a few minutes alone. I think Anya needs a little more convincing."

Boris slides his chair along the floor and walks away from the table. My jaw drops. He doesn't even look back once. Just leaves me with this evident sicko stranger.

And that blood of his runs through my veins, too.

Good God, I'm fucked.

"You're good at what you do, Anya. You fly under the radar, you follow instructions, and you deliver. You handled Vigo, that cocksucker. Escaped without a trace." Conor grins. "I like the blonde hair better, for what it's worth. Sexy."

Bile rises in the back of my throat. "You knew about Vigo?"

"I know about everything," he says in his thick New York accent. "I even know that my own brother and his dipshit sidekick, Dante Villani, were tailing me that night. I have eyes and ears everywhere, even out here." An evil laugh escapes his lips. "You're fitting in well, too. Getting fucked by the enemy."

"He's not my enemy!" I say through gritted teeth. "I know the truth now!"

"You only know what you know." He lifts an eyebrow and sits back in the chair, folding his arms over his chest.

"What I know is that you and my uncle baited me. You sent me out here under false pretenses. He knew I'd never go along with this if he told me the truth about that night."

"Yeah, well, now you know. But guess what? It doesn't make a difference," he hisses. "You've gained their trust and made it possible for me to get close."

"They'll never let you get back in! Heaven doesn't trust you. She told me so herself. So whatever you have planned, it's not going to work!" The legs of my chair scrape against the floor as my body shoots up out of it for the second time.

He looks at me, his gaze hard. "I suspected your loyalties might be a little tangled up, so here's the plan."

"My loyalties are just fine. So shove your plan up your ass!"

Conor raises a hand the slightest bit and two guys appear from out of nowhere, flanking me on either side.

"Sit," one of them seethes. "And don't get up again until you're told."

My eyes skirt around the restaurant. Exactly how much of a scene do I want to cause right now?

My blood simmers as it courses through my veins, my very limited options looping through my mind.

"What do you want from them? Everything is under lock and key," I blurt.

"Not everything." His eyes glitter murderously with repressed hatred.

"What the hell do you want, then?"

"You'll find out in the morning," he says. "But know this. If you don't do exactly as I say, I will expose you. I will play the part of the concerned brother who tells them that it's their 'trusted' Russian au pair who has been plotting against them this whole time under orders from the Volkov Bratva. Revenge for that infamous night in Manhattan. They will kill you before morning. You, not me."

"You're insane!" I yelp. "I'll tell them the truth! They'll believe me over you!"

"Why?" he asks in a sharp voice. "Because you've been so honest with them up till now?" He pulls something out of his pocket... an envelope with pictures. They fall onto the table, one by one, and my stomach sinks further and further into my shoes. Me, walking into Tatiana the night I killed Vigo. Me with Dante and the other guy who looks just like this sociopath Conor. Me, hopping out the window of Velvet Lounge in my sports bra, glasses, and shorts.

With a pounding pulse, I slowly raise my eyes to his.

"Now tell me again what I need to convince them of?" He leans forward. "You feeling a little conflicted right now? Well, let me give you a little more food for thought. Right about now, one of my other guys has your uncle tied up and in the trunk of his car. See, I heard all you said about wanting to get out of this life and wanting respect and blah blah blah. All that bullshit. And deep down, what you really want is for someone to give a damn about you. He does, in his own twisted way, I'm sure. Like you said, you're his only family. And now you have the power to determine whether he lives or dies. Do what I ask, walk away a rich woman, save your uncle, and live your dreams." He shrugs. "Or, ignore my threats and you both die. It's that simple."

"I can't..."

"But you will," he finishes for me. "Tomorrow, Anya. I'll be waiting. And watching."

Chapter Twenty-Two
DANTE

I pace in front of the windows of my apartment, fisting my hair when I hear the key card slide into the lock. Matteo flings open the door, making the walls shake from the impact.

"How the fuck could you leave the restaurant without throwing her into the trunk of your car?" he thunders.

"First, my trunk ain't that big." I level him with a glare, stalking over to him. "Second, I don't cause scenes," I say through clenched teeth. "We both know she's coming back here tonight. If I tipped off Conor and Boris, we could have had an army of thugs all over us. They could be, and probably are, here right now!"

"So you let them have their little meeting," he snarls. "While we're back here, sitting fucking ducks!" He looks around. "Where the hell is Patty? Did you leave him there, too?"

"No, ass. He's out looking for Maura. She took the baby before, remember? I told him to find her and bring her back here. We need everyone in the same place, and that place is *not* gonna be yours."

The door lock clicks again and Sergio walks in. "What the hell is going on?" he says, a look of alarm on his face.

"Anya, the au pair, is in bed with Conor!" Matteo roars, pushing back his hair.

Sergio's brows knit together. "Wait — I thought Anya was in bed with Dante."

"No, she was up against a window with Dante," Matteo mutters darkly before stomping back over to me. "I told you she was snooping around! That should have tipped you off. How the fuck didn't you know?"

"I'm not a mind reader, Matty!" I yell.

"You didn't pick up on anything funny? Huh? Things about Anya, things about the girl at Tatiana, the fucking 'lead' that got away from you?"

"I'm very fucking confused right now," Sergio mutters. "You got any vodka?"

"Paying homage to the Russians, yeah?" Matteo snarls.

Sergio holds up both his hands. "Okay, okay! Forget the vodka. Scotch, it is." He pulls open a cabinet and grabs the bottle and a glass.

While he guzzles the amber-colored liquid, Matteo circles me like a caged lion. "How could you miss the signs?"

"Are you kidding me?" I bellow. "What signs? She's been watching your kid for a few days! Changing diapers, giving baths, feeding her. It's not like we've caught her polishing her knife and gun collection, for fuck's sake!"

"I brought you here to sniff out threats and keep us safe from them," he growls. "And meanwhile, we've been living under the same roof as a Russian assassin!"

"Hey!" I stab him in the chest with a finger. "Your wife didn't seem too swift on the uptake either. She was all like, 'Anya, I love you! You saved us! You're an angel!'" I roll my eyes. "So who's really the one who snoozed on this shit? Seems like there's plenty of blame to go around. None of us are perfect, Matty. That's why there are four of us! We pick up the slack for each other!"

"Right now, there's a lot of slack, and we need way more than four people to pick it the hell up!"

"When does Romo fly in?" Sergio asks. "'Cause then we'll have another—"

"Shut the hell up, Serge!" Matteo yells.

"Sure, alienate everyone," I scoff. "Then you'll really be fucked when shit hits the fan and you're here all by yourself to clean up the mess!"

A loud knock on the door makes me jump. "This might be her," I grumble. "What's the fucking plan?"

"It's not Anya," Matteo says, pushing past me and opening the door. Alek Severinov, the boss of the Severinov Bratva and our partner in the Red Ladro Syndicate, stands in the doorway. His hulking body takes up all available space, and when he walks into the foyer, I can feel the tension his presence brings. His younger brother Kaz follows, equally massive and one-hundred percent more menacing. He's the muscle of the family.

"So Volkov is making a play," Alek says in a deep voice, folding his massive arms over his chest. "Is that why you dragged me over here?"

"They're out here," Matteo says in a choked voice. "Planning something. We were duped by our new au pair. She's one of them, and over the past few days, she's gotten..." His glower points in my direction. "Close."

Alek nods. "We've had a few run-ins with them back East," he says, looking at Kaz. "We ready for their retaliation against our syndicate partners?"

Kaz's blue eyes glitter and the guy practically foams at the mouth at the thought of destroying them. "Fuck, yeah."

"They're after something," Matteo says. "We thought Conor crossed them, that he needed money to pay a debt. But Dante found out tonight that he's working with them...and against us."

Alek and Kaz exchange a look. "You know, I'm just gonna say that ever since you guys took our offer and joined the syndicate, we spend a lot of time cleaning up your crap."

Kaz shrugs. "Eh, it's an excuse to fuck shit up. Besides, we knew it when we let them in."

Alex rolls his eyes at Kaz. "With you around, I'm sure there will be plenty of times they'll have to return the favor.

Kaz chuckles and I press my fingertips to my temple. Matteo still paces, staring at his watch every few seconds.

I walk over to Matteo while Sergio gets Kaz and Alek a drink. I text Patty and Heaven but neither one responds. Tiny hairs on my arms stand at attention. I don't like this radio silence at all.

"They're gonna help us, thank fuck. But it doesn't change the fact that I did miss things. Hell, I missed everything. I blame myself entirely," I say to Matteo in a hushed voice.

Matteo sighs. "Look, I'm sorry for leveling you like that. We all missed things. We knew there was a threat, and we should have worked harder to uncover it. We snoozed on the Conor thing for too long, and that's where we messed up. I was too preoccupied about keeping it from Heaven to really turn this situation on its ear."

I grimace. "What the hell does that sicko want, Matty? Why is he here? And how the hell does the bratva fit in? We didn't want to start a war months ago, and we don't need one now. Are they still out for blood because of that standoff we had at Roman's? Did they use Conor to get close to us? And now that they're inside, what are they after?"

"I don't know," Matteo grunts. "But I would really like for Patty to get back here with the girls. You're sure they looked like they were staying at the restaurant once you left, right?"

"Yeah, but who the hell knows where those crews are lurking? I'm gonna go look for Patty and the girls."

"What about Anya? Will she come here looking for you?"

I nod. "And when she does, we'll handle her. She's about to become our leverage."

I storm over to the door and pull it open, stalking down the hallway as it slams shut behind me.

Anya, her words, her expressions — it was all bullshit. Lies!

It meant nothing.

She never gave a damn about me.

I was just part of a job.

A pawn in her insidious little game.

I grit my teeth.

But she doesn't know that now, I control the board. And her strategy is about to go up in smoke.

Because we all know one thing.

Nobody who tries to hurt us survives long enough to tell their tale of victory.

Victory will be fucking *ours*.

Chapter Twenty-Three
ANYA

Conor puts his hand on my arm just as I'm about to pull the door handle and let myself out of his car. I can't get away from his toxic cloud fast enough, and the longer I sit here, the more it chokes me.

"Remember what I told you, Anya. You'll get my call tomorrow morning. If you pull a fast one before that, your uncle is dead." His lips curl up into an evil smile. "Eyes and ears. Don't forget."

I pull my arm away from him, my throat so tight I can barely breathe. "I heard what you said, you fucking lunatic," I hiss. "Don't ever touch me again or you'll lose that hand."

He chuckles. "Such a badass. I like that fire in you. I'm gonna have to figure out a way for us to work together again. I need someone like you on my crew. Face of an angel and tongue of a viper." His hand grazes the top of my thigh. "I'd like to see what else you can do with that tongue, too."

His touch scorches my skin and not in the good way. "I said take your fucking hands off!" I grab his hand and sink my teeth into the flesh as hard as I can until he yelps and yanks it away from me.

"You stupid bitch!" His blue eyes darken. "I'll kill you if you ever try something like that again."

I narrow my eyes. "Bring it on, asshole. I'm good at one thing. Killing. So try me." I shove the car door open and stomp into the hotel, not looking back once. I keep my teeth gritted because the gravity of the situation I've stepped into is dragging me into the pits of hell.

I've always teetered on the brink, but always managed to steady myself before plunging into the fiery depths.

Tonight, though, I'm consumed in flames, and there's no lifeline dangling over me.

I'm on my own.

Either I figure out how to pull myself out or I perish.

Those are the alternatives.

My shoulders quake as I hurry through the casino and I hear someone call my name.

Dammit.

This is not a good time at all for a little girl talk!

"Anya!" Dottie says, waving me over. "You look like you've just seen a ghost. Are you okay, dear?"

I gasp for breath and shake my head. "No," I whisper. "I'm not."

"You're so pale. Do you need anything?" She takes a tentative step forward as if she's contemplating her next move, and then she wraps her arms around me.

And it feels so nice and warm and comforting.

My life is none of those things, so I bask in the novelty of it all, knowing that I need to have a very difficult conversation in the next few minutes.

I can use all of the comfort I can get since I am on the verge of being alone again.

More loss.

More devastation.

I honestly don't know how much more I can take.

The lies, deceit, and misery — my God, it's killing me, slowly and tormentingly.

I breathe Dottie in, the scent of her flowery perfume filling my lungs. She rubs a hand down my back and I hug her.

The last real hug I had was the day Maks was killed.

I'd had a bad day and I remember him gathering me in for a big bear hug.

My brother always watched over me and made me feel protected.

I haven't had that in so long.

But somehow Dottie knew exactly what I needed before going to find Dante.

I pull away, a smile on my face. "Thank you," I murmur, giving her hands a squeeze. "I needed that."

"Of course, dear," she says with a smile. "I'll be around if you need another. I'm a grandma. It's our specialty."

I blink back tears and give her a little wave as I hurry toward the private elevator bank. I stab his number onto my phone screen and let out a relieved breath when he answers. "Dante, thank God. Are you upstairs? I really need to talk to you."

"Yeah, I'm at my apartment."

I furrow my brow. "You sound tense."

"You could say that."

I bite down on my lower lip. Weird. "Okay, well, I'll be right up."

He hangs up without another word and I run a hand through my hair. After a few agonizing minutes, I knock on his door. When he opens it, I'm not prepared for the scene in front of me.

Lots of glaring, accusatory eyes.

Deadly looking men I've never seen before.

A shudder runs through me and I stare at Dante.

My heart sinks into my gut when I see the same threatening look in his eyes. He grabs me, slams the door closed, and then backs me against the wall. His hand is around my throat, but I can see the conflict in his heavy gaze.

That may be the lifeline I've been looking for.

"Who the fuck are you?" he growls, tightening his grip on me.

"You k-know who I a-am,' I sputter. "You know better than anyone."

His fingers graze the Band-Aid and he tears it off as everyone watches. I wince, the pain nothing compared to the fear of what he's about to do with his new discovery, my five-pointed star tattoo. "I knew it," he hisses. "It *is* you. You're the woman who killed Vigo at Tatiana. I tried to deny it to myself, but then I saw you tonight at Artiste with Boris and Conor and I knew it was the truth. I tried to ignore it and missed the signs," he says in a choked voice. "You betrayed me. You betrayed all of us!"

I nod. "I did. And I'm so sorry. But I didn't know the full story, I swear!"

"What the fuck is that supposed to mean?" Matteo yells, stomping toward her. "We brought you into our home, let you take care of our baby, and all along, you were plotting against us with one of our biggest enemies!"

"Dante, Matteo, please, I know it looks bad, but you have to believe me when I tell you they duped me! They sent me out here to work as your brother's au pair so that I could get information for them. They told me you had a hand in killing my brother to get me out here. They knew I'd do anything to avenge his murder. But it was bullshit," I whisper. "I found out tonight it was just a lie to get me to do their dirty work. I know now that you didn't have anything to do with it."

"Your brother?" Dante asks.

"His name was Maks. Frankie Amante shot him."

"Fuck," Dante mutters. "That asshole uncle of yours has had a grudge against us since that night."

"Yes, and then he hooked up with Conor because he had a grudge too. He wants to destroy you," I say in a low voice. "And he is prepared to pay any price to do it."

"Where the hell are they now?" Matteo asks.

"I don't know. Conor dropped me off here and I didn't bother to ask if he had hotel accommodations," I say with a roll of my eyes. "He just said he'd call me with instructions tomorrow." I look from Dante to Matteo and back again. "He wouldn't tell me what he's after, but I think I know. I think he wants Aisling."

Matteo slams a fist against the wall and turns to Dante. "Where the fuck is Patrick? He went looking for the girls. I want them all back here as soon as possible. And we need to get in touch with security. I want them planted at every entrance and exit!"

Dante nods. "I'll make the calls. I just need a second alone with her." He pulls me by the arm and drags me into his bedroom, forcing my back to the wall. His lips are pressed into a tight line, his eyes heavy with a mix of rage, dejection, and pain.

"I let myself fall for you," he hisses. "And you deceived me and my family. You opened us up to dangers you can't even possibly imagine."

"I know, and that's why I came straight here, to help fix what I've done. I didn't know about any of it, even Conor's involvement, until I met him tonight. My uncle kept me in the dark for days. He ignored my calls and texts. He could have been dead for all I knew. And now Conor has him tied up somewhere, threatening to kill him if I don't do what he wants. Not that there is any guarantee he won't be dead by morning, whether or not I follow through."

Dante fists his hair and stomps across the room. "I want to hurt you so badly right now," he hisses. "For putting my family in jeopardy like this."

"I deserve it," I say in an unwavering voice. "And I wouldn't blame you."

He storms back over to me, his forehead practically pressed against mine. He drags his fingers down the front of my dress. "I can separate myself from emotions, Anya. How I felt about you a few hours ago won't stop me from putting a bullet in your brain if I find out you're playing us right now."

I nod, a large lump lodged in my throat. "I didn't once think when this all started that they'd ever hurt Aisling," I say in a low voice once we're alone. "I swear to you."

"Your word doesn't mean shit right now," Dante grunts.

"I know, but I can help. Please believe me. We can stop him!"

"You said Conor has your uncle held hostage. Are you prepared for what might happen if you cross him?"

I swallow hard. "I care about my uncle, but I want to do the right thing. I have to. I can't sit by and let you and your family get hurt. This is on me, and I'll make it right. Please just give me that chance."

He stares at me for a long minute. "One chance. We take him out and walk away from each other forever. Because you're a fucking liar and I have no room in my life for someone like you."

An icy sensation snakes around my heart and squeezes, but I won't let him see me cringe.

Or cower.

"Okay," I rasp.

He kicks open the bedroom door and stalks over to his brother and the two new guys I don't recognize. They huddle together and I rub my hands up and down my arms.

A heavy fist knocks on the door and Dante pulls it open. "Goddamn, Patty!"

My breath hitches. I recognize him as the other guy from Tatiana. That night, he was sharp, sleek, and sophisticated in his suit.

Right now, he's a hot fucking mess. His dark blonde hair is hanging in his face, his shirt is rumpled, and his face is a mess of panic. But it's the body he's carrying that makes my blood run cold.

Aunt Maura.

Her face is white, her hands hanging limply at her sides.

"Patrick, where the fuck did you find her?" Matteo yells. "She had the baby!"

"I found her lying next to the stroller right outside the pool deck." Patrick lays her on the couch and listens to her chest.

"She's breathing, thank God. Conor isn't a complete maniac. At least he didn't kill her."

"Where the fuck are Heaven and Aisling?" Matteo screams at Patrick, grabbing him by the shirt and shoving him to the floor.

"I looked everywhere for them!" Patrick shouts back, fisting his hair. "I couldn't find them. Not a fucking trace!"

Matteo pulls out his phone and dials a number…Heaven's, I guess. But after a minute of her not answering, he hangs up. His eyes flash with alarm and he flips around toward me. "He's here, isn't he?" Matteo creeps in my direction, speeding up as he approaches. "You fucking did this! You let him in!" He grabs my dress, his grip tight. My hands fly up to his, clutching them before they can wind themselves around my throat. "He has my wife and daughter right now!"

"Matteo, let me help you find him. We will find the girls, I promise!"

"Because you've been so honest up till now? Why the fuck should I trust you?"

"You need me," I say in an even voice. "You may hate me and want to kill me, but you need the backup."

His Adam's apple bobs up and down in his throat, and the vein in his forehead throbs, his face bright red.

"Look, if he's here, we can find him. Lock the place down. They won't be able to get out. We can stop him, but we need to move now, okay?"

Matteo pulls out his phone and stabs some numbers onto the screen. "Yeah, it's me. Code red. Heaven and Aisling." He clicks to end the call. "I never fucking trusted you," he mutters, raking a hand through his hair. "You're lucky I don't kill you right now."

I'm already painfully aware that I have zero allies in this apartment.

"I need a gun," I say. "We're going to sweep the place. All of us. Dante, what do you have?"

He walks back into his bedroom and comes out a minute later with an array of weapons. I grab a Glock 19 and check to make sure it's loaded.

"How's this gonna work?" Dante asks.

"We need to split up," Matteo says, grabbing his own gun from the waistband of his pants. He walks toward the door and pulls it open just as a piercing sound erupts into the air.

The fire alarm.

Sonofabitch!

"He knows we're locking everything down. This is his only way out," Matteo growls. He points to the guys I don't recognize. "Kaz, Alek, get down to the lobby. Keep an eye out for him, and call if you see Heaven or the baby." They head out, leaving me, Dante, and Patrick with Matteo.

"Patty, stay here with Maura. You two, come with me." Matteo runs out of the apartment and heads down the hallway to the stairwell since the elevators aren't running.

"Where are we going?" Dante asks.

"Basement," Matteo says abruptly. "He wouldn't be dumb enough to try and escape through the front entrance."

A ringtone pierces the air and Matteo grabs his phone.

"Heaven!" His brow furrows, his jaw tightening with each passing second. I can hear her tearful voice on the other end of the line. "You're where?" He puts the call on speaker, his face draining of color as Conor's sadistic laugh shatters the tense silence.

"You heard her, bro. We're on the roof. All three of us. I didn't want to take any chances that Anya would foil my plans, so I decided to speed things up a little bit. She was having a weak moment when I dropped her off and I felt like maybe morality was grabbing her by the tits. Now I'm here and it's about time we settled all of the bad blood between us, don't you think?"

"What do you want, Conor?" he says, his fingertips turning white because he's squeezing the phone so hard.

"I want what you took from me," he growls. "What you both took. For the past year, you've made threats against all of my associates, telling them if they work with us, they'll be dead to you. You've destroyed everything, Villani. You and Heaven. And you deserve to be punished. So I'm gonna do just that. And my niece is going to help me."

"Don't you fucking touch her!" Matteo screams.

"Then you'd better get up here fast. We're dangerously close to the edge, Matteo. One little slip, and I shatter your life the way you did mine. But I want you to be here to witness it. I want to hear you beg for their lives, to promise you'll give me everything I want, to make me whole." He chuckles again. "Because that's how this story ends. Happily for me, not so much for you."

Chapter Twenty-Four
DANTE

"Conor," Matteo says, running up the stairs. "We can work this out. Don't do this. She's your blood! They both are!"

"The baby is half Villani," he says. "And I hate the Villani family. I want to crush the Villani family!"

He takes the stairs three at a time until we get to the door leading to the roof. With a quick look backward, he stabs the mute button. "I'm gonna lure him into the open. You take the shot whenever you get it, do you understand?"

Before I can reply, he un-mutes the line. "I'm here. Opening the door now."

"You'd better be by yourself," Conor grumbles.

Aisling wails in the background and Conor yells at her to shut up. Every muscle in my body tenses as my eyes tangle with Anya's.

"I've got your back," she whispers, pulling out her gun. We both cower against the walls on either side of the door when Matteo creeps onto the roof. "But how are you going to get out there?"

"I need a visual," I mutter, peering out the streaked glass. In the distance I can see Conor by the edge of the roof. Matteo is holding up his hands and Heaven is next to Conor. He's got Aisling in his arms, the bastard. How the fuck am I gonna get my shot?

Tiny hairs on the back of my neck prickle and I flip around just as a heavy hand clutching a gun swings around at my head. I grab the guy's arm and twist it around his back, popping his shoulder blade before I fire off two shots and kick him head first down the stairs.

Another guy flies out of a corner at Anya, grabbing her by the hair. Big mistake.

She sweeps his leg, sending him crashing to the floor before she plugs him in between the eyes. "We have to get out there," she whispers. "I'll do it. Let me distract him."

"He'll kill you on sight. He knows you ran straight to us," I say.

She shrugs. "I'd like to think I can take him, but if that happens, so be it. Maybe it'll give you a second to take the shot." Her hand closes around mine. "Please, Dante. Let me do this for you. For your family."

"Are you sure?" I ask.

She nods. "You said we'd go our separate ways, right? Well, this is me...going." With a small smile, she opens the door, her hands above her head and her gun tucked into the back of her dress. "Conor!" she yells. "It's over! You've got one chance to walk away. If you do something stupid, you're gonna die."

He snickers. "Badass! You are such a badass, Anya! I fucking love it! Let me ask you a question. Who's holding all the fucking cards right now, huh? Look around, bitch! It's me!" He waves his gun at Matteo. "And right about now this cocksucker is gonna beg me to save his wife and daughter. He's gonna bend over for me and tell me what a miserable prick he is for ruining my life and my business!" He glares at Matteo, waving the gun in his face. "Do it!"

The door is open just enough for me to see and hear what's going on but for me to remain invisible.

Exactly the way I like it.

My phone vibrates against my leg and I grab it when I see Patty's name flash across the screen.

"It's about to get very fucking windy up on the roof," he says.

"How did you know where we are?" I ask.

"It's Conor. He always goes big. Of course he'd take them to the roof. I made a call and there's a police chopper on the way. Get ready to end this, Dante."

I end the call, my pulse thrumming against my neck. Conor is still yelling at Matteo, forcing him to his knees. Heaven stands against the edge of the roof, hysterical. She can't make a move or Conor will hurt Aisling.

She's his leverage.

For what, I have no idea.

How the hell does he think this is gonna end?

"You forced me to do this," he says, standing over Matteo. "And in a few minutes, I'm gonna be on my merry way while you and my sister grieve the loss of your kid."

"No!" Heaven shrieks. "Please, Conor! She's your family!"

"None of you are my family," he growls.

"Conor, you have no escape," Anya says. "Your guys are dead. You'll never make it out of here."

He grins at her, a leering, lecherous smirk that makes my gut twist. "I've got something better than my guys, Anya. I've got exactly what I came for, right here in my arms." He points his gun between Heaven and Matteo. "And as much as I want to see both of you dead, I'd rather see you miserable and suffering."

A whoosh of air blasts everything in its path, a deafening motor drowning out Conor's crazed words. I keep my foot firmly planted in the doorway as the chopper closes in, hovering next to the side of the roof. I can see one of the guys inside, positioning himself to take a shot.

I have no shot at all from where I'm standing. I'm too far away and there are too many people in my path. I grit my teeth. The only way I get Conor is to charge at him, and if I do that he'll—

"Anya, no!" Heaven shrieks as Anya pulls the gun from the back of her dress and makes a run at Conor, who clearly didn't expect a chopper to show up and cockblock him from ruining the lives of my family. Anya's sudden movement startles him enough that he stumbles backward, tripping over a large metal box. He recovers too soon, though, not giving Anya enough time to pull the trigger.

Bullets explode into the air and Heaven shrieks as Matteo darts toward Conor, throwing himself on top of him. I take that opportunity to race toward them and grab the baby. Heaven runs over to us and I thrust Aisling into her arms. "Go!" I yell.

Gunshots pop and Conor scrambles to his feet, ducking down behind the metal box. He pops a few shots, a few of them ricocheting off the cement wall behind us.

"Fuck you, Matteo!" he screams. "Fuck you and your wife! Your baby will never be safe! No matter what happens tonight! I made sure of that. You are gonna suffer, do you hear me? Suffer the worst fucking pain of your pathetic life!"

Conor's face is beet red as he clutches his gun and points it at Matteo's head. My breath hitches as I squeeze the trigger…at the very same second that Anya jumps in front of Matteo, swinging her arm out to knock the gun out of Conor's hands.

Her body buckles on impact and she crashes to the ground as it goes off.

"No!" I yell, emptying my clip into Conor. His body jerks left and right as the bullets ravage his body. He falls backward over the metal box, his arms limp at his sides, and the gun clatters to the roof.

Seconds later, a medic leaps out of the chopper after it lands and runs over to Anya. Her head smacked against the concrete when she hit the ground. "No, no, no!" I fall to my knees next to her. "She was trying to save your life," I say to Matteo. "She took that shot for you, Matty," I mutter, squeezing her clammy hand and bringing it to my lips. All of the harsh words I assaulted her with only minutes earlier come back to haunt me.

I told her I'd never trust her, never forgive her.

I said we'd part ways forever.

No looking back.

But as I stare down at her listless body, I'm painfully aware that without her, there's no looking forward.

My heart thumps as the medic examines her and checks her vitals. "I've got a pulse, but we need to get her to the hospital now to see how extensive the damage is." He peers at her right shoulder. "There's an exit wound, which is a really good thing."

Heaven runs back outside with Aisling in her arms. "Oh my God, what happened to Anya?"

Matteo grabs her and Aisling. "She was trying to save me from your brother, Conor's gun went off, and she took the bullet."

Heaven's eyes widen. "Jesus." She looks quickly around, gasping when she sees Conor's body splayed over the metal box, full of blood and bullet holes. "Conor…" Her voice trails off and she bites down on her lower lip, clutching Aisling. "With a quick look back at us, she makes a face. "If I say I wish it'd been me to do it, would that be really evil?"

"Yeah, but we already know that poison runs through your veins," I mutter, looking at the medic. "I'm going with you in the chopper."

"Okay." Another EMT rushes over with a stretcher and together, they load Anya onto it.

I climb onto the chopper, holding Anya's hand tight and clutching it to my chest. "I'm here, babe. And I promise, I'm not letting you go. Ever." I swallow hard. "Because I'm in love with you," I whisper.

And when her fingers give mine the tiniest squeeze in return, I know she hears me.

That's all I needed.

A little shred of hope.

Chapter Twenty-Five
ANYA

A groan slips through my lips when my eyes crack open. I'm surrounded by a sea of white — walls, furniture, bedding.

Shit, is this heaven?

Or a really sick twist on hell, since let's face it, I'm no angel.

Then I tune into the bleeping machines around me, and my eyes drop to the wires connecting me to them.

Okay, so I'm not dead.

I try to shift on the mattress and a sharp pain zips down my right arm. "Ahh," I mumble softly because I can't seem to grab any more spare energy to really make my discomfort known.

The room is so bright, I have to squint so I don't get a massive eye headache. I fling my left arm over my face, fuzzy memories becoming more and more sharp by the second.

Meeting Conor and my uncle.

The car ride back to the Excelsior.

Conor's threats.

The hug from Dottie...

I liked that a lot.

It's probably the first time I felt human in a damn long time, the first time in a while that I felt like maybe I could be better... good...maybe even loved.

And then the floodgates open and the rest of the events pummel me like a crushing wave.

Dante's hand around my neck.

His terse voice telling me in no uncertain terms that we're through.

I sweep my tongue over my dry lips.

But I still ran onto that roof.

I still tried to knock Conor's gun out of his hand because I couldn't let anyone else get hurt or see anyone else suffer.

Too much blood has been shed.

Too much rage has destroyed lives.

I couldn't stand by and let something bad happen to innocent people.

Makes me feel like there's hope for me.

A sliver of good I can cultivate.

I've hurt a lot of people in my life. Extinguished a lot of lives.

Some of them deserved it.

But did they all?

I never got a chance to make that determination. I only got the orders, no questions asked.

No ability to decline the instruction.

Someone like Conor? It'd have been a pleasure to put a bullet between his eyes.

But I can't be this person anymore.

I want more.

The good things I've missed out on.

I probably screwed up my chance for that, but I know I did the right thing and that's a start.

I swallow but my throat is drier than the Mojave. "Water," I mumble weakly. "But…I…can't…reach," I whine to myself since I'm alone in this vast space.

The door to my room creaks open and I slide my arm slightly away from my eyes to see who it is. Maybe a nurse? Someone who can grab me a straw?

But it's not a nurse.

It's Dante.

And as I look up into his concerned gaze, I remember something else…

At least I think I do. I was in shock, bordering on unconscious.

Maybe it was just a manifestation of my need to be loved…by him.

He smooths my hair away from my face. "How are you feeling?"

I make a pained face. "Not great," I croak.

"Do you remember what happened?"

"Honestly, it was so fast, I only have little splotches of memories." I point to the water on the nightstand. "Can you please get that for me?" I rasp.

He pours some into a cup, sticks a straw in it, and holds it up to my lips. I drink it down and as it slips down my parched throat, I truly believe that nothing has ever tasted so good.

When I finally finish and settle back against the pillow, I look up at him. "There is one thing that comes to mind," I say in what is almost a whisper. If I didn't really hear it the first time, I don't know if I want to hear it now.

Not if it isn't true.

Dante kneels down next to me, leaning his elbows on the mattress. "Tell me."

"Well," I start, clearing my throat. "It was just a few words and I was barely awake but I could swear I heard your voice in my ear saying them."

"What were the words?" he asks.

"That you were, um, that you were…" My already low voice trails off and I avert my eyes. I can feel a rush of heat splash into my cheeks. "Um…" I peek at him and let out a snort as the grin stretches across his face. "You're a real jerk, you know that? Here I am, lying in a hospital bed, shot, and you know exactly what I'm trying to say but you want me to sweat through it. Not cool."

"Sorry. I guess it was me getting you back for invading my family and pretending you weren't a Russian mafia assassin who was trying to steal my niece." He snickers. "You deserved to sweat."

I roll my eyes and wince as I twist toward him. "Was it true?"

He holds my gaze for a few seconds, then nods. "Yes. One-hundred percent."

I let out a shaky breath. "You told me it was over and I understood why. I rushed Conor because it was the only way I could make up for what I'd done to you all."

"I know."

"I want to be a good person, Dante," I say, tears stinging my eyes. "I don't want to live inside of this empty shell anymore. I don't want to carry any more hate and I don't want to cause any more torment for others. I don't want to live by someone else's rules. I want to make my own choices, create my own happiness because I finally believe I can have it. And for the past week, I've seen what that can be. I had such a strong connection with you and Heaven and Aisling from the first time we met." I giggle. "Not so much with Matteo, but maybe that'll change now."

"Just to be clear..." he says, lacing his fingers with mine. "You're saying you want a new career?"

"I'm saying I want a new life." I smile, bringing his hand to my heart. "Here, with you, if that's still an option."

"I think it can be arranged." He brushes his lips against my forehead.

"And just for the record," I say. "I'm in love with you, too."

"Glad to hear it because you were really leaving me hanging there." He winks at me.

"You could have waited and told me when I was conscious."

"You're right. But I'm not exactly conventional."

I nod. "Understatement of the year."

"So what the hell are we gonna do now?" he murmurs, tracing a finger down the side of my cheek. "Two retired assassins? Are we gonna open a flower shop or something? Or maybe a day care?" he says with a chuckle.

"I love Aisling but I'm not ready for other kids. They're too sticky and whiny."

Dante nods. "I'm with ya there."

"How's Maura?" I ask.

"Good, she's being checked out but everything seems fine. Guess Conor was storing up a few crumbs of humanity in the center of that black and toxic heart of his."

I let out a breath. "I'm glad she's okay." Then I let out a gasp. "Oh my God! Uncle Boris! Dante, is he—?"

Dante nods. "Also fine. We found Conor's car and sure enough, he was stuffed in the trunk. They gave him a pretty good beating, but it's just bumps and bruises. Nothing serious. Although, things would have turned out a lot differently if Conor hadn't followed you in to the hotel. See, he knew you were a good person. That's why he changed his plan." He smiles at me. "If an evil bastard like that can see the good in you, then you know it's really there."

A soft knock on the door startles me and it creaks open. I crane my neck to see who it is, maybe this time a nurse who can get me some pain meds. That's my hope, anyway.

But it's not a nurse.

It's Matteo. And he's wearing a sheepish expression as he walks toward us.

A smile lifts his lips, the first real one I've seen from him since we met. Well, the first one directed at me.

He's actually pretty gorgeous when he's not scowling.

"Anya," he says. "How are you feeling?"

"A lot better now," I say, squeezing Dante's hand in mine. "Listen, I'm sorry for—"

Matteo holds up a hand. "No. You don't need to apologize to me again. You did it once and I rejected it. Yet you still put your life on the line to save me and my family. I'm the one who owes *you*. You saved everything I love, and I don't think I'll ever be able to thank you enough."

"I'm sure you can come up with some things to show your gratitude," Dante scoffs playfully. "Like maybe a couple of cars, a house, some jewelry..."

"Stop," I say, giving his hand a gentle slap. I look up at Matteo. "I don't need anything. I just want to make sure we're cool. I understand if it's going to take you some time to trust me and I can wait." I smile.

"Trust definitely isn't something I give up easily. I didn't trust you when you came into our lives." He smirks. "My instincts weren't wrong, just saying."

Dante snorts. "You had to get the last word, didn't you?"

"Hey, it is what it is. Deal with it." His eyes darken. "But after what you did on the roof...I mean, you took that bullet for me. Nobody except my brothers and my wife would have done that," he says, shaking his head.

"Some of your brothers," Dante mutters with a mischievous smirk on his face.

Matteo flips him off. "Look, what I'm trying to say is I knew in that second who you really were."

Heaven pops her head into the room. "Can I come in now? Did you finish groveling?" she asks Matteo.

"He didn't really grovel," Dante says. "The undertone was pretty much 'I was right, guys. Just remember that.'"

Heaven rolls her eyes. "Jeez, Matty. The girl saved us all. Would it kill you to show a little humility?"

"He's fine," I say with a chuckle. "And we're good."

"Okay," Heaven says, giving Matteo a look as if to say 'I don't believe her at all but I'll let it go until we get home.' "Well, you rest up and when you get home, we'll get you all set up—"

"Ah, yeah, about that," Dante interjects. "You don't have to worry about that."

Heaven furrows her brow. "Meaning?"

"Meaning I'm gonna take care of it and get her all set up at *my* place."

Heaven's face lights up like the Rockefeller Center Christmas tree. "Oh. Well, then, it sounds like that's settled." She can't even help the huge smile plastered across her face as she rubs a hand down my arm. "Do you need anything at all, sweetie?"

I gaze at Dante, tiny flutters in my belly alerting me to the fact that the butterflies are back in force. "Nope, I finally have everything I need right here."

EPILOGUE

Anya

I grasp Dante's hand and lead him down a darkened hallway. "Just listen to my voice and stay right against me."

It's dark for him because I just put a blindfold over his eyes.

But even without a blindfold, I feel like I'm navigating in pitch blackness. I take tentative steps, unfamiliar with this corridor. But I wanted to keep him away from anything that might give away the surprise. As far as he knows, we've driven somewhere.

Unless he realizes I drove his car in a convoluted circle, he won't have any idea where I'm taking him.

I reach out my hand and grasp the brass doorknob, turning it slowly. I silence the gasp that's about to escape my throat when I see the inside of the room.

Our room.

Soft white lights are wrapped in tulle and hung across the ceiling. They look like tiny stars glimmering down on us, stars I've only become acquainted with since moving out here to Las Vegas. The room is private, at least for this part of the night. There is one single table set up in the center, cascades of white roses and calla lilies spilling over the sides of a centerpiece. There are brass candelabras set up around the perimeter of the room, the flames flickering furiously and adding to the aura of the occasion.

It's perfect.

Exactly the way I'd wanted it.

The past few months have been a whirlwind for us. After a lot of discussion, we decided to relocate to New York. It took a visit to Ivan Volkov and a lot of negotiation to release me from my previous role as one of the bratva's hired guns. But in exchange, Matteo offered him a sweet business opportunity he couldn't ignore. One of the stipulations was that Uncle Boris gets to run the new shipping operation. But it didn't take much to convince Volkov since access to the piers in the Villani territory would be huge for business and Volkov is no idiot. And just like that, I became a free woman.

Dante decided he needed a change of pace, too, since we do eventually want to start our own family and a mom and dad assassin team wouldn't necessarily provide the most nurturing environment. So instead, he is starting his own security consulting firm, just like Matteo had recommended. He's already got a slate of clients anxious to work with him, and he'll also partner with Roman to handle the family's businesses in lower Manhattan.

As for me, I just got accepted to the Fashion Institute of Technology.

I'm finally making my dreams come true.

All of them.

And I couldn't be happier.

Lately, I've felt my parents and Maks's presence a lot more, especially at times like this when I'm about to make a big bold move in my life. It's a comforting feeling, knowing they're there in spirit, smiling down on me. I know they always wanted the best for me, even though it took a long time for me to figure out how to make that a reality.

"Okay, we're standing still. Can I take off the blindfold now? Or is there kinky shit I'm not allowed to see yet?"

I giggle. "There's no kinky shit here. But hold that thought for a few hours."

He breathes in. "Smells good. Are we eating? I hope so because I'm starving." His hands fumble with my dress. "Although I could wait on the food if there's something else I can eat in the meantime?"

"You're insatiable!"

"Damn right," he murmurs. "Now are you gonna let me see that gorgeous face or not?"

I bite down hard on my lower lip.

This is it.

I reach around the back of his head and unknot the scarf, dropping it on one of the chairs. "Happy anniversary, babe," I say.

His eyes sweep the room and he flashes his famous sexy smile at me. "You brought me all the way back to our hotel?"

"Yes, but there's a good reason why."

"Don't keep me in suspense," he says, pulling me close and nuzzling my ear. He always knows exactly what part to suckle when he wants to melt me into a puddle of goo.

But I can't melt right now.

Not yet.

I take a small step backward, still holding his hands in mine. My heart thrums against my chest, delicious shivers making my body shudder.

And then I drop to one knee, unable to keep the smile from spreading across my face. "Dante," I say, tears springing to my eyes. "You once told me you were an unconventional kind of guy." I sniffle. "Well, that must mean we're a perfect pair because I'm an unconventional kind of girl. You gave up so much for me, and you're ready to move across the country to help me realize my dreams. I believe that there were a lot of people upstairs pulling strings for us to find each other, and I am so thankful we did. You're the best thing that has ever happened to me, and I want to spend the rest of my life making sure you know it." I swipe away one stray tear and hold out a shiny gold band. "I love you more than you'll ever know. Will you be my husband?"

He smirks. "Is this because I said I loved you before you finally said it back? You wanted to be the first this time?"

I giggle. "Maybe."

"Well, then, you know we Villanis like to have the last word. So..." He drops down in front of me and pulls out a small, black velvet box, flipping it open to reveal a glittering diamond engagement ring. "I'll say yes if you do."

"Oh my God, yes!" My hand flies up to my mouth. "Were you planning this all along?"

"Of course I was. I figured whatever surprise you had planned, you'd never see this coming as the cherry on top."

"You're right, I didn't at all!"

"Happy anniversary," he says, pulling me close. "And happy engagement."

"Well, not yet," I say.

He furrows his brow. "No?"

"You didn't say yes! It has to be mutual!"

"Yes," he says with a wink. "See, I told you I'll always get the last word."

I roll my eyes and let out a huff, but he snakes a hand around the back of my head and crushes his lips against mine. He tastes like spearmint, so cool and fresh and sweet.

"I love you so much," he murmurs against my lips.

"I love you, too," I say, wrapping my arms around him.

"Okay, so are you gonna tell me why you drove me away from here and then back again?"

"Well, I couldn't very well throw us an engagement party at another restaurant, right?" I snap my fingers and the partition slides over, revealing the rest of our party guests, including my new bestie, Tommy Marcone.

Tommy grins, standing aside so we can see the two cakes he's decorated. One says "He Said Yes" and the other says "She Said Yes."

"I've never done a double engagement party where there are two engagements for the same couple," he says in a dry voice.

"You knew!" I exclaim.

"Of course I knew." He smirks. "The chef always knows."

Dante hugs me close and drops a kiss onto the top of my head before everyone rushes over to me to get a look at the huge rock sitting on my left hand. I hold it out, admiring it along with the rest of them. I've never seen anything so beautiful.

Heaven clasps her hands together. "A wedding! Yay! And it's one where you're not being forced to marry the groom!" She chuckles as Matteo snakes an arm around her waist and dips her backward as she lets out a squeal.

"I don't hear too much complaining from you now," he says gruffly.

"Yeah, that's because her husband doesn't suffer from the Irish curse," Kaz pipes in, hugging his wife Lindy close to him. "No more peanuts for you, Heaven. Only Italian sausages." Kaz points to Marchella and Jaelyn, Roman and Sergio's fiancées. "Am I right, ladies?"

"Hell, yeah!" Jaelyn says. Sergio smacks her ass and grabs her close as Marchella spews champagne all over Roman while she chuckles.

Alek and his wife Gianna roll their eyes. "Kaz, seriously? You're about as subtle as a hand grenade," Gianna scoffs.

"Well, I know I can't argue Kaz's point about the sausage," I say with a giggle. "I'm a lucky girl."

Dante smacks my ass. "Damn right," he murmurs against my ear. "And just wait until later for the real celebration."

I lay my head on his shoulder, smiling at the banter between the Villanis, the Severinovs, and the Marcones.

"Nobody made a better borscht than my grandmother, you fucking guinea bastard!" Alek snips, rolling his eyes at Tommy. "Don't even insult me by saying that!"

"So now you're challenging me to make a better borscht than your grandmother? Game on, Ivan Drago!" Tommy bellows.

"Wait, wait," Dante says, chuckling so hard he can barely get the words out. "Tommy, you remember that restaurant review you got awhile back? About how your gnocchi...wait, lemme get this right...'resembled a saggy ball sack?'"

Tommy's wife, Gemma, doubles over with laughter. "Oh my God! I found that article and framed it for him as a joke."

"Yeah, not one of your funnier ones," Tommy mutters.

I spit out my champagne. "Wait, somebody wrote that?" I gasp through the laughter.

Tommy shrugs. "Yeah, and when he came to my restaurant, I fucking threw a chair at him."

I can't even breathe right now because my body quakes with hysterics.

And it doesn't stop there. The groups laughs and goads each other for hours.

They are one-hundred percent family first, business associates a far second.

They all have each others' backs, no matter what.

A tight-knit group that I am thrilled to be part of.

A real family.

I haven't felt as connected and so much a part of something since I lost my parents and Maks. It's been a long time, and I'm going to cherish it forever.

Dante holds me tight against him as we toast again with bottles of Veuve Clicquot champagne.

I really do have everything I could ever want.

I let out a soft giggle as Dante's lips assault the back of my neck. "I can't get the key in the lock," I murmur. "You're distracting me."

"You need to work on your focus so I can get you inside...and then I can get inside *you*," he whispers against my hair, his low voice full of wickedly delicious promise.

It is so damn hard to concentrate right now, with his demanding tongue trailing a path around my ear. I gasp, sliding in the key once more and doing an inward cheer once the lock beeps. I turn the door handle, drop everything in my hands, and wrap my arms around my fiancé. He gathers me in his arms and carries me outside to the balcony, letting me down in front of one of the day beds.

He reaches around my back and unzips my dress, then he slides the shoulder straps down so they fall to my wrists. The dress slips off easily, falling to my feet. Dante's eyes take on a predatory look as they run over my almost-naked body. I swear I hear a growl rumble deep in his throat and a shiver runs through me, despite the heat.

Even at night, the temperatures out here are sweltering.

I take a step toward him and unbuckle his pants as his fingers reach behind me to unhook my bra.

"You know you made me the happiest guy on the planet tonight, right?" he murmurs, kicking off his pants once I finally get them to his ankles. He pulls off his shirt and tosses it behind him.

I look at his massive, stiff cock and grasp it, stroking it as I nod my head. "And I'm the happiest girl."

"What the hell kind of fate is this, huh?" He reaches behind my head, fisting my hair and drawing me toward him.

"It's twisted, that's for sure," I whisper with a soft giggle. "Just like we are, I guess."

"Twisted and crazy and fucking hot," he says, his lips lifting into his signature sexy grin. He gives my ass a smack, and I squeal before he tears my thong right from my body. "Sorry, I hope you didn't love that pair," he says with a chuckle.

I roll my eyes. "*We're* some pair, huh?"

"And we're gonna have some life," he says, pulling me down onto the day bed. He straddles me from behind on his knees, reaching an arm around me as his cock presses into my pussy. He pulls me against his chest as he thrusts inside of me, his fingers flicking my clit.

"Dante..." I choke out, my breath hitching. "Oh God, oh God, oh God!"

His movements speed up, his dick sliding all the way out and then driving into me, sliding against my clit with every movement. His thick cock pulses and throbs deep inside of me and my quiet whimpers quickly morph into wails for release.

My gut clenches as I squeeze my muscles, pulling him deeper. A tingling sensation in my core shoots out to my limbs, deliciously numbing every cell in my fingers and toes as the orgasm tears through me. My head falls backward onto his chest and he clutches me tight as his movements speed up. His body trembles, slow at first until full-blown tremors make him tense up. A guttural roar erupts from his chest as he makes one final thrust inside of me.

We sit there for a minute, plastered against each other, panting, sweaty, and swimming around in our little bubble of erotic bliss.

I peek up at him after a few more seconds pass. "Thank you," I say quietly.

He winks at me. "For that massive orgasm? You know you're always welcome."

I shake my head. "No, for giving me back what I thought I'd lost forever. For giving me a family. You, me," I smile, biting down on my lip. "And hopefully a baby of our own," I say, rubbing my belly.

"Is that what you want?" he asks, trailing his fingertips down the side of my face.

I nod. "Yes, because it'll be us. And there's nothing more perfect than that."

"Perfect," he says. "And forever."

Yes, forever.

I really love the sound of that.

THE END

THANKS FOR READING!

Can I Ask You A HUGE Favor?

Would you be willing to leave me a review? I would be so grateful as one positive review on Amazon is like buying the book a hundred times. Your support is the lifeblood of Indie authors and provides us with the feedback we need to give the readers exactly what they want! I read each and every review. They mean the world to me! So thank you in advance, and happy reading!

CLICK HERE TO REVIEW

MEET KRISTEN

Kristen Luciani is a *USA Today* bestselling romance author and coach with a penchant for stilettos, kickboxing, and grapefruit martinis. As a deep-rooted romantic who loves steamy, sexy, and suspense-filled stories, she tried her hand at creating a world of enchantment, sensuality, and intrigue, finally uncovering her true passion. Pun intended...

Follow for Giveaways
Facebook Kristen Luciani

Private Reader Group
The Stiletto Click

Complete Works On Amazon
Follow My Amazon Author Page

VIP Newsletter
Click Here To Join My VIP Newsletter

Feedback Or Suggestions For New Books?
Email Me! kristen@kristenluciani.com

Want To Join My ARC Team?
Join My Amazing ARC Team!

Want A FREE Book?
Click Here To Download!

Instagram
@kristen_luciani

BookBub
Follow Me on BookBub

facebook.com/kristenlucianiauthor
twitter.com/kristen_luciani
instagram.com/kristen_luciani

Printed in Great Britain
by Amazon